Dr. Feelgood

Dr. Feelgood

Marissa Monteilh

KENSINGTON PUBLISHING CORP.
http://www.kensingtonbooks.com

This is dedicated to the one I love!

Acknowledgments

Hello again! I've wanted to give birth to a book called *Dr. Feelgood* for quite some time now, and here it is, resting in your wonderful little hands. I want to thank the "doctor" who had the *Dr. Feelgood* nameplate on his desk when I was very young. That name stayed in my innocent memory as one who made people feel good medically, but now that I'm older, the name has a new and pleasurable meaning. And feeling good ain't bad!

As I did before and always will, I thank God for my gift, for my journey, for my health, my family, and my relationships.

My loving children—Adam, Ron, and Nicole, my son-in-law Darrien, my heart-stealing granddaughter Alexis, my devoted brother, Greg, my wise and wonderful Ma Bette, my special Kelvin, big-F Friends—Annette, Ollie, Charles, Tami, and Pamela.

My closest and beloved author buddies—Victoria Christopher Murray, Mary B. Morrison, and Carmen Green, author and the owner of Book-remarks.com Cydney Rax.

My girl Marjorie Coley Davis at KISS 104.1 radio in Atlanta, Angela Jenkins at KBMS radio, Cheryl Robinson with Just About Books (Harambeeradio.com), Radiah at Urban-reviews.com, Shunda Leigh at Booking Matters Magazine, Carol Mackey at Black Expressions, Curledup.com, Romanceincolor.com.

Cherished bookstores who allowed me to add them to my tour like Black Images (a VIP shout-out to Emma Rodgers), Black Book-worm, Nubian Books, B's Books, Howard University Bookstore, Urban Knowledge, Sepia-Sand-Sable, Karibu, Medu Books, Horizon Books, Pyramid Books, Truth Books, Barnes & Noble Palmdale, Waldenbooks CNN Atlanta, Waldenbooks Cumberland Mall Atlanta,

VIII   Acknowledgments

Bernard Henderson at Alexander's in San Francisco, Bernardsbook shelf.com.

The 2006 Make Me Hot contest participants, each and every valued Make Me Hot contest sponsor, the Make Me Hot contest winner Pamela Bell-Melton.

My charming and wonderful agent Maureen Walters and her assistants Christina Morgan and Jenny Fitzsimmons.

My phenomenal Kensington family—Karen Thomas, Nicole Bruce, Latoya Smith, Walter Zacharias, Steven Zacharias, John Scognamiglio, Stacey Barney, Adeola Saul, and Lydia Stein.

Those devoted Myspace.com readers.

Invaluable book clubs—Special Thoughts, Ladies of Color Turning Pages, Turning Pages in Oakland, Sisters on the Reading Edge in Antioch, Chapters Book Club L.A., The North Carolina Bookfest, Angel Reid and the Imani Book Club Atlanta, and Moe.

Curtis Bunn with the National Book Club Conference, the North Carolina Black Book Festival, the Antelope Valley Writers, the African American Literacy Awards for the *Make Me Hot* nomination.

My pastor for saying, "If you can't get something out of it, put something into it."

And last but not least—my faithful and down to earth readers—for all you do, this book's for you!

Always and in all ways,

Marissa Monteilh aka The Diva Writer
www.myspace.com/divawriter

Prologue

Dr. Feelgood is getting his ass kicked but good, curvy Salina Alonzo Woodard thought to herself with her emotions running high as she braced herself for the worst. The sexy doctor's engraved metal nameplate hit the speckled Berber carpet like a rubber ball and bounced faceup upon the polished hardwood entryway floor of his eighth-floor medical office. *Dr. Feelgood* it read.

After many years of saving the lives of other people, tall, dark and handsome, Dr. Makkai Worthy, aka Dr. Feelgood, literally begged for his own life at the hands of a muscular white man whose beautiful Hispanic wife had just been caught cheating on him with the educated, gifted doctor.

Nationally known as attending cardiac surgeon at the Cedars Sinai Medical Center, Dr. Worthy had repaired many ailing hearts over the course of his illustrious career. And over the course of his thirty-seven-year life, he had broken many as well. He was a heart-breaker extraordinaire. Only, repairing those hearts was not on his list of daily duties on this sunny morning, but perhaps, from the intensity of the firm, strangling hold around his neck, it should have been.

"Please, honey, stop it. Please, let him go." Salina Woodard begged and pleaded with her jilted husband to release his gargantuan grip from the neck of her handsome lover. She stood nervously behind her husband, bracing herself upon her tiptoes, peering over his shoulder while pressing her golden acrylic nails into his clothing, pulling toward the back of his flexed upper arms.

With his medium brown complexion now suddenly reddish cinnamon, Dr. Worthy gagged and choked as he forced himself to speak with bugged eyes. "You have the wrong man. I don't even know her," he retched while Salina's husband continued to squeeze, pressing his manly thumbs into the wealthy doctor's Adam's apple.

"Don't even know me?" Salina replied with frantic coated words. Surely her ears deceived her.

She relaxed her stance, releasing her hold on her madman of a spouse. She stood up straight, adjusting her white cotton blouse, smoothing it with her hands and then straightening out her crisp starched collar, securing her leather purse strap along her shoulder. She folded her arms across her chest. A sudden blanket of numbness visited her from head to toe. She held her head up high even though her thoughts sped up. She wanted the attack to end, but she was also insulted by Dr. Worthy's blatant denial. In an instant, part of her wanted to cheer her husband on, hoping he could snap her man-on-the side's neck with one jolt. But, the other part of her took a quick trip down memory lane to the happy times she'd had with this heartbreaker of a man, Dr. Feelgood.

Normally, it was just about raw, bucket-naked nasty sex, but one day, one special evening just last summer, the couple held hands while walking along, checking out the shops in the popular Farmers' Market. She and the brilliant doctor decided to sit at a tiny wrought-iron table at a little outdoor French café. He pulled out her chair with a chivalrous nature. She wiggled her ample hips into a comfortable spot and femininely lifted herself ever so gently as he scooted the chair toward the table after she sat. She felt like a regal queen, proud to be with her lover in public and happy to receive such undivided attention. A feeling she hadn't had in her marriage in a long time.

They sipped on chilled chardonnay while feeding each other French bread dipped in warm olive oil. The night air was still and calm as he wiped the corner of her mouth with his long index finger, following up the gesture with the soft, sweet deliverance of a peck on the lips. She gazed at the good doctor as he sat looking ever so good with his jet-black, freshly tapered, faded haircut. She gave him an approving eye and smirked warmly, crossing her brown legs that were shown off so perfectly, extending from the hem of her sheer royal blue dress.

He took possession of her left hand that rested on her lap. "You're very special to me, Salina," he said.

"And you to me," she replied, wearing a smile. For the first time, words of caring were exchanged while vertical, as opposed to horizontally.

They talked and laughed and flirted through dinner as though it were a first date. Then they leisurely strolled along the trendy Grove under the moonlit sky and shining stars, hand in hand together, as if she were just as single as he was.

But, the only person seeing stars now was Dr. Worthy. He flailed his hands about, trying to fend off his jealous attacker. He lay on his back upon his own oval mahogany desk in the middle of his office. Important papers flew onto the floor, as well as an array of pens, paper clips, and framed photos.

Salina snapped out of her moment of reflection, coming back to present time. Again urgency took over her adulterous mind.

"Help," the attractive woman screeched as she anxiously glanced toward the door and then back. "Honey, stop," she yelled with her hands now pounding on her green-eyed monster of a husband's wide back. At the same time, she heard the sound of a siren from the paramedic unit.

Within what seemed like two seconds, they burst into the office, and it took three strapping men to pry her scorned husband off of the prestigious doctor. Dr. Worthy squinted his dark brown eyes tightly and put his hand on his ravaged throat to chase away the raging pain and ease circulation. He leaned up with one arm as he stood from the desk and panted until he could steady his pace. And then, he propelled his fit body toward his attacker and sucker punched him dead in the face.

"Makkai," yelled Salina.

Barely flinching his head, Salina's husband took the blow with ease, cutting his eyes as though he wanted to chop off the doctor's head with a meat cleaver.

Dr. Worthy shouted through his windedness, "Punk. You messed with the wrong man. You'll never see the light of day again. I promise you." The doctor rapidly shook out his throbbing million-dollar hand.

The paramedics literally turned the other cheek to the punch and took the man away, handing him over to the authorities who'd just arrived down the hall.

Salina simply stared at the doctor from the doorway, breathing heavily while shaking her head. "I can't believe you denied me."

"Who the hell are you?" Dr. Feelgood cut his eyes and leaned over his desk, massaging his clean-shaven, classic jaw, and rubbing the back of his perfect head.

"You're the asshole."

He pointed that same long index finger that had lovingly dabbed the olive oil from the corner of her mouth, the one that had penetrated her depths on many an intimate evening. He thrashed his words her way. "Get out of my office before I press charges against you, too."

Salina squeezed her stare through tight eyes. She spoke with authority and certainty and promise. "I speak for all of your dick-whipped flock when I say this. One day, you'll pay for what you do to women, Makkai Worthy. One day, you'll pay all right." She sliced him with her eyes and gave an about-faced, runway pivot just before his vengeful words stabbed her in the back.

"You were just another pussy that got hooked. Get over it."

Chapter 1

Georgia

I love me some Dr. Makkai Worthy.

"Mommy, can I have some Junior Mints?" my oldest daughter, curly headed Treasure, asked with a major clump of sleep in her eyes. Considering it's just after six in the morning, I don't think so.

With a large mug of my full-strength, morning wake-up brew in one hand, I stood in the kitchen wearing leopard baby doll pajamas and fluffy black house slippers, stirring a simmering pot on the stove with my other hand. "No, it's time for breakfast. Now go ahead on and wake up your sister so you two can eat this oatmeal while it's hot. And then go wash up your faces. Now go."

Treasure flashed an innocent, hurt, eight-year-old pout. Her three-year-old, big-eyed sister was in zombie-mode as if sleep-walking as she came out of her room wiping her right eye with one hand, dragging a Dora the Explorer blanket with the other.

"Mommy," she cried with a soft, slow whine. "I wanna watch Sponge Bob." With her long, jet-black hair and Indian skin, cranky was her middle name until the time of day hit double digits, which would be nearly four hours from now.

I banged the ceramic mug down on the tile counter and scooped two big spoonfuls into their bowls, adding some brown sugar and butter. "No, not this morning, now don't play with me. We're running late. We only have time to eat and get dressed. Now, come on and get in your high chair."

"I want the big-girl chair."

"Sit somewhere, just come on." I pointed in the direction my youngest needed to place herself right away.

My heart-shape-faced baby's name is Love Jones, named after her tired-ass daddy, Rydell Jones. I still can't believe I actually gave her his last name. He acts like he'd rather see us on an episode of "Maury Povich" than say one word to me ever again in life. After being with him for years, he accused me of some tired-ass shit two weeks before I found out I was pregnant. Once we broke up after a dramatic and almost violent scene, I only contacted him when Love was born to ask him to sign the birth certificate. He did, but then called up here starting some mess, trying to deny paternity once he saw the girls and me in the Del Amo mall with Makkai. We're always ending up in the same places. Whatever. Makkai named her, even though he's not her father.

I met Mister fine and studly Makkai when I was four months pregnant while coming from a doctor's appointment at Cedars Sinai hospital.

"How are you?" He was wearing his black designer suit like it was a ten thousand dollar bill. He lifted his five hundred dollar pair of smoky-gray sunglasses and presented me with a strong, lingering handshake. His wink lingered, too.

I replied, "Fine, and you?" The blush I'd applied earlier that morning was no longer necessary. I sucked in my belly and poked my chest out all in one fell swoop.

He nodded and looked me up and down, glaring at my chest. "Not as fine as you."

That's normally one tired-ass line, but this man walked and talked and smelled and looked like he was somebody. Before I knew it, I handed him the digits and it was on.

He seemed to get off on doing me with a baby on the way. He'd back me up and hit it from behind, digging in deep while I lay on my side. And then he'd love to suck on my wide, tender nipples, trying his best to milk me like I was a dang cow. My poor baby would be jerking like she was having a conniption fit. I think doing that man on the regular brought her on eight weeks early. I'm blessed to even have her. She only weighed three pounds.

At first, he was right there. He was even in the delivery room. He checked in on my older daughter when she stayed with my mother while I was in the hospital. My mother seemed to fall in love with him.

"Now that is a good man," she'd declare like she'd have dibs on him herself if she could do it without stabbing me in the back.

Yes, he can charm us all, young, old, gay, straight. But, being that I was on screw lockdown for six weeks after Love was born, I didn't see Makkai much.

Anyway, enough about my kids. Right now I'm not even trying to focus my energy on telling you anything other than what Dr. Makkai Worthy is all about.

See, by the time Love was maybe three months old or so, Makkai and I got back to our regular routine of him coming by after work, usually around midnight or one in the morning while the girls were sleeping. He'd crawl into my bed and work his magic. Like Charlie Wilson, he'd perform his tricks on me.

Now, I'll be the first to tell you he has a reputation for throwing down in the bedroom. You could say he's an animal in bed. Yes, my Makkai has this way about him. It's a way that no man in my life has even been able to come close to. It made me fall in love with him.

"I love kissing you, baby," he said as he planted his lips on mine, looking me dead in the eye with a provocative longing to please.

I was drunk with lust. This man stole my will every time he'd come near me. The scent of him fucked me up, but good.

"Your skin is like milk chocolate." He said he loved the fact that

I had meat on my bones. Everything about me is thick, from my lips to my ass. And what I loved about him was the fact that he was long and strong and down to get the friction on. He's giving and good-looking, and he always smells like the manliest scent of musky, peppery testosterone juice I've ever sniffed. It was like a drug. It was absolutely fucking intoxicating.

I lay on my back upon my cream colored sheets as Makkai gave me a slow tongue bath. I slyly tossed the fluffy, in-the-way pillows onto the floor and focused my attention on his handiwork. His perfect mouth traveled to the right side of my neck, one of my most sensitive spots, and then to my goose-bumped breasts. He has a way of twisting my nipple with his thumb and forefinger while lightly flicking the other nipple with his tongue, and then adding just enough saliva to make it super slippery as he meets my nipple with his nipple. It's so damn erotic to watch and feel. Almost as if he's playing with my erect clit.

He never rushes, always takes his time when he's about to . . . go down. He moves to my belly button, sticking his tongue inside, and then over to my hip bone where it almost tickles, it's so sensitive, doing all of this while parting my legs with his hand, making sure to rub around my entire area, and slowly slipping one finger inside to check for wetness. He sticks that drenched finger in his mouth and moans, "That is the sweetest taste in the world." Makkai kisses my upper thighs and then moves in toward my middle, but just as he senses that my wide hips are sending a hurried signal of anxiousness, he travels back down my thigh, still fingering me lightly. He's the damn tease master.

He glances up at me with those long eyelashes and big brown eyes, and then looks directly into the crevice of my vagina as if it has eyes, and approaches it slowly. The treat that I'm about to receive is one that makes me want to burst already. My heart races, and all I can do is lean my head back and enjoy, while shutting my eyes to brace myself.

I feel a hot, wet tongue, traveling around my outsides, and then flicking my clit. I feel my vulnerable peak pulsate with pleasure. He licks my outer lips, bends my legs back and secures himself in that position, lying flat on his belly with his head in between my legs. He then takes my stiffened clit into his mouth, and he sucks it in a way that makes me look down to get a visual peek at exactly what this expert is doing. If I were gay, I'd want to know how to do that shit. How does he make me feel like I could cum in his mouth within two seconds? Dammit.

I feel my ass tighten, and the blood starts to flow from the minute he secures it in his mouth. His tongue is doing something . . . some kind of magical, secretive trick that most men would pay money to learn. Hell, their women would fork over the money themselves in a heartbeat. His teeth are in on it. His lips are in on it, too. His tongue is the ringleader. And then he stops, traveling to my sweet sticky hole, sticking his tongue inside while using his long, wide index finger above my mound. He then moves up to the clit again and lowers my legs straight so that he can get a direct hit. I point my toes and flex my quads, and he separates my wet lips with both hands, the same hands that have repaired ailing hearts his entire career, and rests his elbows on my thighs.

This shit is what he does that no other man can do. This shit is what no other man takes the time to do. No other man gets it quite right because their asses are lazy. No one can compare to the hard work of Dr. Feelgood. "Ahhh, Makkai, I love the way you do this, baby."

He inserts three fingers inside of me while he sucks in a swirling, flicking motion, yet the brotha can still speak. "I know you love it. Tell me what it feels like." He speedily moves his head from left to right with a deep groaning sound that's almost barbaric.

"It feels like I'm going to explode."

"Go ahead and explode then. Explode for me now, baby. Give it to me. Give it to me good." He holds steady, focusing on my build up, taking it all into his mouth while saying, "Uh huh, uh huh." He's even a damn cheerleader.

"Aahhhh, baby, I, I . . . Ooooooo, aaaawww, ahhh, Makkai." I try my best to keep it down, but hell, fuck the dumb shit. "I love you, Nigga." I tighten up and then I literally collapse. I could have sworn I heard this talented pussy master chuckle between my legs.

Yet and still, knowing I'm in sensitivity mode, he tickles me with his tongue and then gives it a fond farewell kiss goodbye.

I jump and flinch, still coming down as I turn to the side in an effort to escape.

"That's my baby. Now it's ready." He moves up, reaching over to the black lacquer nightstand for a condom. "That clit throbs in my mouth like nothing I've ever seen."

I reach down to the floor to now grab that same discarded pillow just as he lies on top of me. I scoot back to rest my sweaty head on the pillow.

He lifts my legs up and back, as I take on the pleasurable role of missionary wide receiver. All of his thickness and width enter me as he grunts. "Yeah. This is the best pussy I've ever had. Damn, it's nasty wet."

The feeling is intense and almost illegal. He should be arrested on the spot. Well, maybe after he's done. "You do it so good, baby. Only you."

"Only me?"

"Yes, only you. It's all yours."

"This is my pussy."

"Always, Makkai, always."

He pulls out as he speaks. "Oooh, shit. I don't want to cum yet. Put your leg over my shoulder."

Like the master he is, he scoots me to my side and enters me again. His position is at an angle that's hitting something. Call it a G spot, or an XYZ spot, but it is making something heat up and throb and rush. I squint my eyes, trying to fight it, but the faster he pumps, the faster it comes, and it makes me dizzy. The room is spinning all around me. I put my own hand over my mouth as I release a burst of throbbing and wetness that's almost frightening.

"Get that nut, baby. Damn," he says as I feel his thickness expand and go deeper, and then expand again. "Oh, yeah, that's my baby." He freezes and his tip seems to hit my deepest point. He then gave way on top of me.

He moves my leg flat, climbs off of me, and turns over on his back. He breathed hard and looked over at me. I breathed hard and looked over at him. And we shook our heads at each other. Damn, that man can sure make a woman cum.

Okay, so now you know. The situation with him has served me just fine, actually. I get the oral sex of the century, and he gets, from what he tells me, the best pussy he's ever had in his entire life. That man loves to fuck him some Georgia Mae Manley. Me, to be honest with you, even though he is packing, I could take or leave the dick. But, I have to give him his props because he is the only man to get enough of a deep, continual rhythm going to ever give me a vaginal orgasm. Truly, I could fall asleep right after I came in his face and feel totally fulfilled. Like my name, I like it dirty south thank you very much. Anyway, he's already snoozing, and I need my sleep before these two girls wake up in the morning, driving me crazy. But, of course, he'll be gone by then. But, it's all-good. For now anyway.

Chapter 2

Monday

Here's my deal. I'll tell you as I drive toward the Marina for my weekly wax and electrolysis at Sheena's Spa and Salon because I'm always on the run. It's a beautiful day and the sun is shining, a slight breeze is blowing, and all is sweet.

See, I am a wealthy, attractive, sophisticated forty-year-old woman. Okay, I'm forty-four. I like men who are actually and factually one step away from being afraid of me, yet who can stand up to me anyway. I let em know I don't have time for no childish ass games.

The love of my life, my mom, died years ago and left me executor of her twenty-million-dollar estate. She owned a chain of Cajun restaurants called Mondays, named after me, of course. I drive a tan Jaguar to match my skin, the Creole in me. I live in her seven-bedroom, exclusive home in Palos Verdes with my little black Shitsu named Soul, who's like my child. I don't have kids. I have never been married and don't want to be married, and basically, I don't think I've ever even been in love. Men are a trip. Love is a four-letter word worth about as much as that other four-letter word that starts with an *F* and ends with a *K*. I say the *L* word to get what I want. Hell, I say both words to get what I want. Mainly to attract men and get what they've got. I never knew what it was like to be in it, love that is, so I stayed out of it. Basically, I say fuck love. I'm doing just fine, thank you very much. Sex for me is simply recreational.

Mr. Smooth Operator Makkai Worthy calls me Delicious. He tells me my stuff tastes like a warm-ass, apple dumpling dessert, and he crawls all up inside of it like he'd be fine if he never, ever came out. That man craves it on a regular basis. Tells me it's the best pussy he's ever had in his entire life, yes he does. And I ain't mad at him.

I heard someone say that if you screw a skilled lover too often and have too many grand orgasms, you'll bond. Must be that I was the last lady in line when they were handing out estrogen because I could give a damn about bonding. I'll give you one and take mine and get to steppin. I don't want to see your ass in the morning.

I met him while he was doing his rounds in the intensive care unit at the hospital. What had happened was, my ex-lover, this sixty-two-year-old man who had heart trouble, was Makkai's regular patient.

One night my "old man" started getting short of breath while I straddled his burly face. I thought he was blowing on me like it was some new sex trick, but he was damn near doing a Lamaze breathing technique, trying to catch what he didn't want to be, his last breath. He started choking and he actually turned blue. I sighed major attitude for feeling shortchanged, but calmed down and peeled my cheated vagina away from his lousy face, and then I hopped up to call 911.

Once we arrived in the emergency room, I saw that tall, debonair hunk of a doctor standing there in his white coat with that shiny stethoscope around his manly neck. At this point I needed oxygen myself. I followed the glorious looking doctor out to the nurses' station.

I stood within an inch of his essence as he typed notes into his tiny electronic keyboard. Shifting my weight to my right side, I crossed my arms and flashed my legendary smile. "Being that my friend here might be on his last leg, not to give you the impression that I ever got any of his third leg anyway, but with all due respect, I need someone not only to satisfy me orally, but who can get rock hard, too, more than once every blue moon. I haven't had a big stiff one up inside of me in a month of Mondays. By the way, my name is Monday Askins. Basically, I'm really sorry if I'm offending you and this may not be an appropriate time, but I'm horny as Samantha on *Sex and the City*. His attention was all mine.

Actually, he didn't look one bit offended. He kept his dark brown eyeballs attached to my vanilla chest and smiled. I gradually turned to my side with purpose, shifting my stance. As I suspected, his eyes darted to my bodacious booty view. As always, men will be men. We screwed that night . . . all night. Now, I will say one thing . . . that Superman lover needs to get an *S* tattooed on his chest because if ever I met a super hero in bed, it's him. He's gotta have a cape hidden in his house somewhere. Lover boy talks more shit, but he can definitely back it up. We've been fucking ever since. Gotta go. I'm two minutes late for my three o'clock appointment, and that's just plain old tacky. Ciao.

Chapter 3

Allow me, Makkai J. Worthy, to break it on down for you. Red-boned Monday had me at hello. She sports a sexy gap in her teeth that turned me the hell on. When you see it you just envision her . . . oh well, I've digressed. She is tall and thick and fine, and she looks like she should be on a runway in Paris, even with her being well into her forties. But, the folks in the modeling world would've had one problem with Monday's body, which the brothas have no problem with whatsoever. They actually call it a blessing. The most impressive asset about this woman is the size of her healthy gluteus maximus. You could say her ass is set, if you get what I'm saying. I mean Serena Williams has nothing on this amazon queen.

And the years have been kind to her butt, figuratively. Her hips are wide and her cheeks are large and high and firm and yellow and soft and heavy. Playing with her rear end is like winning the booty lottery. She has the ass of life—all other asses should have come from this ass. Cheeks are too deep to get my dick through the depth of her meat to find her pussy from behind, and I'm not at all lacking in that department, so most times I just lay her on her damn back. And the funny thing is . . . her last name is Askins. I call her Ms. Asskins, and apparently folks called her mother that as well. They all come from a long line of behinds, and they joke to each other about it. They add an extra *S* to their last name on purpose.

No wonder she smothered that old man. She's not sitting on my face for all the ass at Mardi Gras.

Okay, so I guess you can tell that I have a fetish for her Asskins, but even with all she's got going for her physically, the woman's a trip to deal with.

She's a pathological liar. She has some serious secrets, and I have no problem telling you what they are. But, I'll just enjoy letting her make a fool out of herself a little bit longer. You'll find out. And by the way, we met as she was coming out of a private, residential swingers' club and I was going in. I knew she looked familiar. She didn't approach me at the hospital to tell me about how she needed to get some lovin' because she was starving. I saw her in the hospital, but she never told me the bold-faced lie about her being love starved. She was already getting plenty of the shaft.

It was an underground, after-hours spot early one Sunday morning. Folks called it *Sex in the Suburbs*. It was a three-story Miami Vice–style house in Holmby Hills, which was owned by an ex-pro football player. Mainly it was people who'd swear they'd keep the goings-on to themselves. What happened there stayed there. Some were famous, most were just horny. I only stopped by maybe twice a year to watch. I tried to be an incognito-Negro. Didn't want folks who violated the privacy rules talking about me in the paper the next day, so I kept as low a profile as I could, being that this was the hottest secret freak castle of Los Angeles.

All you had to do was pay your hundred dollars and you were in. It had hidden rooms everywhere, all decorated in some wild color scheme. Soft, cushiony, loud colored lounge chairs with netlike canopies filled the bedrooms, game room, den, and living room. Security monitors were visible so folks tried their best to behave, and huge plasma televisions played the hottest brown sugar porno you'd ever want to see. Dim reddish lights, candles and soft jazz set the mood. The smell of jasmine incense hit my nostrils when I stepped into an enclosed sunroom.

I saw a woman grinding her hips as she sat on the edge of a violet and black sofa, and then I saw a head between her thighs. My eyes widened, but considering where I was, I knew they were not deceiving me. The head was braided down like Iverson.

As I zeroed in on an available love seat nearby, I turned back to see the attractive, smiling woman, looking me dead in my eyes.

"Hello there, Doctor," she spoke loudly with lust eluding from her vision.

"Excuse me?" Maybe it was my ears that were deceiving me now. Shouldn't she be focusing on her nut?

"Fancy seeing you here. But, I'm not surprised." She continued talking without even blinking. Her hips kept up the sensual grinding without hesitation. And the gentleman who was on his knees pleasing her with closed eyes, didn't skip a beat.

My mouth was wide open, yet I replied, "Why do you say that?" I hadn't even taken a seat yet. I couldn't budge. But, my little buddy was at full attention.

"I know a stud when I see one. White coat or not."

"How about if we continue this conversation a little later on. Like when you're done." I looked to the side, semi-embarrassed for her, and for him. And I wasn't about to cock-block.

"Oh, I'm just about done," she responded, slowly shutting her bronze eyelids and giving out a sexy moan, grabbing hold of the armrests and turning her head from side to side. She squeezed her thighs so tight around her giver's head that he jerked, and then she jerked, and then I jerked, and then she gave a lengthy, throaty sigh. In a split second, she spoke as if having gotten over it. "Can you pour me some gin?" She pointed her long, curved nail to the cherrywood side table where a lead crystal pitcher rested upon a tray.

"Sure." Sheer shock put me in slow motion. My hardness started to settle.

Her young man of a partner stood up, adjusting his baggy jeans and nodding my way. I nodded back. He wiped his moustache with the back of his hand and headed outside. Brotha lit up a blunt, staring out over the hillside view of the city lights.

"Oh, I'll get it," she said with a sweetness to her voice, standing up pantiless and pulling down her cocoa silk skirt to pour her own drink.

"I would have gotten it."

"You're too slow." She brought the glass to her red lips and sipped and swallowed the liquor like a pro.

"Excuse me, but you didn't give me time to move."

"Slow is good, sometimes. I'm not complaining. Monday's the name." She shook my hand. We each squeezed a tight grip.

"Makkai."

She still had on her silver, ankle-strapped heels. Her round breasts winked from behind a silvery bra that shimmered from underneath a dark coal blouse. The matching short skirt looked like it was pulling from behind, just from the pure width of her backside. Her legs were bare and tanned and firm. A wide, gold belt cinched her small waist. Her reddish-brown hair was hanging along her slender shoulders. Her scent was gardenia.

"You are very beautiful."

"Thanks." She softly squeezed my bicep, offering a snuggling embrace, flashing her sexy gapped teeth.

I gazed into her mouth and then examined her thick, supple looking lips. I felt as though I might have been staring a little too long. I swallowed and breathed out and then looked around toward the patio area. Her giving friend was gone. "I see you didn't waste your money getting in here."

She popped her lips. "Please. I don't pay to get in here."

"Oh, excuse me." A pregnant pause took over. She continued to absorb the dark liquid while giving me her full-on, seductive, inviting eyes. Her full-on, inviting, seductive eyes. "Hey, what do you say we get out of here," I suggested. I felt my little buddy start to rise again.

"Lead the way." She grabbed her Chanel bag and took my hand, one step behind me.

"Hey, Laurinda," an older, scantily dressed woman said, as we exited the front door and she went in.

Monday did not reply.

The woman asked, looking at me like I had a pork chop hanging from around my neck, "Damn, who is he? Can I come with you two?"

Monday shook her head no without looking back.

We stepped down the front stairs, and I said, "That's good because I don't party with any more than two, including myself." Even though I felt that maybe just watching her get eaten couldn't hurt. "Hey, I thought you said your name was Monday."

"Laurinda's just a name I use when I'm here."

"You say so."

And that was our first night together. The first of many more to come.

Chapter 4

Mary Jane

My name is Nurse Mary Jane Cherry. I was born a Cherry. I've never been married, though I was proposed to by a really sweet, shy, kind of square man who could have been everything I'd ever wanted if I'd been ready. But, he was like twice my age and I was only twenty-five. He had grown children and agreed he was too old to raise a kid all over again. And I definitely want kids.

I'm thirty-four now, and if I ever want to have those kids, I need to find a husband. I love children. I have two younger brothers who really look up to me. I try to set an example for them. My mother and father both died last year, so my brothers and I are even closer now. See, my mother was admitted into the VA hospital after having shortness of breath, and before we knew it, she died of kidney failure. I felt so bad because obviously I think we should have seen it coming, but I never encouraged her to go to the doctor. I just thought she was out of shape when she'd start breathing hard after walking up a flight of stairs. I do go through a lot of guilt over that. She was only fifty-two years old. She never seemed sick with more than a cold her entire life. My dad had a fatal heart attack three months later.

Now I work in the cardiology department at Cedars Sinai hospital in West Hollywood, California, but also as an RN in the pediatric emergency room. Both of my brothers still live in San Francisco. I don't want to be too far from them, so I wouldn't consider relocating too far away, but they're both married and my youngest brother, the twenty-seven-year-old, just became a father. I'm now Auntie Mary Jane to little Yardley Cherry. I told him that girl will have some serious problems when she submits a resume. Folks will think she's an adult porn star.

Anyway, I'm here to talk about Dr. Makkai Worthy. He's sort of my boss but not really. My real boss is a powerful sister named Dr. Lois Taylor. She supervises three units, oncology, cardiology and pediatrics. But, the reason I know Dr. Worthy so well is because we've gone out and, well, here's what happened.

"Why were you so reserved when I said good night to you this evening?" I asked, riding in the passenger seat of his fancy whip. He'd just picked me up at my place.

He gave his eyes to the southbound lanes of the San Diego freeway. "Just wanted to be discreet. That nosey little male nurse was all ears."

"And would it be so bad if they knew we went to dinner every now and then?" I stared out of the passenger window with my arms crossed.

"Maybe not for you, but for me, definitely."

"Why, because you're dating every woman in the place." I looked over at him. He did not smile. "I'm just kidding."

His eyes still belonged to the road. "No, you're not."

"Where do you want to eat?" I flipped down the visor mirror and checked my lip gloss.

"I thought we'd go to Lawry's in Beverly Hills."

"That works."

"So, how was your day?" he asked casually.

"Cool. And yours?" I closed the mirror and looked inside of my purse for a breath mint.

"Cool."

"Why are you making small talk with me, Makkai?"

"I just have a lot on my mind."

"Does it have anything to do with that man who came after you in the hospital the other day?"

"No. Word travels fast, huh?"

"You know it." I popped a spearmint lifesaver into my mouth without offering him one.

He cracked a slight glimmer of a smile. "They should call it Peyton Place Hospital, or Desperate Doctors and Nurses."

"Cute. But, what's really up with you?"

Then he just spilled it. "Mary Jane, I don't think we should see each other anymore after this."

"Why?" I turned my head towards him, lowering my chin with an edge.

He still looked straightforward. "It's just too risky for me. I mean, I really like you and everything, but I don't think we're on the same page as far as keeping this to ourselves. I think you're a lot more casual about it at work than I am."

I was blinking like I had a spastic twitch. "Just because I said good night to you in the hallway when I was leaving?"

This time he did glance over at me. "You stood there like you wanted me to walk out with you."

"I did not. I was waiting for your reply."

"It just felt weird."

"That's just your paranoia. So you're saying you don't want to see me anymore?"

He answered quickly. "I want to, but I've worked too hard to risk this by violating the rules."

"The hospital doesn't have any rules about dating coworkers."

"Yes, but I do."

My arms assumed a crossed position again. "Fine, Makkai. No more fooling around. But, are you sure you want to be seen with me out at dinner? God forbid a patient or an administrator walks in."

"Actually, I think we need to just cut the outings and only kick it at night when we're both feeling the need."

My hand flexed in his direction. "Not. Why don't you just take me home? I'm not some cheap floozy, Makkai." I put my studded purse onto my lap.

"I want to take you to dinner." He signaled and made a lane change.

"It'll be like the darn last supper. I am not desperate, you know. I am a quality woman, and since you don't know that, trying to only take part of me won't work. Take me home."

He sped down the wide-open freeway with his *DR FG 1* vanity plate proudly perched upon the rear end of his flashy Benz and headed back in the direction of my apartment in the Palms area. He coolly slipped in a Stevie Wonder CD, playing *"You've Got It Bad, Girl."* I wanted to scream.

That man gave me my first orgasm ever. I'd thought sex was good before, but he taught me how to explode with a rush like a bomb. The very first time it happened he used his doctor talk just before by whispering in my ear while stroking me. "Fear and anxiety are shut off during the female orgasm, you know. You can't be afraid of letting go. There's a strong deactivation of the cortex of the brain." Damn him.

And I'll be darn if that medical mumbo jumbo didn't work right in the middle of busting a rush that scared the crap out of me. Hell, I did indeed need to be afraid of letting go. It almost hurt. That was unheard of, that kind of ex-rated sensation.

Anyway, after the conversation in his car, I stopped being his nurse and went back to working in ICU, but the stress of what you see in that department on a daily basis is wearing me down and burning me out. My desire is to work full-time with the babies in the obstetrics department, where the newborns are, the ones that are in need of critical care. That's where I can give one hundred percent of my energy with pleasure. Energy that deserves to be given to the sweet innocent ones who didn't ask to come into this crazy world. They schedule me up there every now and then, but for now, I'm usually on the eighth floor assisting Makkai and the other doctors.

I'm not the one to play cat and mouse with this man, even though he does deserve every letter of his nickname, Dr. Feelgood. No wonder that lady's husband came up here trying to kill him.

Chapter 5

Now, don't get me wrong, creamy terracotta complexioned Nurse Cherry is fine, you know, cute face, slim waist, just the way I like em. She's a triple threat, face, ass, and chest. I can hear that song *"Mary Jane"* by Rick James playing in my head when I see her. She has a sultry strut without even trying, kinda like that waitress in the movie *Car Wash*. At least I don't think she's trying, but if she is, she's all right with me. And even better, she is sweet, sweet like candy. She always smells of a sexy scent like she's recently bathed in Perry Ellis body wash for women. Kinda reminds me of the scent this private dancer used to wear years ago.

Anyway, she looks like she could be Beyonce's older sister. She has about a twenty-inch difference between her waist and hips, and her waist is twenty-one inches as it is. She's shaped like a hard, brown Coke bottle. And I'm sorry to go there but I'll be dammed if Mary Jane doesn't have the biggest damn clit I've ever seen in my entire life. That's all I'm going to say about that for now.

And I know my buddy Carlos is trying to get at her. I have to be cool with it, though. That's been our deal since college when we'd end up sharing women. The deal was that if anyone started catching feelings, he could throw up a stop sign and the other would honor it. But, I can't say that I'd throw one up regarding Mary Jane Cherry. She's cool and all, but it's not that kind of party. I've found that she's not very experienced, but definitely willing to learn.

However, believe it or not, I'm not willing to risk my job just for some lovin', no matter how good it is.

And speaking of my job, I'm constantly thankful and amazed that I'm blessed enough to be able to do what I do. My true priority my entire adult life, though, has been my career. There has been little time for a social life. My dream was to be a cardiac surgeon, and thank God I achieved that dream, even though it seemed like a long shot. Surgical residency was time consuming and stressful, but I kept the faith and kept at it, knowing that once the right opportunity came along, the rest would unfold, as long as I was prepared.

Truth be told, back in the day when I was only fifteen, no one believed me when I told them I'd end up being a heart surgeon. That is, no one but my faith-filled mom.

My mom moved us to California when I was in the tenth grade. My younger sister Fonda, who was named after my mom's favorite actor, Henry Fonda, and I were born and raised in a small town in Florida called Wildwood. It's what some would call country. Okay, it's what everybody would call country. Our two-bedroom place looked more like a shack than a house, but it was home. Fonda and I shared a tiny room with an old, beaten down wooden bunk bed.

We'd hang out in the kitchen or else in the front yard, usually with my mother, but sometimes just my sister and me. And we'd dance, barbecue up a feast, and listen to oldies. Mom got us hooked on old school. I adapted a love for anything that's Stevie Wonder.

I can hear Mom now, snapping her fingers to "*Signed, Sealed, Delivered*" like it was yesterday. "Here I am baby," she'd bolt out loud like she had a lucrative record contract, tightening her hand into a fist beneath her chin as if it were a microphone. She'd mix up her fancy footwork and shake her hippy-hippy-hips to the groove, grabbing our hands and twirling me and my sister around like we were her dance partners at a local corner juke joint. Those cherished memories are etched on my heart like a forever tattoo.

A lot of times I'd play baseball in the open field next door. I'd toss the ball in the air as high as I could and catch it with my too-tight, tattered glove. I'd never miss. I had an eye for the exact spot it would land, most times not even having to take even one step back or one step forward. Or, I'd pretend to throw the ball as far away as I could, never releasing it, just testing out my upper arm strength.

Yeah, the field of dirt with the broken down chain link fence and homemade bases made of cardboard was my field of dreams. Sometimes I'd just sit on home plate and dream about what life would be like if I were looking outside of my own estate one day, seeing a few tall tress on my very own property.

Those were my grand and rare alone times when I was young. But, most times I'd hit a few balls with my dad's cousins, my "play uncles" when they'd come over. They were quite the characters . . . my Uncle Leroy and Uncle Milton. I'll never forget them.

Uncle Leroy was patient. "Hey there, boy, now place your feet parallel to the width of your body."

"Dat boy's body's bout as narra as a strang bean dere," Uncle Milton joked at my expense. His beer belly shook when he chuckled.

Uncle Leroy continued, using physical gestures as examples. "Like I said, about the width of your body. Straddle that poor excuse for a home base. And keep your elbow up. Grip the bat, like this, with your right hand higher than your left."

"Jus let him hit the dern thang. Or miss it, hell, he'll learn soon nuff."

Uncle Leroy insisted, "Will you let me do this? This could be our next Hank Aaron, right here. Makkai Worthy, the professional baseball player."

"He's Makkai Worthy the strang bean ret now."

"Cut it out, you two. Just let that boy have some fun. Hit the ball, sweetheart," Mom said as she stood on the sidelines with Fonda, cheering me on. Mom always spoke as though she was born and raised in California. She was college educated even though she didn't graduate, but perhaps it was from her early days of being an English tutor, until Dad made her quit working.

"Mama, can I try?" asked Fonda, with her tall self. She was wearing her peach colored, frilly dress. She always wore dresses, with big bright ribbons in her long, braided hair.

"No," said Uncle Milton. "Dat sports deres fa boys."

"I want to play, too." Fonda was adamant, flashing a sour face.

Mom looked at her. "Baby, let's go inside and leave the guys to themselves."

"Hit it hard, Makkai. I know you can do it," Fonda said as she turned toward the house with her girlie voice cracking from her hurt feelings. She looked back at me as Mom had her hand on Fonda's back. Fonda's wide eyes said, "Show em, big brother."

I couldn't help but give her a thank you smile, and then I looked forward, centering myself over the cardboard, remembering everything my Uncle Leroy told me. My elbow was up. My feet were resolutely planted, and my grip was not too tight, but firm.

Uncle Milton looked at me, eye to eye. I looked at the ball. He looked at me. I looked at the ball. He wound up and then threw the pitch underhanded.

The ball made its way along until, a wham-bam, I slugged the dang sucker. The wooden bat met that dirty white hardball with a loud thud, and it traveled up and up and up, journeying over and over and over across the street and right into . . . Mrs. Pope's brand new stained glass living room window.

"Damn, dat dere boy has an arm fo sho," said Uncle Milton, scratching the scalp beneath his salt-and-pepper afro.

Uncle Leroy stared at the direction and distance the ball traveled and then looked at me. "I told you he could do it."

Uncle Milton replied, "Yeah, but can he start makin dat money now, cause once dat old bag come out here yellin', it's gon be all bout fiddin' her windapane."

I stood there, half smiling and half scared as hell, looking back at the front door where little Fonda stood, wearing a big grin with my name on it.

"Good job, Makkai," she yelled. "Good job."

Mom nodded with pride, flashing her signature warm smile. Mom was always there.

Chapter 6

Yes, those were the days. They say you can take the boy out of the country, but you can't take the country out of the boy. I disagree. I am a city boy through and through. The country can't do anything for me now. But, it was my life back then.

Yeah, you could say my mother, Corrine Cotton, raised us by herself ever since she left my father. She's my heart. Tall and dark-skinned and strong and heavyset, she's always been one loving woman. I suppose she woke up one day and realized she was through with doing it all alone after getting tired of an empty bed on a regular basis, so she filed for divorce and decided the best place to go was sunny Los Angeles where my mom's best friend lived. She wanted to be as far away from my dad as she could. I don't think my mother ever quite got over my father, that's what I believe anyway. But, she hid it with her usual anger when we'd say his name . . . Roosevelt Worthy.

Perhaps the anger was because Poppa, Roosevelt Worthy, was a through and through, player to the bone, rolling stone. Truly, wherever he lay his hat was his home. The only problem was, he never wore an actual factual hat when he should have . . . on his popular penis.

He drove big rigs for a living and was always on the road. Yeah, Dad loved to drive. The final woman to call the house was just before we left. Mom had never raised her voice when there'd been confrontations before, but with this woman, Mom went totally off. However, there was one thing that Mom and these women seemed to agree upon after all was said and done . . . that Roosevelt Worthy was the throw-down, get the job done, turn-you-out king in bed.

Sometimes we knew Dad had done something shady just by the look on Mom's face, but usually it was because we overheard them late at night. She hoped that my sister and I didn't notice his indiscretions, and since I was the male, I believe she definitely didn't want me to adopt his irresponsible ways. Oh well, who knew?

Anyway, I attended Westchester High School in California. Somehow I managed to stay on the honor roll, and then I accepted a baseball scholarship to the University of Santa Barbara, but only stayed there for one year. The truth is, compared to all of the athletically gifted kids at my school, I sucked at baseball at that level, but what I was good at was learning and remembering without having to study. You tell me something once and I get it. I think I have a photographic memory for everything.

After battling between whether to go to Moorehouse or Yale, or staying local, I got accepted to USC, where I graduated with honors, and where I also earned my medical degree from USC's School of Medicine. I spent the next five years of general surgery residency at Stanford University School of Medicine, and then three years of fellowship in cardiothoracic surgery at Loma Linda University. I'm an attending cardiac surgeon, so I am a faculty member, and it pays very well. But, my goal is to be the chief of cardiothoracic surgery, still an attending surgeon so that I can keep up with clinicals, but also in charge of financial and administrative aspects. That's where the real money is.

My mother took a stenographer course when we moved to L.A. and made fairly good money working for the courts downtown. And she even ended up marrying about ten years ago, so now she can think about retiring since she's creeping up on sixty. I take care of her financially anyway, whether she can pay her bills or not, so I don't know why she doesn't just quit her job. This dude, Mr. Cotton, had better look after her a little bit better because she sometimes complains about pain under her left arm and terrible headaches, but he stays in the garage working on his vintage Studebaker. He's a retired manager for the auto club. He can make that car more important all he wants. I'm keeping an eye on both of them.

I'm glad that Mom found a mate actually. Even though I think she could have done better than that old geezer husband of hers. But, who am I to talk? At least he's tied the knot.

I never had a steady girlfriend while in high school or college, but I was popular with the ladies. I experimented with Asian and white women, whom I liked just fine, and sexy Hispanic women are cool, too, very close to black women, but my preference is for my dark and lovely or light and fine, ladies of color . . . my hot and sassy sisters.

No desire for kids really. I've managed to remain childless. I always wear my hat, unlike my father. No one is going to claim that I'm their father, some adult child coming up to me at the age of twenty, telling me I dated their mother and that I owe them something for missing out. I heard that my father went through that enough. After he got older and stopped driving rigs, I heard that a few scorned members of his female fan club would sometimes call the oldies radio station where he worked part-time as a disc jockey, confronting him on the air. He'd calmly disconnect them, saved by the profanity delay switch. He always seemed to get away with his philandering ways.

You see, even though my father was only married twice, dude has fifty-six sons and seventy-eight daughters . . . that he knows of. And he even casually claims to have dated some three hundred forty women, and admits to impregnating over one hundred of them, some more than once like my mother. And the sad part is, as if that's not bad enough, rumor is, that he has some children he doesn't even know about. Yes, Rolling Stone Roosevelt is the name he answers to with misdirected pride.

Speaking of a true player-player by the way, excuse me. "Yo, boss man, what's up?" I asked my buddy Carlos Jenkins while headed past the front door of the hospital. It sounded like he had me on speaker.

"I can't call it. You tell me, bro."

I adjusted my Bluetooth, waving to the security guard. "I'm just headed up the elevator to begin an operation. How about you?"

He spoke on the heels of a yawn. "Man, I'm just getting out of bed, and might even go back for a couple of hours. I'm not leaving the house today, even for a minute. Superwoman Alice just left, and my ass is spent. My rear end is sore, just from pumping it all night long. That girl is a nympho from way back."

"You always did like the ones that had stamina."

"Oh, you know it." He bumped a full-volume Jay Z tune. "So, any word from your Latina lover, Salina, with the jealous, deadly husband?"

"Yeah, I saw her not long ago."

A passerby in the hallway offered a nod and a smile. "Good morning, Dr. Worthy." Tall and sturdy, with a broad jaw and damn near a shaved head, Dr. Lois Taylor walked by looking stern, a far cry from the friendly tone of her greeting.

"Good morning." I swore she needed a good enema, or a tight vagina. She had to be swinging or swung, one of em.

Carlos continued. "You're still hitting that, dude? Salina I mean." The word *astonished* best describes his tone.

"Man, somehow it's even better now than it was before. I can't figure it out."

"You're the man. Must be that revenge thing. So old girl can get down, huh?"

"You always worry me when you ask that. Hey look, dude, let me hit you up later. I need to chill for a minute before I get started. I'm just now walking into my office." I tossed my briefcase on my desk.

"No problem, do your thing. I'll get back. Hey, if you see that babe named Mary Jane, tell her I'll give her a call this afternoon."

"Later, C."

I've known long-dong Carlos since college. We were room-mates. He's the product of a Hispanic mother and a black father. He brags with pride that anatomically, he takes after his father. For some reason, he always felt like he had to compete with me, and it drove me crazy. For so long he tried so hard to hit on the women who liked me, that I just had to accept the fact that we were going to duplicate efforts. We've traded, passed along and shared stories. But, in a way, that crap grows tired. There are enough women in this world to go around without sharing, for sure. It just seems that we'd always end up in the same places.

Like here at the hospital. He's an on-call engineer who services the scanners and x-ray machines, so I see him while I'm here more than I see him outside of work. I knew he was eyeing my curvy Mary Jane. It's so like him to let me know that maybe there's some interest by telling me to give her a message for him. I ain't telling her a damn thing. If she's interested, that's between them. If he knows me at all, he knows I am or was getting that. Maybe that turns him on even more. And now dude is asking about Salina. I just know he'll find a way to date, or should I say screw, her, too. That's just how Carlos rolls. They say your friends say a lot about you. And I guess they're right. Yes, unfortunately, I guess they're right.

Chapter 7

After performing a successful bypass surgery on a forty-year-old male, I took a moment to sit and just be still.

That was the whole point of my regular meditation . . . to breathe and concentrate, attempting to gain mental focus and clarity. You have to have some way to balance your life with the complex procedures that I perform. I learned that in medical school.

I looked over at the grease board on my wall. The date rang of familiarity. I closed my eyes, but for some reason, all I could think about was my baby sister. I remembered. Today was the twenty-second anniversary of her, and her baby girl's, my niece's, untimely death. A few months before that, she and I had a conversation I'll never forget. It went something like this.

"Makkai, do you hear that?" her youthful, thirteen-year-old voice whispered from the lower bunk as though she were hearing things.

"Yes, I hear it," I spoke downward toward my baby sister.

She was snuggled under the denim blue comforter, tucked in to just under her china doll chin. "I can't sleep."

I slept on top of the covers, lying on my stomach, feet hanging off the twin bed. "Just relax. You'll be fine. You'll doze off in no time." I leaned down to get a night-light view of her.

Suddenly, my young ears filled with a loud, yet garbled sentence spoken by my mother.

"What's going on with Mama?" Fonda was curled up in a fetal position.

I looked toward the door. "She's obviously upset."

Mom ranted boisterously, "Don't you ever call this house again." And then instantly, her tone downshifted. "I don't need you to tell me anything. That's between my husband and me."

Three long seconds went by and the sound of a receiver slammed to its base took over.

Fonda simply spoke. "Makkai, Daddy is weird."

"Why do you say that?"

"He just is." She turned over to lie on her back, resting her hand over her swollen belly. By this time, my baby sister was well into her pregnancy.

"He's gone so much that it's hard to figure him out. But, I know that he breaks Mom's heart by not being around."

"He's not true to her, is he?"

"I don't think so, Fonda. But, you don't need to be worrying about anything. You just need to take care of yourself so that baby can stay in there as long as possible."

She played mute. "I like it when Dad's not here."

"Corrine, I'm home." Dad slammed the back screen door. Fonda jumped, and then resumed her fetal position.

Mom spoke to accompany the sound of her own sturdy, fast-paced footsteps. "Roosevelt, one of your little floozies just called here. I'm not taking this too much longer."

"Oh, woman, that's somebody just trying to start some stuff. I told you misery loves company. And I'm telling you again to stop listening to all of that stuff."

"Where were you?" It seemed as though she was purposely clanging pots and pans.

"I was driving that rig all the way from D.C. to back down this way. I'm exhausted and in no mood for this nonsense in my own house. Now, what's for dinner?"

Mom sounded different. "Nothing. You missed dinner. It's one in the morning."

"Next time, you need to put something in the icebox for me. I keep telling you that, woman."

She spoke with a tight jaw. "There won't be a next time, so you don't have to worry about me doing anything for you ever again."

"You are really talking trash tonight, woman. You'll snap out of it. You're not going anywhere."

Fonda spoke with reserve while they continued their verbal sparring. "Makkai, don't go to sleep tonight. Let's just talk until the sun comes up. Please."

"Hey, what are you two doing up?" Dad asked after the door creaked like the sound of an intruder entering a dark room in a horror movie. "Go to sleep, Makkai."

"Yes, sir."

"Good night, Fonda."

She gave a soft-spoken, "Good night."

Dad turned his right ear in her direction. "What? I didn't hear you."

"I said good night."

"All right, then."

As the faint bit of light faded, Fonda and I then heard their bedroom door close.

She still whispered. "Please, Makkai."

"Okay, Fonda. But, we have to keep it down. What do you want to talk about?"

"Anything. Just keep talking. That way, I'll know you're watching over me."

In an instant, my reflections halted into reality. It was like it was yesterday, but it was decades ago. My stomach panged and my throat swelled up and my heart actually ached. Knowing I had about thirty minutes before my next procedure, I suddenly grabbed my car keys and walked right back out of my office door, got into my ride, and headed down the street to the West Hollywood Cemetery, less than two miles away. It was my sanctuary when I needed to be reminded of the really important, basic things in life, like family.

I gazed over at my sister's light brown granite gravesite and fell to my knees with the warmth of the sun at my back. *Fonda Renee*

Worthy, it read . . . *daughter, sister, and mother.* I put my hands together and lowered my head.

Hey, Fonda. I've been thinking about you a lot more these days for some reason. I miss my baby sister. Things are okay with me. They'd be a lot better, though, if I could come to your house and visit you and your family. I wonder what type of man you would have married. I hope you got a healthy impression of what a man is, surely not from Dad, but maybe from me, maybe from someone. God took you and your daughter, my little niece, home when He wanted you, but that seems pretty selfish to me. Too young to die, so much life to live. Truth is, you don't have to go through this madness we deal with down here. Jealousy, hate, prejudice, poverty, anger, lust and sickness. Yeah, can't imagine why I'm sad for you. You've got it made. I'm the one left here with all of this life stuff.

But, memories of your innocence, and quietness, and kindness, and giving nature ring in my head every day. What if? What if Fonda had lived? The sweet-natured, square, straight-A student who was taller than me, with your thin self. But, as you can see, I grew taller after all. Eventually, I passed you up. I always wanted you to look up to me so I could watch over you. Now I'm looking up to you in heaven. I'll keep talking from time to time like you asked me to. I love you, Fonda. Always will.

Chapter 8

Salina

"Salina, you are one trifling, skank-ass wife if you won't bail your own damn husband out of jail."

I sat at my dining room table sippin' on a watermelon wine cooler with my juices flowing and my blood boiling. I swigged a major gulp and took a deep breath, forcing myself to gently place the bottle down on the table without shattering it into little pieces. Her dumb-ass comment rambled about in my head while my thoughts sped up. I squeezed and squeezed the cordless phone.

See, *mi esposo* is still in custody for his little choking incident and has a court date soon. They could release him on five hundred thousand dollars bond, which would cost me about fifty thousand. But, I decided not to when his little black chicken-head hoe called my house after she heard he was locked up.

One more sip. One slow swallow. One more inhale. One more exhale. I switched the phone to my other ear, but not before thinking perhaps I should hang up on this silly-ass freakazoid. Yet I replied. I just had to. "Why? So you can sneak around with my husband at my expense."

She blasted back. "Look, chica, isn't that what they call dirty Mexican girls?" She laughed at her own tired-ass sense of humor.

"I'll tell you one thing, from what I hear, you and your man both have a hankering for chocolate. So don't even trip."

"Bitch, you can kiss my Mexican ass."

"No, I wouldn't want to turn you out like your little boyfriend the doctor did."

"Look trick, you're just as pathetic as my husband. You two belong together." I stood and approached my patio, sliding the glass door open for some air, glancing out onto the deep-green blades of grass and colorful rosebushes that were blooming under the bright morning sun. The image, however, was not enough to turn my screwed-up mood around. "In the meantime what are you going to do, come over here and kick my brown butt? Both of you are foolish. He's so stupid that he tried to beat somebody up for fooling around when he was creepin' anyway. But, what your skanky little nappy headed ass needs to remember is that if you had it going on so tough, and if he was so into you, he wouldn't have cared about who I was with in the first place. Case closed, Hoe-Chica."

"Well, he sure as hell doesn't care now. He's coming home with me when he gets out."

"Yeah, after he gets done being somebody's bitch in that jail cell. He wouldn't be able to survive being locked up too long, any more than he'd be able to survive a day in your little hometown slum. He'd be better off being a little white homo in jail than living amongst you and your pet rats. Shouldn't you be feeding Ben?"

"You've got it all wrong."

"Don't fucking call my house again." I slammed the patio door shut and headed back toward the half-full wine bottle that called my name.

"Don't fucking fuck my man again."

"You can have his tired, soft dick ass," I told her, half yelling.

"I don't need your permission for that. Besides, he was always hard when he hit this."

"Goodbye, Shaquonda, or whatever your name is."

"My name is Sha-nay-nay."

I let out a single serious chuckle. "I knew it. Ghetto Queen." I clicked off the phone.

"Oh, Papi will stay in jail, that's for sure. Hoochie can *basa mi cuda* for all I care," I said out loud, slapping my own butt with one hand. I then guzzled the remaining wine and forced a swallow. "I don't give a shit."

A shattering crash of breaking glass sounded as my empty wine bottle met the kitchen wall. The cordless landed with a thud and then a crash, cracking into three pieces as it met the kitchen cabinet. My ass met the dining room chair as I covered my eyes and screamed up toward the ceiling. "Why? Shake it off, Salina. You can handle this. You don't need his sorry butt anyway." I sat back and reluctantly remembered.

I've been married to Tom Woodard for six years, since straight out of college. He was one pretty-ass ex-quarterback white boy, I'll give him that much. He never went any direction other than white back then, but I straight turned him out for real. I brought it on, sucking him down and fucking him up the right way.

And now, he has the nerve to be out there doing a hood rat sister and then get mad at me. Hell no, his butt is staying right where it is. Here I was dealing with my desire for a black man, feeling all guilty and shit, and he went off and got him a black woman, and a down-home ignorant one at that. Ain't that some bull?

Fool was always cock-blocking though, even back in college. I had a thing for this fine-ass, chocolate triathlete named Richard, but the women loved to call him Dick. Dick Perkins. I snuck away from Tom one weekend, and I'll be damned if Dick Perkins didn't get me hooked. He could fling that caramel dick like he could fling the very shot put he'd received a scholarship for. Tom showed up and pulled me away by my hair. Fool even threatened to kill Dick back then, so I had no choice but to let Dick go. By then, Tom and I were engaged, twenty thousand dollars into my mom and dad's pocket. But, I never forgot about what that shit felt like when Dick was all up in me. It was soulful and deep and nasty and intense, just like a porno flick. Black dick is a motherfucker.

But, damn, neither one of them could ever eat the pussy right like Dr. Makkai Worthy. So while Mr. Woodard is on lockdown, I'm going to keep letting Makkai do his thing. Hell, we hit it the night after my dumb excuse for a husband got arrested. It was some straight on, crazy ass, room smelling like booty and pussy, make-up punishment sex.

Grabbing my dustpan and broom, I swept and swept, and picked up the pieces of my husband-gone-astray tantrum. If only my man shit could be cleaned up that easily.

Chapter 9

Salina Alonzo Freak-mama Woodard . . . I hear her talking. But, I've always wondered why when a married woman fools around on her husband, it's the man she fools around with who is called the dog? Doesn't that make her a cheating, philandering cat?

So I see now that I'm not the first black dude that she'd "cliterally" come after. She's the type that if her best friend told her about a man she met who could toss the dick, Salina would hunt him down and show up at his doorway wearing nothing but a smile. I don't know why she's married anyway. In my opinion, she's not wife material. But, I'm at least glad she admits to loving the black dick because I've never seen a girl ride it like her. She's a sexaholic and she's as eager as any woman I've ever been with. She'll instantly take the damn lead, and once you put her in a position, she'll switch up on you just to gain control. She is triple-jointed limber and has a few different accents to go along with it—well, check this out from the night after her husband was arrested.

To straddle a horse vault in gymnastics with an end-to-end split that lowers one's middle point flat to the surface would have a lesser degree of difficulty than what Salina Woodard can do, even when standing on her head. I give her an eleven out of a possible ten. She spreads her flexed legs so wide and so parallel, with her perfect, fire engine red toes pointed west to east, flashing that sexy purple tattoo on her ankle, only so I can stand over her and do as I please. And I do aim to please, with my mouth and my hands and even my weapon if I want to go deep sea diving. And I do want to go deep sea diving. And I did. I guess she told you that we hit it the night after the arrest. But, allow me to take you there.

Her acrobatic demonstrations of her limberness amaze me every time. She can spin and sit and flop and flip and bounce and twirl and even squeeze herself so tight around me that I feel like I could be sucked in.

One warm evening, atop a California king-sized bed in room number 402 at the Ritz Carlton around the corner from her home in Torrance, I grinded my way inside of her, inch by inch.

"Salina, I don't know how that pipsqueak of a man handled you." The song on the radio channel on TV was *"I Need a Girl to Ride, Ride, Ride"* by Usher. How appropriate.

"He didn't."

"Well, I'm sure having fun trying."

"You need to take all of this pussy so his crazy ass is assed out. Don't leave any for anyone but you."

She smelled of Poeme by Lancôme. Her scent took a little trip through my senses, ringing a bell to remind me that this was the insatiable one. "Oh, I'm not."

"Is it good?"

"Yes."

"Yes, what?" She had the nerve to frown.

"It is good."

"Is it the best?"

"This is the best pussy I've ever had."

"I'll bet you say that to all the girls, Besides, didn't you say I'm just another pussy that got hooked? Isn't that what you said yesterday?"

"I said that because you were . . ."

"Because I was what, dammit?" She pumped like she was on a mission.

"You know I had to get you back for . . ."

"For what?"

I fully invaded her with every fierce grind. "For the fact that your man loved this pussy enough to try to kill my ass."

"You're damn right. Now who is it that's hooked tonight?"

"I am?"

"Who?"

"I am."

"Who the fuck are you?"

"Makkai."

"And Makkai belongs to?"

"Salina."

"Say my name again."

"Salina."

"Say my name. Louder."

Damn she fires me up. "Salina," I belted out as I probed her fleshy cavity.

"Your ass is going to have to deliver tonight, Dr. Feelgood. You were a bad boy. Now what's my name again?"

"Salina." Dampness coated my skin and hers. The wetness seeping from her lower hairline smelled spicy and sweet.

"You're never going to forget who am I again, are you?"

"No."

"No who?" That's my bad girl. The increasingly slushy sound of juices could be heard in between her every command.

"No, Salina."

"Now pull out and bend down and put you face up against my Spanish ass."

Just call me her soldier and call her my drill sergeant. I made my exit and my nose met her golden asshole within two-point-two seconds.

"Inhale. Smell it."

Sniffing was my pleasure. My dick was so hard from the visual that I could have cut raw diamonds.

"Now stick your tongue inside like it's a dick. Tongue-fuck me in the ass."

The point of my tongue penetrated her tightness and entered with a wet stiffness that sent her into moan-mode.

"Stick it so far inside that your eyes start tearing up. Do it right. I don't feel it deep enough."

Oh damn. "I know you feel that."

"Don't say a fucking word until I ask you to."

Aye-aye, ma'am. No wonder her husband went nuts.

"Now lick around my asshole until my pussy starts dripping. Stick your fingers inside so you can test it to see when it's ready."

Her cream met my middle finger, and then two more fingers begged to join in.

"Pull out so I can see. Do it now."

She eyeballed my middle fingers.

"No, not yet. Make it wetter."

Back in they went. Deeper.

"Lick it with more spit and flick your tongue like it has wings. Now kiss my asshole with a loud smack so I can hear it. Louder. Louder. You denied me and I want you to never forget this most valuable pussy again. Don't you know I'm the MVP? Oh I forgot. You're some hot-ass renowned doctor and you think you can just fuck with me like I'm some useless whore for you to disrespect. Suddenly, I forgot your name now. What's your name again? Say it."

"Makkai."

"Makkai, huh? Okay Makkai, now take those fingers out again and show me what comes out. And it had better be greasy."

The liquid sugar juices shone, with some of the heated glaze creeping down in between my fingers.

"Yeah, Look at that. See how turned-on you've got me right now? Is that how turned on you were yesterday when you denied me. Was your dick hard when you kicked me out of your office?"

My dick throbbed like it begged to answer. "Yes."

"I should have known. Bring that big hard dick up to my tight pussy hole and stick it in fast. Do it now."

I found her hole and inserted myself. "Like this?"

"I didn't ask you a question. You still don't have permission to talk. Do you think you're deep enough into Salina's pussy, huh?" She shoved herself deeper toward me. "Now you can answer me."

"Yes." I sped up my pace.

"I want every inch you can give me."

I flexed my ass muscles tighter and pulled all the way out, and then dove in deep and rough, aiming straight back, even feeling like I was moving some stuff around up in there. She didn't even flinch.

"Deeper."

I swear I was in her uterus.

"Deeper."

That shit talking was sure to lead to a major burst within only a few more pumps and she knew it.

"Oh, hell no. I feel that swelling up. You don't deserve that. You know what, Papi, I'm about to finish this off, but I need you to do what you do best. Now pull out."

I stopped my pumping frenzy and froze in place, squeezing the base of my dick to keep myself from shooting my load just in time.

"Put that mouth on my wet pussy. Do you hear me?"

"Si."

"Smart man. Then get down there and make it melt."

I exited her as slowly as I could and immediately put my mouth within two inches of her meaty vagina. The heat hit my face before my mouth ever touched her sensitive, rosy skin. I moved her vertical lips aside to allow for easy access. Her tip was dark pink and glossy and swollen and at stiff attention. I was amazed that she was actually quiet for two seconds. Her eyes were closed shut. I inserted my middle finger and kissed her tip and then swirled my tongue around it, making a flicking motion. And then I sucked it. She started to shout her x-rated verbalness again. The throb of her tiny muscle was powerful.

"Aaayyyyyy, Papi, oooouuui, yes. Suck that sucker. That's it, it's so good!! Yes, yes, yes!" Her head flung back, her long hair swung from side to side, covering her face, and she erupted like she was about to pee on herself. Her walls gripped my finger tightly. I could feel her insides contract and release, contract and release, contract and release. Now that is an undeniable orgasm. That, you can't fake.

She didn't let me get mine.

But, I will.

I deserved that, I guess.

That release of hers was good to the last drop.

Yes, that Salina is on fire with her controlling ass. Now as you can see though, I can handle a little nasty, horizontal shit talking. Makes it all the wilder with that carnal edge. And to be honest, I'll continue to hit it every now and then, if for no other reason than to get back at that psycho gargantuan husband of hers. Fool tried to kill me. That's wild and dominating Salina knocking on the hotel room door right now. Gotta go.

Chapter 10

Georgia

My mother lives about three miles away, just south of my neighborhood. When I need to go out, or when I'm having company in the early evening, she baby-sits for me with pleasure. I'm an only child and my mom is an only girl, too. Girls run in our family. She would have loved me to marry my deadbeat baby's daddy before he started trippin'. He accused me of some bogus shit right in front of my daughter. He accused me of being gay. I told that sorry excuse for a man that I love the dick too much to be gay. I just got tired of him being the one-minute man, one day per month. But, anyway, since he tripped like that, I cut him loose. I figured giving him six years of my life was long enough.

While he was with me, he seemed to be someone I could communicate with and someone I had a few things in common with. Like we both love to write. He was a sportswriter for a local news program in Los Angeles. Now he's an assistant producer for this well-known, forever bachelor sportscaster at NBC. They hang out after work all the time and that's what takes him to the strip clubs and nightclubs six nights a week. And so, Stardust came into the picture.

See, I met her first. I was sitting at this bar waiting for my girl to meet me for a drink after work, and this tall woman came over and sat down right next to me. Her generous backside devoured the bar seat while she crossed her long legs. She smiled, flashing picture perfect white teeth against her full, shimmery, ebony lips.

She spoke to the bartender. "The usual."

"Yes, ma'am."

A smile spread across her toffee-colored face.

She searched her Gucci bag and glanced over at me.

I gave a nod and looked over toward the front door. And then I looked back at her.

On the bar in front of her, the bartender placed a frosty drink topped with whipped cream. It was a combination of swirled green, with red and brown. She immediately took a huge sip through a wide, black straw, and laid a twenty on the bar. She gave an approving nod.

She took me into her sights again. She was already in mine. "Are you thirsty? You look like you could drink this with your eyes. It's called a Knockout."

I giggled. "Looks like it can. Knock someone out I mean. Sorry to be staring."

She spoke while stirring her drink counter-clockwise. "No problem. I just noticed you noticing me, that's all. I'm just here to enjoy a little relaxation juice."

"Relaxation juice?"

"You'd better know it. For real." She stretched out her words.

"Okay?"

She giggled. Her pretty breasts giggled too. Her hard nipples were pointing at me from under her low-cut tee. "And what are you drinking?" Her baby brown eyes were glued to my mouth.

I looked around the room again. "Oh, nothing. I'm waiting for a friend. I'll order when she gets here." I scratched the back of my neck.

"My, aren't you polite?" Her long, thick eyelashes curled up to her eyebrows.

"No, I just don't drink alone."

"You're not alone now." She flashed her smile.

"I guess I'm not."

"Your lips are beautiful. I love the way your tongue moistens them after a sentence."

Oh shit. "Oh really?"

"Really."

My eyes focused on the front door again. I tossed my bangs to the side, noticing a few beads of sweat along my forehead.

She spoke to the approaching bartender, shoving her money closer to him. "She'll have what I'm having."

I shook my head to both of them. "I don't know. I'm driving and that looks pretty strong. I was just gonna have one glass of white wine and get back home."

"Oh, lighten up. Just try one. Plus, you've got a friend coming who can be the designated if need be."

I nodded as I spoke. "Oh she's definitely not the designated type. But, I guess there's no harm in having just one."

She cracked a grin.

"But, what about you?" I asked her. "Aren't you driving?"

She looked at an area near my waist as she spoke. "I live right next door. My name is Stardust. Push comes to shove, you can crash at my place if you'd like. If you've had too much to drink, that is."

"Like I said, I'm just having one. But, my name is Georgia."

"Nice to meet you, Georgia."

My friend stood me up and never called. I ended up having about four Knockouts and eventually, before it was all said and done, four clit-busting orgasms courtesy of Stardust. Needless to say, the down low did come out that night.

But, from what Stardust tells me now, weeks later Rydell came in all by his lonesome and met her while sitting at the same bar. He mentioned me by name and cried on her shoulder about his daughters. Small world. Seems she was a regular. Next thing, he was at her place, too. Turns out she only gives head to the dudes. She only had dick up inside of her once before and that was a guy she tried out in high school on a prom date her parents set up. She did it just to see if the feelings she was catching for the girls were bogus or not. Turns out they weren't.

After that, she had a woman for a few years who broke her heart by going back to dick-land on her. I can't say that I blame her. Now, I guess she just assumes that once a bisexual woman she's interested in has bonded to a penis, they'll eventually go back to men anyway, so she doesn't even trip. She knows me. I already told her.

Yes, Stardust was good, even without letting the guys inside. Shit, head-wise she was maybe even better than me. No wonder Rydell never tried to come back to me. There's so much damn temptation for the men in this world. Hell, there's a whole lot of women out there willing to give it up after just one drink. I guess I should know.

I work as a freelance writer. Sometimes stations call me in and sometimes they don't, but to fill in money-wise, I had to get creative. So I came up with a name on the Internet called Cook4U, which gets em every time. Folks love to eat. Only I log into the ladies-looking-for-ladies chat rooms. I'd never let my nosey baby's daddy know, even though he was on to me, or even let my best friend know, or my mother, or Makkai for that matter. He's discussed how he hates women who act straight and then sneak to be with other women. He'd rather they come on out of the closet and be one hundred percent gay. Well, call me on the down low if you want, but no matter how much I try to fight it, I need the touch of a woman every now and then. It's simply recreational, no big deal. However, I definitely don't want a relationship with one.

But, right now, being with women is a way to pay my bills. That's because my old boss, Tucker Hill, who was my news director when I worked in Orange County, pays me to hook him up. And it's easy, because these girls think they're getting me, when they're really getting him, too. But, by then they're stripped down and raring to get their freak on with me. And even if they don't let Tucker "in," it's fine with me. I still get paid.

But, of course, like I said, Makkai doesn't know a thing about it. And if I have my way, he never will.

Chapter 11

Every now and then I get a chance to get out and get all dressed up to attend an award ceremony. As it turns out, I have a formal event coming up soon. It's a ceremony sponsored by the NAACP that honors accomplished professionals in our community. One category is contributions in the field of medicine, and I have been selected as this year's recipient. I really don't want to go alone, though. Most of my peers are married or have had longtime mates. When it's a company function I usually take my mother, and she gets a kick out of it.

This time it would be great to have a nice-looking lady on my arm. Don't want to bring anyone I work with. That'd be too close for comfort. The decision lies in which one will not see it as a marriage proposal, and which one will be classy enough to be seen on my arm. In spite of what we do behind closed doors, can they be class in the streets?

"Don't you have a birthday coming up soon, too? Who are you spending that with?" my mom asked me as I bounced my dilemma off of her, sitting at my desk at work.

"First things first, Mom." I could hear Pastor Paula White's ministry in the background. Mom didn't go to church in California like she did when she was in Florida, but she did know the Bible, and she did love her spiritual shows on Trinity Broadcasting.

"Baby, bring the girls on by here. I'll pick one out for you."

"Mom, it's not worth going through all that trouble."

"Actually I was just kidding, son. But, heck, it would be nice to just meet someone who's in your life, just on general purpose. I can't remember the last time that happened."

"I brought Patricia, that fifty-year-old, by a few years ago for Thanksgiving dinner. You don't remember her?"

"You didn't bring her by. You invited her and she drove herself over here and ate, and then you announced that you had to leave, so she left first."

"Well, still, she's someone I was dating. And I remember implicitly, I had to leave because I got an emergency call at the hospital."

"Okay, if you say so. Whatever happened to her anyway? Was it that she was almost old enough to be your mom?" Mom joked. I could hear her smile.

"Mom." I sat up and began scrolling through some appointments in my phone book.

"Son, I know you have nothing against older women, but she looked older than me."

I cleared my throat. "Anyway, Mom, she caught a case of the wife-wannabes. She kept suggesting we buy rings and then kept leaving things over my house to make excuses to come back."

"Oh, you actually brought her to your house? That was serious then."

"Contrary to what you think, that's not unusual. But, she just wanted to move too fast, and when I told her my feeling about wanting to slow things down, she cursed me out, called me a commitment-phobic jerk and slammed down the phone. And then she called to say she was sorry. I don't go backwards. Not often, anyway. You know that, Mom."

"Yes, I do. But, have you ever thought about her question?"

"Mom."

"Really, Makkai. I've asked myself that question, too. Don't you think I want grandbabies one day, boy?"

"You'll have grandkids, Mom. I'm only thirty-seven. I've got time." I leaned back again, rocking in my high-back desk chair.

"Yes, but you'll be forty before you know it."

"Excuse me but I've been a little busy in case you haven't noticed."

"Oh, I see what's going to happen. You'll end up with some sweet young thang half your age, I just know it."

"Not necessarily."

"I don't know too many forty-year-old women who want to push a baby out of their wombs that late in life. That is, if their eggs have any juice left anyway."

"Mom, stop. Besides, I might marry someone who already has kids."

"True. But, you've got to have a son of your own. I picture you being a father to a cute little boy you can play baseball with and do guy things with. And as brilliant as you are, those genes just can't go to waste. Surely you got your brain from my side of the family." She laughed out loud for a few seconds. "Anyway, you'd make a great dad."

I followed her laugh with a chuckle. "Yes, I got my smarts from you. But, you know it's not like I need to carry on the Worthy name. Lord knows there are enough Worthy males on this planet."

"I won't argue with you on that one. All I'm saying is, you've got that big old house in Hollywood Hills, you make all that money, you have two fancy cars, you've achieved all that success, and there's no one to share it with. Don't end up finding out that it's a lonely way to live. You need love in your heart too. That's what you need, Makkai."

I stood up and took off my suit jacket. "I've got enough love for you to last my entire lifetime and yours, Mom."

"Well, that's sweet. I'm talking about a woman of your own."

"Anyway, I'll pick you up this weekend so you can get a dress to wear. Is Mr. Cotton going?"

She snapped her tongue like she was from the hood. "Why do you call him Mr. Cotton? His name is Al."

"Is he coming?"

"He'll be in Charlotte that weekend, seeing about a car he wants to buy."

"Good."

"Makkai, stop. I'd say 'Mr. Cotton' has been in your life long enough for you two to bond, even a little."

"Mom, don't get me started. That man is living in that house I bought you without even showing enough motivation to repair a leaky faucet. And the next time he doesn't go with you to get the results of a biopsy, I'm going to corner him and give him a piece of my mind. He's hardly a father figure to me."

"I'm not with him so he can be a father for you. I'm with him for me, to be my mate and my companion. And besides, I told him he didn't have to go with me to that appointment. I wanted to be alone"

"That's not something a wife should be able to keep you from going to, whether she wants to be alone or not."

"What would you know about what a wife needs?"

"Oh, low blow, Mom. But, I'm just saying."

"I hear you, Makkai. I was just kidding. But, you know that the one thing that comforts me is just knowing you're there for me."

"Always, Mom." I turned off the light to my office.

"I love you."

"I love you, too, Mom. I'll check on you later."

"And I'll be glad to meet whoever you end up choosing. I'll see you this weekend. I should be back from church at around eleven."

My girl.

Chapter 12

Early in the morning, I headed down the hall to scrub for an eight-o'clock open-heart surgery on a middle-aged female with a ruptured aorta.

I walked into the overly bright operating room once I got all gloved and masked for surgery. The patient's body was cooled, and the perfusion technologist placed her on a cardiopulmonary bypass machine, which does the same job the heart would do, but allows us to operate on a heart that is still, as opposed to one that is beating and moving. Modern technology gives us more time to do what we need to do. But, the hours do fly by.

As I made the lengthy and deep incision, I was suddenly amazed at how routine surgery had become. As much as I remained focused and deliberate, I was still able to perform yet think. Think about my life, and my family, and my future. Here I was, using my talent and education to repair damage to an organ. A vital, major organ that served as the most important, central focal point in the body, aside from the brain, yet and still, each needed the other in life-sustaining ways in order to function. Kind of like a man and a woman, I suppose. This patient had high blood pressure, and the years of strain on the heart muscle had enlarged her heart to double the size with so much pressure that the aorta had swollen, and the damage needed to be manually repaired. Stress in life can do that to anyone. Life is challenging and beautiful all at the same time.

Before I knew it, I was suturing her up, and again sustaining her system by allowing her heart to take it from there. And it did. The technician gave me the thumbs-up look. It was an awesome responsibility, yet from where I sat in my life, it was a once fulfilling job that just wasn't quite enough anymore. I loved it. But, more and more lately, I was feeling as though I was the one who really needed heart surgery, perhaps to open up my heart.

After a long day of two successful major operations, I was glad to finally be able to shut it down and head home from a nearly twelve-hour, marathon shift. I wanted to make a decision about who to invite to this award dinner, but the more I thought about it, the more I was leaning toward going unescorted. It just seemed a whole lot easier.

Since Salina freaks out, even though we still kick it, she's not even a consideration. I dare not call Patricia back after the way we ended our short run. She's the one who bought me that nameplate, having branded me Dr. Feelgood in the first place. It's a shame I wasn't ready for her because whether she was fifty or not, we really were compatible. Mary Jane and I are just friends, but being that she's a coworker, probably still mad at me, and kind of shy anyway, I'd better not. Monday is professional and attractive and sophisticated, but I'm not sure I'm ready to bring Miss Freak of the Week around this crowd. Plus, they know she was dating a patient of mine anyway. Besides, she comes off a little strong sometimes. And she just doesn't come off as the girl-on-the-arm type.

But, for now, I'm thinking Georgia might work. Even though she could have starred in L.L. Cool J's video for *"Around the Way Girl,"* she does have some class, I think. Every time I hear the lyrics "I wanna eat you like a cookie when I see you walk," her sexy strut comes to mind. Okay, but the point is, she's pretty, she's intelligent, she's personable, and I've known her long enough to where I don't believe she'd think it means something.

"So, what do you think?" I asked from my mobile.

"I'd love to. I'd be honored actually. Hold on a second, please."

Georgia tried to muffle the sound. "Girls, get in that room and close the door until I tell you to come out. Can't you see Mommy is on the phone? What did I tell you about that? Go in the room, now. I'm so sorry, Makkai. Yes, I'd love to go with you." She shifted from sweet, to wicked, to sweet again in no time flat.

"Okay, so do you have anything to wear?"

"I'm sure I have something in that closet." She giggled, sounding kind of unsure.

"How about if I drop off some money in a little while and you can go shopping for something formal? I'm wearing a black tux with a white shirt and tie, so I'd say all white or all black would be good. Keep it sophisticated."

"Okay."

"Fine then, I guess I'll see you in a little while. I've got a quick stop to make to catch the tail end of a USC alumni get together, but I'll be by after that. Maybe in a couple of hours, maybe less."

"I'll be up. See you then. And, Makkai, congratulations."

My boys sat at the long, double-sided, catch-action bar at Magic Johnson's Fridays in Ladera. It was standing room only, as usual. To find a seat in this place is like winning the California lottery. I used to take time to make this my regular hangout, but it had been months since the last time I stopped by. Tonight gave me a reason to definitely stop on by, if only for a minute.

Turning from the bar to eye me as I walked up, Dr. Hightower, the chiropractor, asked, wearing his three-quarter-length camel suit, "So, you're getting the NAACP award, huh, Doctor? What up, man?"

"Yeah." I gave handshakes as I walked in and stood behind him and another doctor.

"Oh, you're big-time now, huh?" asked Dr. Winton Humphrey, a dentist who owned his own practice in the Crenshaw area.

"Not even. What's happening?"

"It's all good. Just don't forget about us down here while you're flying high."

"Anyway, how'd the alumni banquet go?" I asked.

Dr. Hightower half replied, rubbing his goatee, eyeing a stallion-looking lady who walked by. "It was cool. The new president spoke." He looked our way. "Boy was as bland as a medical book."

"I'll bet."

Dr. Humphrey continued. "He even tried to tell an x-rated joke about how the tongue is the strongest muscle in the body. It was just the way he said it, being that the brother looked so square that no one even went there with him."

Having heard Dr. Humphrey's every word, Carlos's female friend asked as she and Carlos walked up, "Is that true, Doctor? About the tongue I mean?"

Dr. Humphrey replied, "Not that I know. But, it can be a powerful tool. Though, it's not *the* tool, if you know what I'm saying." He gave her the eye.

"Hey, bros, what's up?" said Carlos, high-fiving and smiling big. "Man, I was told that some lions mate over fifty times a day."

Carlos's friend said while grinning wide, "I wanna be a lion in my next life."

"Hell, a pig's orgasm lasts thirty-minutes," Carlos added.

Carlos' female friend corrected herself. "Cancel that, I wanna be a pig." She laughed.

"I'm with you," Dr Hightower said, inspecting her from her forehead to her ankles. His eyes licked her up and down.

Carlos looked at his friend. "What are you laughing at? You women don't deserve thirty minutes. A female praying mantis can't make love to the male until after she rips his head off."

Everyone laughed together.

Dr. Humphrey responded, "Sounds the closest to a woman in my opinion. That's a sister's problem today, always tearing the black man down."

"No comment," I said. With nowhere to sit, and knowing Georgia was waiting on me, I just had to excuse myself. "On that note, I've gotta get going."

"Yeah, me, too," Carlos replied, looking at his watch.

"You two just got here," said Dr. Humphrey.

"Yeah, but we've got places to go," said Carlos. Both of us waved, as we headed toward the door. He left his female friend sandwiched in between the doctors.

"Where are you headed?" he asked.

"To a friend's house."

"Don't hurt her, man."

I looked back at him as we exited the front door together. "Never. Hey, I thought you came with that girl."

"Yo, what up, Dr. Worthy?" a gentleman asked whom I'd never seen before in my life.

"Hey now. Nothing much."

Carlos told me, "No. She's just someone who runs the switchboard at the office. Actually, she just pulled me aside and asked me about your ass."

"Oh, she's cute, believe me, but I've got my hands full."

"Like I said, don't hurt em." He pulled off in his truck, me in my Benzo. That's my boy. He'll surely hit that eventually. That's just the kinda brotha Carlos is.

Chapter 13

Georgia

"This means something," I told my mom the next morning from my cell phone. Makkai left at five. I had a quick writing gig that I was headed to at the radio station, just from ten to two o'clock. Makkai didn't get any sleep, and I've only had a couple myself. I'll be good for nothing today.

Mom's tone was drab. "What are you talking about, it means something? That man has a whole lot of responsibilities and hasn't come out and said anything of the sort. You told me the way it is with Makkai is just fine with you anyway."

"It is, but for him to ask me to his award show after all these years, I think he's coming around."

"Coming around to what?"

"To the idea of taking this to the next level."

"Georgia, he didn't ask you to marry him. It's just a date."

"Mom, I'm going to get to meet his mother and his coworkers during a very special occasion in his life. He must see a future with me. And I know I'm the only one he's seeing."

"Oh, I say unless you've talked about monogamy, don't ever assume that. Besides, don't get your head all up in the clouds. Come on back down to reality. Now, where are you going to buy that dress from?"

"Probably Nordstrom. Can you watch the kids tonight while I shop?"

"No problem."

"And how about them spending the night on the twenty-seventh, the night of the event? I think it's at like seven o'clock."

"Sure, they can."

"Thanks, Mom."

"No problem. By the way, your dad's coming over tomorrow night." Suddenly, she sounded upbeat.

Suddenly, drab owned me. "Mom, not again. What's goin' on with you two?"

"We're just talking."

"After twenty years of him leaving you and hooking up with some other woman, you're just talking to him?"

"Georgia, honey, he left because I stayed out all night, remember?"

"Yeah, but he could have forgiven you and kept his family together. If you ask me, he was looking for an excuse."

"Georgia, not all men are dogs, you know."

"If you say so." I took a quick peek into the rearview and my frown lines were talking louder than I was.

Mom said, "I'll talk to you later. Those little girls are all ears right about now, I'm sure. They don't miss a beat. Especially since you're talking about their grandfather."

"I already dropped them off, Mom."

"Good. See you tonight, dear."

"Bye."

The main entrance to the W Hotel in Westwood was absolutely fabulous, with huge, life-sized silver trophies and black balloons aligned all up and down the canopy-covered driveway. We stepped out of the black stretch limousine where there was actually a red carpet set up.

"You look so pretty," I told Makkai's sweet, friendly mother, who had on a black knee-length dress with a black fishnet shawl and low-heel velvet pumps.

She eyeballed me from head to toe, putting her hand on my shoulder. "Child, you look like you could be in one of those *Ebony Fashion Fair* shows. She's beautiful, Makkai." She put her arm through his.

"Thanks, Mom. You both look beautiful. I see you wore red," he whispered to me from the corner of his mouth with a glimmer of a forced smile.

"Yes, red goes with everything."

Flashbulbs went off, shining upon Makkai like he was the president or something. But, the president had nothing on him this night.

His suit was Armani black, his satin tie was pearl white, his shoes were shiny new patent leather Hugo Boss, and he looked like a million bucks. He stood in between us as we walked inside and were escorted to our table.

"Hello, Dr. Worthy," said a distinguished-looking man, the head of the NAACP. "We're honored to have you here."

"I'm honored to have been chosen. This is my mother, Mrs. Cotton, and my friend, Georgia Manley."

"Hello," he said to us both, slightly bowing our way.

We responded simultaneously, "Nice to meet you."

He spoke again to Makkai. "The work you do is simply amazing, Doctor. And you're a role model for so many young people all over the country."

Mrs. Cotton smiled, taking her seat beside her renowned son.

Before long, main course meals were served that included a red leaf vinaigrette salad, shrimp-covered salmon and asparagus spears, and a buttery yellow rice covered with hollandaise. The mood was upbeat and the company was great. Sharing our table was Dr. Lois Taylor, who worked with Makkai.

"So, Dr. Worthy, what's next on your list of accomplishments?" Speaking in a smoky voice, she grinned at only him, sitting there with her broad shoulders, wearing a low-cut, sunny yellow taffeta pantsuit. She didn't have very much on top, and her medium brown face wasn't much to write home about, but she spoke as if one had better get to writing. Anyway.

"Nothing planned, Dr. Taylor, just enjoying each day as it comes."

She took a sip of her red wine. "You seem to have your bases covered."

"What do you mean?" Makkai took a small bite of his vegetable and chewed like he had a large piece of tough steak to deal with.

"A great career, voted-for awards, a beautiful mom and a beautiful lady by your side."

"I could say the same about you, Doctor."

"Yes, but there's no man at my side. I'm working on that, though." She raised her glass and took a bigger sip.

"You won't have a problem," Makkai said without looking at her, only cutting his fork into his baked fish.

"No, you won't," said Mrs. Cotton, giving a nod to signal her agreement, or to deliver her son from Dr. Taylor's clutches.

I said nothing. Dr. Taylor looked at me with a wink and nodded. I immediately delved into my vanilla crème brûlée.

"And this evening, the recipient of our distinguished Daniel Hale Williams award, named after the great black surgeon who performed the first prototype open heart surgery back in 1893, is a gifted specialty surgeon who works in the field of adult heart surgery. He chairs several organizations, as well as being the vice-president of the Society for Thoracic Surgeons. He has pioneered efforts on the national health-care scene advocating research into heart disease in the black community, being that cardiovascular disease is the leading cause of death amongst African American men and women. Ladies and gentlemen, please welcome, Dr. Makkai Jerome Worthy," said last year's recipient, Dr. Robert Anderson.

"Jerome?" I asked his mother as we all stood in unison, while I sort of snickered.

"That was my father's name," Mrs. Cotton said with pride, putting her hands together for her accomplished son.

"I see." I felt as though I should not have said it like that. But, dang, I guess I really was making fun. Makkai did not look like a Jerome. Bad girl, Georgia, bad girl. Surely his mom had at least one strike against me already.

As Makkai approached the podium, Dr. Anderson handed Makkai the bronzed statue. Makkai stood smiling like a winning politician, slightly bowing until the applause ceased. Dr. Lois Taylor was the last one at our table to take her seat again.

"Wow, I am so honored to be acknowledged in this way. You go through life just doing what you do and in no way do you ever expect anything in return. I enjoy helping people and treating patients who look to me for my training and knowledge. You pray that you make the best decision, because it really is all in God's hands. We, as doctors, don't have as much control over the outcomes of our patients' health as people think we do. It's just about making timely medical decisions and letting God's healing hands do the rest. I get a chance to go to work and perform the very same surgeries I watched being performed from those observation galleries while I was a junior and senior in medical school. And now I get to share my commitment to provide the best medical care possible, and interact with patients and families and my fellow colleagues in the medical profession. I'm living a dream come true. And it's only just begun.

"I'd like to thank a team of so many people, first being those fantastic folks who I work with, who I've learned from, who have helped me, and who have supported me. But, mainly I could not possibly do what I do without my beautiful mother, Corrine Cotton, my rock and my roots. She always told me that greatness is on the other side of inconvenience. And that there's no elevator to success, you have to take the stairs. Thanks Mom, for raising me to believe I could do anything."

She smiled and blushed, humbly and demurely looking around at everyone who applauded.

Makkai delivered a respectful nod her way and placed his hand over his heart.

She blew him a major kiss, and wiped her right eye with her napkin.

"I'd also like to thank God for my many blessings, for my health, and for my family. And I'd like to thank the NAACP for this prestigious Daniel Hale Williams award, and for the greatness that his name and the organization stand for. As a whole, the NAACP serves a great purpose in the advancement of our race. So I thank you again. May many, many blessings come your way. I'm honored and humbled. Good night."

As Makkai moved away from the podium, not one person remained seated. He held tight to the statue, taking the few steps down from the stage and back toward the table, stepping along with the sound of many clapping hands and loud whistles. He approached his mother who had tears in her eyes. He hugged her and then stood next to me as the applause dissipated, taking my hand and squeezing it firmly as we took our seats at the same time.

Next thing we knew, after a few more awards were handed out, it was time for a little booty shaking, grooving to everything from "*Boogie on Reggae Woman*," to the latest cut by Ludacris.

"Go ahead with your bad self," I said to Makkai's mom as she danced next to me, working it out with the gentleman who was the head of the NAACP. He actually taught her how to step in the name of love.

"Don't think I can't get my groove on now," she told me, allowing her smile to take over her face.

"Mom's dropping it like it's hot," Makkai said, looking thrilled by her joy.

He danced with everyone, including doing the cha-cha with Dr. Lois, Gotta-Find-Me-a-Man, Taylor. But, I snatched him away when "*I Don't See Nothing Wrong*" by R. Kelly began. It was time to slow dance and she needed to back up. One song is my absolute limit for sharing. There'll be no bumpin' and grindin' with my man.

I must admit that the evening was a blast.

My belly was full.

I looked good.
And I ended up barefoot with a buzz.
Dancing with the finest man in the world.
The man of my dreams.
Dr. Feelgood.

Chapter 14

Georgia

"It was nice meeting you," I told Makkai's mother as the limousine pulled up to drop her off first. We sat across from her in facing seats.

"Nice meeting you, too, young lady. You're a beautiful girl. And, Makkai, I'm proud of you, son. You looked so great up there. Thanks for allowing me to tag along."

"You'll always be front and center, Mom."

"You two have a good evening." She put her hand on her son's knee. "Makkai, I'll talk to you tomorrow."

"Not so fast. I'm walking you to the door."

"Makkai, I'll be fine."

"No, Mom. I know Mr., sorry, Al, is gone and you're home alone, so I don't think so." He moved from beside me and slid over across the pewter-colored leather seat and toward the door. He stepped out first and offered his hand. She grabbed on and stepped out, and they talked all the way to the door of her yellow house with the white picket fence.

When Makkai got back in, he sat across from me. "Did you have fun?"

"I did. That was a great ceremony and the food was great, too."

"It was, wasn't it?"

I slipped off my jeweled high-heel sandals, wiggling my toes. "And your mother is the nicest woman in the world."

"She's pretty special."

"I showed her pictures of the girls. She said she wants to meet them one day."

"Oh, she did? They are some cutie pies."

"I told her you'd met my mom, too."

"Okay."

I rubbed the souls of my feet. "So, Makkai, how do you know Dr. Taylor?"

"Dr. Taylor is in my department. She's a coworker, why?"

"Just wondering."

"Georgia, you can just cut that right on out. I had a great evening and want to keep it positive."

"So do I."

"Good."

A while later, after the driver turned up the oldies station at Makkai's request, the car pulled into the driveway and up to Makkai's front door.

"Do you want to come in?"

I was a little bit surprised, but you know I had to play it off. "Come in? Sure."

Unlike the first-lady treatment he gave his mother, he got out and headed straight to the driver to give him a tip.

I carefully stepped out, looking toward my car, which was parked in the circular driveway.

"Your car will be fine there."

This man's Hollywood Hills house is a magnificent sight to see. Makkai had it going on. It was huge, with a flat roof, but it was tri-level, with white stone columns along the front door that led to two, twelve-foot-tall double doors. Lion's head doorknockers hung in brass.

We went in through his four-car garage and stepped into a spacious sunken kitchen with gray and black granite countertops and matching floors. He had a walnut island in the middle of the kitchen that was bigger than a king-sized bed. All of his appliances were shiny black, and the faucets and lighting fixtures were stainless steel.

"Can I get you something to drink?"

"Oh, no, I'm fine."

He placed his grand award statue on his marble entryway table. "Make yourself at home. My bedroom is upstairs and to the left, two flights up to the top floor. Or you can take the elevator, right here." He pointed toward the hallway.

I just stood and stared from the doorway of his kitchen to the sprawling living room with white carpet and toffee brown leather furnishings. He had a formal fiberglass table that sat twelve. Beyond the dining room was a panoramic view that spanned from the Hollywood sign, to most of the city from downtown to Century City, and almost to the shoreline of the Pacific.

From the back, his home sat on stilts, high on a hill. And down below, far below, was a black-bottom, Olympic-sized swimming pool, with black and white outdoor furniture, a circular bar, a light green tennis court and a red clay basketball half-court.

My jaw remained dropped. "Makkai, this is absolutely beautiful."

He spoke as he led the way. "I got this house for a steal years ago. I've made a lot of improvements. Believe me, it didn't come like this. Here, I'll show you the rest of the house, including my office and guest rooms, and I have a weight room if you want to use it in the morning. But, I hope we head up to that bed in a minute. I am dead tired, Georgia."

We were both tired actually, finding ourselves lying down as soon as everything but our underwear came off.

I lay still on my back, checking out his massive bedroom with floor-to-ceiling beveled mirrors everywhere, a black marble fireplace, two huge suede sofas and a headboard that spanned along the entire wall.

In an instant, Makkai was snoring. I didn't even know he snored. Maybe because I'd usually fall asleep before him, just in postorgasm mode. But tonight, there was no sex . . . just being together.

Before I knew it, I was up standing up in my coral panties and staring outside of the sliding glass door that led to a beautiful, large balcony.

I wondered if the alarm would go off if I went out there for a little air. I looked back at Makkai, sound asleep, and as my eyes made it back to the view, I saw his Sidekick on his oak end table next to the sofa, illuminated by the tiny lights of his headboard. The bad girl in me told me to pick it up. The good girl in me told me to take my ass to sleep.

As I scrolled through, my heart started racing frantically. With every number that appeared, a beat pounded just as strong as the curiosity grew and more panic started to rise. What am I doing? But, then again, who are these women? Same area codes, different area codes, unfamiliar area codes. I just had to know. I picked up a Post-it and pencil from the end table and started to write. My jealous hands were shaking. The incoming calls were frequent. The outgoing calls were similar. I carefully and quickly replaced his phone on the side table, tiptoeing all the while, and made my way to my purse beside the bed, taking out my cell. I headed to the enormous ebony bathroom and closed the door, locking it behind me. I pressed star sixty-seven so my number wouldn't show up and I dialed.

This is Royale. I'm not in right now.
This is Magenta, I promise to call you back.
This is Salina.
This is Monday.
Hi, this is Mary Jane.

Damn, why do women now leave their names on their announcements? They make it so damn easy. So if there are men living with all of these women, where are they, are why aren't their voices on the recordings? What am I doing? Surely these are just friends. And he'll say that I'm a stupid dumb bitch for violating his privacy anyway. Yes, that is what this will be all about. Oh, hell, I had to call just one more.

"Hello?" a soft, sexy voice answered.

"Hello."

"Who's this?"

"Who's this?"

"Hello? Who is this?"

I shut the phone. The voice sounded familiar.

Why is it that when people are busted, they blame you for the violation? Point is if there's nothing to find, there's nothing to worry about. He'll tell me he doesn't go around snooping through my things, so how dare I go around snooping through his, and that I can't come to his house anymore. But, the point is, this is not about what he would do. He would say it doesn't matter to him, just so it won't matter to me. He wants you to chill like he has chilled. He's not jealous or insecure because it's not like that. Well, maybe it's because you haven't given him a reason to think there's someone else. And, you're not him. You're you. You know right from wrong. And this is wrong. But, two wrongs don't make a right, and what you won't tell me, this call log will.

The real deal is . . . men are fucking dogs. They are never satisfied. They are greedy. They lie. They are running around in a world of so many women per man that the thought of having ten women to choose from at any given time just causes spasms of pumped blood from their brains to their dicks. Hence, a hard-on. He can have a fine-ass Halle at home and still check out a hottie, wondering what it feels like to be inside of her. He can be with her, and take her to lunch, and talk to the other throughout the day, and sneak by her house in the afternoon, and see her for dinner, and make a run by her house at around midnight. And call you to say he can't wait to see you the next day. I'd rather you be with someone else, missing me, than you be with me, missing her.

How come I'm not enough for Makkai? Oh, that's right, he's Dr.

Feelgood. Well, Dr. Feelgood is every man who is a liar, a player, a flake, a punk, a mama's boy, a hound, a weirdo. Just like my no-good daddy.

I am so damn angry I could lose my mind.

With way too much running through my head, I had no choice but to get out of his bed at seven in the morning because Makkai's alarm went off since he had to get up early. I didn't get a wink of sleep, and I didn't get to slip on some of his clothes to work out in his weight room either.

He made a slow trek to his bathroom, brushed his teeth, and then threw on some boxers. After washing my face, I slowly put my clothes back on, and then we headed downstairs.

"What's up?" He read my face as we walked outside.

I rubbed my eyelids. "Just tired." I tried to play it off, unsure how I would approach him just yet.

"Okay, well, try to get some sleep at home. You'll be fine. I'll talk to you later." He gave me a weak peck on the lips as he closed the door to my car, and then watched me pull off, up the driveway and out the electronic double gate.

I rode way past the posted speed limit, still wearing my red slinky halter gown, tapping my French manicured acrylic nails along the steering wheel, and singing along with the full-volume words to "*I Hate You So Much Right Now*," by Kelis. I rolled down all of the windows, breeze blasting through my hair and against my face, and screamed at the top of my lungs, "Oh yeah, I forgot, Makkai . . . we were only fucking, right?"

Chapter 15

"Today, we are honored to have a few distinguished guests in our midst," said baritone-voiced, afro-wearing Pastor Smith. Later that morning, the applause at the mega-church dissipated.

Pastor Smith wore a wheat-colored, double-breasted, three-quarter-length, three-piece, tailor-made suit made with the finest gabardine material, accented by a pink silk handkerchief, and two-tone cognac David Eden alligator and crocodile shoes. He was beyond clean; he was Mr. Clean.

The arena-styled church with deep rose-colored theatre-style seats was large and packed.

Pastor Smith spoke as smooth as he looked after the congregation had heard the gospel choir sing a moving spiritual rendition of Hezekiah Walker's "*Jesus is My Help*."

"First we have Ms. Tanya Hart, well-known entertainment news anchor and, from what I hear, an awesome singer. Please welcome Ms. Hart." He led the applause. "Maybe one day you'll come and sing with our choir. I'm sure our congregation would love that. And we have Mr., or should I say Dr. Makkai Worthy, renowned heart surgeon. This man has been performing complicated heart surgeries for many years, and he's a past president of the Black Surgeons Foundation. Ladies and gentlemen, please welcome Dr. Makkai Worthy."

I sat back down as quickly as I stood. The churchgoers clapped. Someone heckled and made inaudible noises.

"I just know I didn't hear someone whistle. And don't tell me it was the Lord. Ladies, see now, you need to come to our next *Women Thou Art Loosed* conference conducted by Pastor Jakes next month.

The churchgoers were amused.

"Well, thanks for coming, both of you, Ms. Hart and Dr. Worthy. We're glad to have you. And to all of you, thanks for blessing *yourselves* with your presence today. The message this morning could apply to that little whistle blower in the back row. The sermon today is about fulfilling your life by walking with God now, rather than later. If the world should end tomorrow, have you lived your life today? Not just the life you think you want to live, but the life God wants you to live. Many of you have loved ones who have passed on. So you know how short life can be.

"I want you to turn to Isaiah 57:15, *I live in a high and holy place, but also with Him who is contrite and lowly in spirit, to revive the spirit of the lowly and to revive the heart of the contrite.* So no matter what is going on in your life, no matter what sins you've committed or how low you go, God lives among or within His people. *He lives with humble people to give hope and confidence.* Mind you I said humble people. Now, let's talk about the word *humble* for a moment."

I listened to Pastor Smith talk about the contrite and the humble, but my mind wandered to when we were in church on the day of Fonda and my little niece's funeral. A large and a small casket, both in white and chrome, sat up front for both her and little Rosie. It was the same spiritual message.

The elderly Reverend Hornaday spoke. "Here is a young woman, and a tiny baby girl, who have gone home to see the Lord in what some would say was far too soon. But, in God's time, and with God's will, whether you live a day or a hundred years, the bottom line is, once your life experience is done, you pass on. But, your soul still lives on because spirit never ever dies. And so this vessel of a body ceases to function, but in spirit, you will meet Fonda again, and you will see little Rosie, but only if you're ready when that day comes. In spirit, they live on. In memory, they are still in our hearts. Fonda Renee Worthy lived a life as a true child of God. She loved the church, she loved her mother, she loved her brother, she loved her daughter, and she so loved the Lord. She always had a smile on her face and a helping hand to lend, even at the tender age of thirteen. But, she's with the Lord now, resting in peace."

Dad sat beside his cousins two rows behind us. I looked back, and his pain, the agony of losing a child was written all over his face. I held tight to Mom's hand. She put her weary head on my shoulder and wept like a baby. My heart was broken in two.

The reverend spoke again. "Yes, you'll see her again. And on that day, will you be ready when you stand before the Lord? Ask yourself if you can answer God's question affirmatively like Fonda answered. Have you served the Lord? I say to you, come up now and tell us that you accept Jesus Christ as your Lord and Savior."

The present-day voice of Pastor Smith spoke louder in my head once again. "I suggest that you come up now. Don't be shy. So while heads are bowed and eyes are closed, those of you who are ill, who have addictions, who have lied, who have stolen, who are in need of money, or of a friend, or of peace of mind, please stand up. Stand up now. Stand up and come up to the altar. Christ stood for you so now you can stand for Him."

My feet wouldn't cooperate with my head. My thoughts were to go up to seek peace, but my actions were that it could wait, as if tomorrow were promised. Here I was this playboy sinner of a big brother to a saint of a little sister, who the Lord let live longer than she. Maybe, just maybe, He wasn't done with me yet.

It's Sunday night and I've heard it said that nothing good ever happens after three in the morning. It's already three-oh-two and there was a knock at the door. I opened it after looking through the peephole. I must be drunk or dreaming.

I pulled the door open and stood in amazement.

"What the fuck is up with all those bitches?" Her frantic voice slapped my eardrums.

I stood stunned, still trying to open one eye. Surely the other eye was deceiving me. "What the fuck is up with you, Georgia? It's three in the morning."

"All of those damn calls on your cell." She stood without make-up, no purse, no jacket, resting her weight on her right leg with her arms crossed like she actually deserved something.

"All of what calls? You mean to tell me you went through my cell phone? You had no right."

"You have no right to keep a harem like you do, Makkai."

I stepped out into the chilly air, pulling the unlocked door closed behind me. "First of all, I never told you anything to the contrary. Besides, most of those calls are from patients anyway."

"Bullshit. How about Royale and Magenta? Sound like hoes to me. And Mary Jane? Must be a stripper." She rolled her neck and her eyes.

I dared not tell Georgia she needed a Tic-Tac. "You dialed those numbers last night?" My eyes were fully functioning now, expanded so wide they were bulging toward her forehead.

"You're damn right."

I pointed in her jealous face. "You know what? You are fucking crazy. Are you trying to ruin my reputation by bringing my drama into my patients' lives? What did you say to them?"

She glanced down at her light-blue tennis shoes and crossed her legs at the ankle. "Nothing, I just hung up." Her gear shifting moods reeked of instability.

"Damn, Georgia. What's wrong with you all of a sudden? This is my reputation you're screwing with."

Her pissed-off eyes found mine. "Oh, so I get it. You're more worried about you being protected than my broken heart."

"Broken what? What did I do to break anything? I never promised you anything."

"What about those things you say in bed, Makkai? Don't even try it. You always tell me I'm the one and that I'm special. And then you take me out to let the world know about me. You introduce me to your mother and now I find this out."

"You're kidding me, right? I let the world know who you are? I let a small group of people know your name is Georgia, my friend. I didn't introduce you as my woman, my fiancée, or anything other than a friend."

"But, they know I must be someone special to you."

"You are, or should I say you were. But, not any damn more, I'll tell you that. This is a side of you I've never seen and don't want to ever see again. Now go home."

She stuck her neck out toward me. "No."

I pointed toward who knows where. "Go home to your kids and calm the hell down."

She planted her feet firmly, folding her arms. "No. I'm not going anywhere."

"Don't make me." I inhaled.

"What? Call the police?" She stood firm. "You surely wouldn't do that."

I let out the long-held-in breath. "What do you want from me, Georgia? Why not just go home and let's call this thing off."

"I want to stay here tonight." Her eyes spelled the word *please*.

Surely I looked stunned. "Why?"

"I'm feeling some real serious hurt here, Makkai, okay? Not that you would even begin to know what that's like. Lord knows no one has ever gotten close enough to your heart to hurt you. God forbid."

"You don't know that."

She raised her hand to wipe her tear-soaked cheek.

I leaned down to connect with her eyes. "Georgia, why did you have to go snooping around when I let you in my home? We had a good evening and now this?"

She sniffled. "Makkai, are you that good at making love like you're in love but you're not? I just thought you felt something for me."

"But, even if I did, you don't expect this to be a way to bring us closer? I'm sure you see and talk to people and I have no right to intrude or question you. That's your business."

"If you cared, you'd make it your business."

I reached back to find the doorknob. "Well, you can't make mine yours. Not like this." I took a deep breath. "You know what, fine, Georgia. Come in. You shouldn't be out in the street this late anyway. Crash here, right on my sofa. It'll be time to get up soon anyway." I stepped back to make room for her to cross the threshold.

She looked stunned for a moment. It seemed as though a cat had her tongue and I hoped she'd never find it. But, dang it, as she stepped inside I realized this woman just couldn't seem to keep her mouth shut. "I really did enjoy being invited over here with you. It took years to get here, though."

I tossed a blanket and a pillow her way. "I'm never even here myself."

"That's a shame. It's a beautiful home." She stood over near the wall where my awards hung. Did she really have two personalities? Okay, maybe three.

I spoke to her back. "Good night. And don't touch anything."

Chapter 16

Georgia

I didn't dare. Watching him walk away looking like a stud of a male model, the only thing I wanted to touch was him.

By five o'clock, the first morning light of day had not shone yet. Makkai's house was dark and still. I lay on his playpen sofa in my nylon sweat suit and bobby socks, with his velour blanket over my body, trying my best to close my eyes and doze. It had been my second night without sleep. I never even went to my mom's house to get the girls. I promised my mom I'd be there in the morning.

Before I knew it, I was on the third flight of stairs. And this time, I wasn't worried about Makkai's phone, or other women. This time, I wanted him to feel me, and remember me, to remind him how I made him feel. I wanted to make love to Makkai, whether he loved me or not.

"Baby, wake up."

"What?" he asked his clutched pillow.

Under the glow of dim mood lighting, I stood next to his huge bed and removed every stitch of my clothing, releasing them onto the bedroom floor. I climbed on top of the unmade side.

He peeled his eyes open. "What are you doing?"

I crawled toward him like a lioness, naked and ready. "I want you. I want you just like this. I want to wake up to you and be the first person you talk to and touch in the morning. Baby, lay back." I pulled the covers toward the foot of the bed.

Makkai laid his head back. I felt his upper body surrender. He was quiet and very warm. I moved my body downward, down to his penis, and it was limp. I kissed it through his clothes. I pulled down his gingham pajama bottoms, and he assisted me by lifting his backside. I took him into my hand and placed him inside the wetness and warmth of my wide-open mouth. I swirled my tongue and kissed his tip and inserted him in and out, over and over again, guiding him with my hand, adding major saliva to make the handling extra slippery as my thick lips sucked his length. Slowly, he started to extend, expanding inch-by-inch. Before I knew it, he was full-grown within my mouth and moaning.

I spoke seductively on purpose, looking up at him while giving wide, nasty eyes. "Can I sit on it, Makkai?"

"Yes," he answered with a moan.

I moved up, preparing to rest upon his exact spot, when he reached over, rummaging through the bottom drawer of his chest. He secured a Magnum condom upon himself, and it stood straight up, totally cooperating, waiting for me to take it in.

I straddled him and eased it inside of me, circling my hips and grinding straightforward and back, listening to the sound of the skin friction from our bodies pumping together.

"I want to have your baby," I whispered directly into his left earlobe.

He sounded lost but didn't miss a beat. "Uh huh."

"We'd be so good together. Having one for you would make it perfect."

"Uh, huh," he said again. "Georgia, uuuh, yes, oh, it's so good. Do you feel that?"

"Yes, I do."

He opened his eyes. "Are you gonna cut out all of this crazy shit you've been talking?"

"Yes, Makkai." I stared straight back at him.

"It would be a shame if we couldn't do this anymore, if I couldn't feel your insides like this. It would be a shame if I couldn't cum inside of, of, cum inside of you like this. Oh, Georgia. Uuuuggggppphhh. Dammit!" His grunt and stillness symbolized his ejaculation.

He broke our stare. The sound of him receiving the pleasure I brought him was such a turn-on. I wasn't even worried about mine. I lay my breasts down upon his defined chest and hugged him tightly, with him still inside of me. I was still bouncing my ass like I was in a big booty movie, contracting until I had every bit of his final throb.

"We're so good together," I whispered as I felt him deflate inside of me.

He then moved me, scooting out from under me, and he walked into the bathroom to remove his sperm-filled condom. I got up from his grand bed and approached him from behind, checking out his fine, toned body. I planted kisses on his wide back, following the definition with my tongue, then down to his trim waist, and then on down to his firm, strong ass. I took each cheek in my hands. He made an about face, and before I knew it, his hardness met me and he was deep in my mouth again. I released him and stood straight up, keeping one hand on him below, and led him back to the bed where I got up an all fours. He grabbed another condom and placed it on himself before plunging straight on into my deepness. After a few good pumps and him feeling me clapping loose-booty all up against him, he buckled on top of me and was still. That was two for him, none for me. But, that was just how I wanted it.

"Baby, here, take that off. I've got it," I said as I rolled him onto his back.

"No, I'm cool," he said. He covered his dick with his hand and started to doze.

I got up and went into the bathroom where I turned on the copper faucet and closed the door. Boy even had the tops of his Versace cologne bottles engraved with his initials *MW*.

I didn't want him to hear me pee. But, the pee wouldn't come anyway. I sat on the toilet and looked around at the manly towels, the contemporary wallpaper, the beautiful black art on the walls, and then I looked down. The first condom he'd placed inside of the toilet stared at me. I reached inside and grabbed it as tepid water dripped from my hand. I lowered the lid and sat on the toilet, leaned back, bending my knees up toward the ceiling, and inserted the condom deep inside of me.

I exited the bathroom, found my sweat suit and got dressed. "I'm going to go ahead and get home. It's almost six, and I need to pick up the girls soon. I'll let you sleep."

With half-open eyes, he glanced over at me, almost looking like he'd hoped he was dreaming. "Okay."

"I'll lock up."

His eyes widened. "No, I'll walk you out," he said, coming to a stance, slipping on his pajama bottoms. He went to the bathroom and flushed the other condom, washed his face and hands, and proceeded to take my hand as we walked downstairs to the front door.

I stood before him. "Will I see you again, Makkai? I really am sorry."

He gave long blinks. "We'll talk about it."

"You're mad at me."

"I'm tired, Georgia." His chest looked so good.

"I'm sorry. I think I'm about to get a visit from Aunt Flo. You know, just hormonal and stuff."

"It's cool." He put his hand on my back. "Go home, Georgia. And be safe."

"I will. I love you."

He closed the door as my sentence ended.

I rummaged through the white pages and there it was.

"Hi, Mrs. Cotton. This is Georgia, Makkai's friend. How are you?"

"Oh, I'm fine. How nice of you to call. To what do I owe this pleasure?"

Oh, hell. As I sat at home one afternoon more than one week later while the kids were in school, I realized it was her voice I'd heard that sounded so familiar when I called the number I took from Makkai's cell. She must have been sleeping then, because now, she didn't sound sexy, or groggy, or pissed off. I can't believe I did that. "I just wanted to tell you how nice it was meeting you the other night."

"It was my pleasure. You seem to be a very sweet girl."

"Thank you." I played twirl and roll with my hair.

"How was your day? Did you work today?"

"No, I wasn't feeling well."

"What's wrong?"

"I'm not sure. Just feeling a little nauseated, that's all."

"Well, take it easy and perhaps you can try some Pepto Bismol. That works for me every time, especially when I eat food that's a little too rich for me."

"Okay. I'll remember that."

"Did you eat anything different lately?"

"No." I didn't tell her that I hadn't been eating at all.

"How are the girls?"

"They're fine."

"I still can't believe how gorgeous those girls are. The two of them together in that picture is just priceless."

"Thanks. You know, I was going to ask you, do you mind if maybe I stop by tomorrow? I have an appointment for Treasure and Love to take new pictures, and it's in the Crenshaw mall right around the corner from you."

"That would be great. What time would that be?"

I flipped through my day planner. "Around noon. We should be done by then."

"Okay. Do you know where I am?"

"I know you're in Baldwin Hills. I know we dropped you off on Cloverdale, right?"

"Yes, it's 3802 Cloverdale Avenue. It's at the southeast corner of Cloverdale and Coliseum, just west of La Brea."

"Sure, I remember where it is."

"That'll be so nice. Thanks for thinking of me. My husband Al should be here, too. Makkai is coming by at six tonight to take me to dinner. Are you coming?"

"No. I haven't talked to him about that."

"I see. Well, Georgia, thanks for calling. I'll see you and those baby dolls tomorrow."

"Okay. See you then. Have a good night."

"You, too."

Chapter 17

"I don't want her coming by," I told my mother as we sat at her favorite restaurant, the Red Lobster.

"Why?" The waiter had taken our orders for the Ultimate Feast. Mom loaded up on garlic bread, and we asked that our salads be served with our main course.

"She freaked out after that night, actually showing up at my house without calling."

"Why?"

"Does it matter why?"

"No, but what happened?" she asked, biting into the buttery breadstick.

"She scrolled through my cell and started calling women."

"Oh, no, son. You can't have that. You've got to straighten her out on that one. That is a bad sign."

"Don't I know it?"

"And she seemed so sweet the other night. What am I going to say when she comes by?"

"She's not coming by, Mom. You gave her your address?"

"She knew where it was already. She was in the limousine the other night. I was just so impressed that she was so sweet to call and want to bring those girls by."

"Oh, Lord." My eyes hit the ceiling.

Mom leaned in to deliver her words closer. "Well, you need to be careful."

The young waitress placed our glasses on the table. "I brought water for both of you. And here's your white wine, ma'am."

Mom leaned back. "Thanks so much."

"Your orders will be right up."

"Sounds good," I replied before speaking to Mom again. "I don't think she's going to trip out. But, really, she's got some serious issues."

"Probably man issues. Obviously she doesn't trust." Mom sipped her ice water from a straw.

"Obviously. But, I'm not her man. She doesn't need to trust me."

"What you need to do is call her and straighten her out before she comes over and I embarrass her."

"I will."

"Good." Mom exchanged her water glass for her wineglass.

The waitress approached again. "You know, I'll have a glass of wine, too."

She placed our lobster tail and crab platters in front of us. The aroma of seafood and garlic butter convinced us to focus on our meal, as Mom said grace.

Over an hour later, just as I said goodbye to Mom, I grabbed my cell and stepped out of Mom's front door. The number I dialed was ringing by the time I stepped into my ride. I took off and honked as Mom waved goodbye. I secured my earphone. My outgoing call was answered.

"Hello." A young, high voice greeted me.

"Where's your mom?"

"She's in the bathroom."

"May I talk to her, please?" I said, speeding onto the main highway.

"Who's this?"

"It's Makkai, sweetheart."

"Hi, Makkai," Treasure said with an exclamation point.

"Hi."

"Mom said you were coming over. Are you?"

"Not tonight, Treasure. Now, please put your mom on the phone."

She yelled into the phone. "Mom, it's Makkai."

I heard Georgia yell in the background. "Okay."

"She's on the toilet, you know."

I smirked in spite of my deliberate focus. "Okay, thanks."

I heard Georgia's voice becoming clearer. She sounded half embarrassed, saying as she approached, "Treasure, give me that phone. Go check on your little sister."

Treasure's voice sang, "Bye, Makkai."

"Bye, honey."

"I said give me the phone. Hello." A muffled sound followed.

A Prince cut blasted through my speakers. "Georgia?"

She spoke loudly. "Yes. How are you?"

"Not so good."

"What's wrong?"

"Georgia, my mother tells me you're coming by with the girls."

"Yes, tomorrow. Why?"

"I don't want you doing that."

A double pregnant pause occurred. "Why?"

"Georgia, it's not like that with us and you know it."

"Not like what?"

"We already talked about this. Like tight enough for you to be going by to see my family."

"Makkai, I met your mother at your event and we talked. I can go see her if I want to."

"No, you can't."

"Makkai, you're tripping." She gave a minor laugh.

"Georgia, I want you to stop calling my mother."

"You are totally blowing this out of proportion."

"No, I think you are."

"Hold up now, I talked to your mom, and she wants to meet the girls."

"No, I don't want you taking them over there."

"Then I'll talk to your mother."

I turned down the CD volume. "What is wrong with you? I'm telling you no. If you go by there, I'm going to have my mother and her husband call the police. I will file what I have to if necessary."

"Makkai, you cannot be serious."

"I am serious."

"Makkai."

"Goodbye, Georgia." I snatched my earphone and ended the call.

Damn, that girl is hardheaded.

Ring.

Ring.

Ring.

Ring.

Fifty unanswered phone calls later, she gave up.

Thank God some time had gone by without a word from Georgia. I saw that as a good sign. She didn't show up at Mom's house. I was beginning to believe she got the message. But then, one night my cell rang while I was in my home office upstairs checking email. I didn't answer it. My voice mail tone sounded.

"Makkai, I'm at your door. Pick up the fucking phone. Makkai. I have to tell you something. I know your ass is in there."

Carl Lewis had nothing on me. I sprinted downstairs to the front door, still with my cell in hand. I flung open the door. "How did you get past the gate?"

"Same way I did before. It opens when you drive up, with or without a remote." Her face was red as well as her eyes.

I made a mental note to fix that as I spoke, "Georgia, you can't just show up here again without being invited. You did that once before and got away with it. Now, I want you to leave. If you don't, I will dial 911 with you standing right here." I held my cell phone in front of her face.

"Makkai, I'm pregnant and it's yours." She said it like she was actually delivering good news.

Why was I not shocked? "That's not possible."

"Why, because you wore a hard hat? That means nothing. You're the only man I've slept with, and I'm pregnant."

"But, you told me you were about to get a visit from 'Aunt Flo' as you said."

"Well, I didn't."

I shook my head. "Georgia, I want you to leave."

"No."

"We'll talk about this over the phone."

She stomped her right foot. "How can you be so cruel to me? When did you start being so mean?" A tear welled up in her left eye.

"When you showed up the last time having gone through my phone. I see you with new eyes now. I'll never see you the same."

"And I'll never see you the same either. I'm going to have this baby."

"Fine."

"And? You don't care?" Her right hand was framing her hip.

"Leave."

The tear traced a path from her eye to her cheek as she wiped it with the back of her hand. "Goodbye, Makkai. I never thought after all these years you'd end up being so cruel."

"I never thought after all these years you'd end up being so crazy."

"Good riddance," she said as she stepped quickly to her white Sebring and slammed the door, turning the ignition and then pulling off in the same millisecond, barely waiting for the gate to open.

That woman is not even telling me the truth. Either way, it can't be mine. There's no way. Besides, Lord knows she's got more kids than she should be allowed to have anyway.

Chapter 18

Monday

He gave me that, "You had me at hello," crock of corny bull. Run for the hills if a man ever has the nerve to run that line on you. Makkai is using me just like I'm using him. He takes me to fancy restaurants, he buys me nice gifts, and he gives me money to get my hair and nails done every now and then. He says he doesn't do that for anyone else. Probably because no one else makes it mandatory. But, his generosity is the only reason he's getting this gold card pussy, because he has money. What can a poor man do for me other than eat my pussy and spend my money?

He devoured me. "Damn, Delicious. It's so pretty, all clean-shaven and perfect, like a fleshy peach."

"I love it when you call me Delicious." Lust filled the room. And a few shots of tequila filled my head.

"It is. You taste like butterscotch with whipped-cream."

"I do?" I asked, watching him enjoy himself.

"It has a sweet taste that I can't even describe."

"Then why don't you share it with me so I can taste it, too."

"I bet you would taste it if you could."

"Come on up here."

He moved upward and brought his lips to mine. I licked all inside his mouth and smacked his lips loudly as we pressed mouths together. I inhaled.

I said, "Oooooooo, more please."

He worked his way from up high to down below again and tasted inside for a while. He came back up and gave me what his taste buds were covered with.

While kissing me, he managed to secure a ribbed condom by touch, and he placed his size inside of it. I looked at him as he leaned up, flashing his total erection, preparing to enter me. He looked at me with serious eyes. I smiled.

He told me, "Damn, that gap in your teeth is so sexy."

Once he was deep inside, he kissed my lips and sucked on my bottom lip. Then he grabbed my backside while handfuls of ass spread in between his manly fingers.

"Damn, this is heaven."

"Get all you can, baby," I encouraged him. "Make yourself at home."

"Oh, I am." He was lost in me.

Perfect timing. "You gonna take me to get that bracelet I wanted that I told you about?"

"Yes, Monday."

"When?"

"As soon as we're done. I'll get you anything you want."

"Oh really?"

"Really. Now turn over."

I moved my leg from around him and rolled to my left to lie on my stomach.

"Bend your hips up."

I propped up on my elbows. He separated my heavy cheeks and found his way to my entrance.

"Who am I?" he asked with authority.

"Makkai."

"Is this my pussy?"

"Yes."

"Damn, this is the best pussy I've ever had."

"Is it?"

"Yes."

"Is it delicious?"

"It is delicious."

"Is my pussy deep enough?"

"Yes."

"Is it tight enough?"

"Yes." Boyfriend pulled back his flat hand and popped the hell out of my right cheek.

I loved it. "Ooooo, yes."

He then popped it again.

I felt the sting. "Yes."

"How about this?" He let go of my waist and simultaneously popped each cheek with each hand while he rode me like a jockey.

I bucked. "Oh, Makkai."

"Is that how you want it?"

"Yes."

"Like this?" He yanked me back toward him and did it again.

"Yes, yes." My heartbeat pounded as I squinted my eyes. I balled up my fists.

"That ass is turning so red, but you like it, huh? You want my handprint to be there until next week, right?"

"Yes, that hard." My eyes were still closed.

"How's this?" he asked, doing two full hand slaps and pressing his hand into my cheek as he hit it.

I fucking erupted. I popped my eyes open as I gushed in a fast rush, jerking my butt up and back to get through it. "Dammit, Makkai. Oh, yeah." I sighed and lowered my hips to the mattress while he still grinded up against my butt as quiet as a mouse. And all of a sudden, he grunted, extended his head up toward the pine headboard and pressed all up through me, and then he jerked over and over again.

"Is it good?" I asked him, turning back to look over my shoulder at him. His sweaty face rested on my back.

"It is the best," he said as his throb subsided.

I said, still panting, "That's how it should be. Now, I'm going to take a shower so we can get to that jewelry store." He slowly rolled off me and I stood up.

"You are a hard one to figure out. It's all about what you can get out of it, right?"

"And you should know. I'm not sweating you or stressing you, so, I think you need to get dressed, too, and keep your word." I stepped into my bright red panties and walked toward the bathroom door.

He surrendered. "I'm right behind you. Damn, that ass is pretty," I heard him say.

Chapter 19

I had an account at the blingity-bling 14Karats store in Beverly Hills on Beverly Drive. Usually, I get my gold watches and sterling diamond-cut chains there. And I have a ring, almost looks like a bowl ring, but it has the medical community insignia in raised gold. It cost me an arm and a leg.

The store's private second level had smoked-glass and plush black casings. The owner, an older gentleman with white hair, approached while extending his hand. "Dr. Worthy, it's great to see you. To what do we owe this pleasure?"

"Just want to pick up a little something for Ms. Askins, here. She's looking for a bracelet."

"Hello, Ms. Askins. The pleasure is all mine. What type of bracelet, if I may ask?"

"A tennis bracelet," Monday said, peering from behind me, wearing her white tinted shades while holding my hand.

I had no problem correcting her immediately. "No, a gold bracelet."

"How about a bangle?" the manager asked.

Monday acquiesced with less of a twinkle in her eyes. "Okay, a bangle."

"Can you show us what you've got?" I asked.

"Sure. Right this way."

A tall, trim, tanned, brunette female salesperson walked up. "Can I get you anything to drink?"

"No thanks," I replied.

Monday inquired further. "Like, what do you have? Like water?"

"Water and whatever you'd like."

"Whatever I'd like?" She removed her sunglasses.

I looked at her like she'd better not say Dom P.

"Whatever you'd like," the salesperson assured her.

"Well, actually, I'd love a dirty martini."

"Dirty martini it is. I'll be right back."

Monday beamed, lagging behind. "I love this store. I've got to hang out with you more often."

I pointed in the direction of the owner. "Monday, do you want to look at the selections or not?"

"Yes. I'm coming." She flung hair about and secured her red purse strap along her shoulder.

The owner said, standing behind a glass case, "I think this would look nice on your wrist, especially with your beautiful complexion. It's a yellow and white gold swirl. We call it a rope of gold. It's brand new. We just got it in yesterday."

"It's beautiful."

"That's a lot of gold." First thing I did was ask, "How much?"

"Only fourteen hundred dollars."

"That's not bad," Monday said as she held out her hand. He gave her the piece.

"What else do you have?" I inquired.

"We have solid gold bangles that are polished, and some others that would possibly fall a little under a thousand, or maybe a Figaro style."

The lady returned with Monday's drink. It was in a lead crystal martini glass with two, toothpick-speared olives.

"He'll hold it," she told the lady, nodding in my direction with her eyes on the jewelry.

"I want this one." She secured the first bracelet on her wrist and clasped it as if to stake her claim. She then took her glass from me. "Thanks."

She posed for me while she took a sip. She licked the rim of the glass and batted her eyelashes. She then took one of the green olives into her mouth, and bit down with her sexy gapped teeth, while the liquid squirted from the meat of the olive. She chewed and smiled.

The owner cleared his throat. "Will you be taking the rope of gold, sir?"

"Yes, we'll be taking the rope of gold."

Monday shook her hips and giggled but did not spill a drop. She kicked up her heel behind her as she hugged me, sipping from behind my back, raising her glass to the owner.

"Great job, sir," she said. "We'll be coming back."

Her sentence was premature. But, I really didn't mind that little arrangement. Fourteen hundred wasn't a bad price. Monday was good, and she was right; she minded her own business, and once she got what she wanted, she ran off back to her life until I called again. She was no drama and no headache. And to be so damn fine, I wasn't about to complain.

We exited the store. Monday wore the bracelet and carried the black and silver 14Karats designer bag in her hand.

She admired her new gift. "You are way too good to me."

"You are way too good, period."

She slipped her arm in mine, strutting like America's next top model. "When we get back to the hotel, what do you say to celebrating?"

"Not today, Monday. I've gotta get going after I drop you off."

"I understand. I'll just make a hair appointment. You know that'll take all day."

"I'm sure."

"Well, you let me know when you're available again. I'll be around."

"Sounds like a plan."

"And Makkai, I'll cherish this gift forever. You are very generous."

"No problem."

She squeezed my arm and moved in closer. "Makkai. Do you think you can give me like one-hundred cash? I left my credit cards and debit card at home. I don't want to drive that far after you drop me off. Besides, my hairdresser is near the hotel."

"I've got it." I pulled out my wallet and a bill in one fell swoop. "Here."

She took the money and folded it into quarters. "Thanks. I'll give it back to you." She stopped as we approached the car and gave me a quick kiss.

"No need."

She tucked the bill into her purse. "You are the best. I appreciate it."

I smiled as she stepped toward the passenger seat and sat down. I closed the door and walked around the back of the car. As I opened the driver side door and stepped inside, a young white man walked by and stared all through Monday's very being. She noticed, and I noticed.

She looked stunned. "That's rude."

"He has good eyesight." I started up the car.

The man even looked back twice.

I told her, "I can't say that I blame him."

I pulled off while she rested her right arm along the open window. The eighteen-carat gold, gleaming bracelet was blinding under the rays of the sun. Her left hand was resting along my lap, making its way toward my crotch, then rubbing in between my legs. I reached over and squeezed her thigh just above her knee. This woman deserved whatever she wanted. My hard-on lasted the entire way back to the hotel.

I'll call her next week.

Chapter 20

Mary Jane

I flipped open my cell as I stood in the hallway on the eighth floor. "This is Nurse Cherry."

"I just love that name, Cherry."

Carlos Jenkins is Dr. Worthy's best friend. He comes around the hospital every now and then. He's bright and he's charming, but he's Makkai's friend and that bothers me, even though it doesn't seem to bother either one of them. Heck, forget Makkai anyway. He basically kicked me to the curb.

I crossed my arms with the phone between my chin and shoulder. "Let me guess, this is Carlos."

"The one and only."

"And what makes you the one and only?"

"I suppose you'd have to talk to a few of my ex-lovers to find out."

"Ex-lovers, huh? So do you have any ex-wives or ex-girlfriends?"

"Oh, no, never been married before. But, of course I've been in relationships."

"Well, that's good, at least."

On his end, I heard the sound of a door closing.

He said, "So, enough talk about my legendary status. That was back in the day, anyway. I'm different now."

"Oh, you are?"

"Oh, yes. I'm looking for a good woman to settle down with."

"That's a good thing."

"And you, Nurse Cherry, in my opinion, fit the bill in every way." He spoke in a voice that reminded me of Mack Daddy Mack.

"How do you know that?"

"Well, I see virtue in you. And you know that's what men fall for when they're ready to say goodbye to their bachelorhood . . . virtue."

"And when they're not ready, what do they require?"

"A pulse. No, just kidding." He chuckled all by himself.

"There's probably a lot of truth to that, I'm sure."

"Nothing further on that one."

"Smart move. So to what do I owe this call?"

"I was just hoping I could catch you on this number to see if you wanted to have lunch with me."

"Lunch when?"

"Today."

I noticed the male nurse taking a peek at me from his station. I turned my back. "I can't today. I'll barely have a chance to run down to the cafeteria and grab some yogurt the way this day is going."

"That's too bad. So is that how you keep your gorgeous figure, by eating yogurt?"

"Oh, that's not even my usual, so don't get me wrong. I eat ribs, and smothered anything."

"I see. I'll remember that when I take you to dinner one day. There's this great rib joint in Santa Monica called Dem Bones. You'd love it."

"Sounds like a possibility."

"So you'll come?"

"We can talk about it."

"Just say you'll come."

"I will say I can't make lunch today. But, we'll see what happens. I might be able to come with you."

"Coming with me is exactly what I want. Once you come with me, you'll never want to come with anyone else."

"Carlos, excuse me, but, I get the feeling you're taking this conversation to a place where I'm not comfortable. Please don't do that."

"Oh, woman, I'm just kidding."

"I've always thought of kidding as a way to excuse the truth. I'm not feeling respected when you do that."

"Enough said. It'll never happen again."

"Good. I'd appreciate it."

"A lady of virtue you are."

I glanced down at my watch. "Carlos, I'm going to have to go and assist a doctor down the hall. Thanks again for the lunch invitation."

"You're welcome. I'll be in touch. That you can count on."

"Okay. Take care now."

That man is fine as wine, kinda looks like Eric Benet, with his twisted hair and fine features. But, he's as crass as a dirty old man. I know he's dying to get in my pants and nothing else. For that reason alone, I'm bound and determined that will never happen. He'll treat me like a lady yet, that is if I don't cuss him out before we even have a chance to have a first date.

I walked into a patient's room. The doctor walked in behind me.

He spoke my way in a whisper. "You were down there chatting on your cell phone like this is some social gathering."

I didn't even look back at him, releasing words from the corner of my mouth. "Why are you all in my business, Dr. Worthy?"

"One doesn't need to be in your business to see you talking on the phone all sneaky like you're making an illegal crack deal."

I turned to face him. "I was not." I cleared my throat and gave him the eye to stop.

"All hunched over like you were speaking in code." He actually imitated me as we walked over to the patient.

I said, "Hello, Mrs. Reynolds. This is Dr. Worthy. He'll be giving you a quick once-over today."

She nodded to him with a slight smile.

"Hello, Mrs. Reynolds. Your regular doctor, Dr. Pratt, asked me to see you today. He had an emergency and I told him I would be glad to stop by and see if we can figure out what's going on. Nurse Cherry is here to assist me with your exam. Now, how long have you been having chest pain?"

I told him, "Doctor, she's also coughing up blood, and has shortness of breath, and her temperature is 100.6."

"Okay, thanks, Nurse," Makkai said with a tinge of sarcasm. "I see that right here in her paperwork." He looked at Mrs. Reynolds.

Her voice was raspy. "My chest has been bothering me for about a couple weeks or so. But, I just started coughing up blood this morning."

"I see. Well, let me ask you this. Have you been exposed to any hazardous substances that you know of?"

"No. I don't think so."

"How long have you been hoarse, and had the wheezing?"

She cleared her throat. "For a few months, I guess."

"Any weight loss?"

"Yes, but believe me, I've welcomed that," she joked with a smile.

I replied, placing one hand on her back. "You look good, Mrs. Reynolds."

"Yes, you do. Do you smoke?" he asked.

She nodded. "Oh yes, I've been smoking for about twenty years now, Doctor."

"Okay."

I watched this beautiful, educated, well-achieved, wealthy, generous, empowering man do his thing. That alone was a major turn-on for me. The way he wore his white coat, the way the starched collar of his white shirt stood stiff and proud around his muscular neck, the way he held that lucky pen when he wrote. I wondered what it would be like to excuse ourselves for five minutes and take him into that bathroom so he could pull my skirt up to my ass and work his expertise while banging me up against that bathroom sink, and then he could get down on his knees, and kiss me from the top of my white thigh-highs to the middle of my girlie split, and . . ."

"Nurse Cherry, did you hear me?"

"Yes. I mean, sorry, Dr. Worthy. What did you need?"

"I need you to order a helical, low-dose CT scan of her lungs." He handed me her chart.

"Oh, sorry. Yes, Doctor."

"My lungs?" she asked.

He replied, "Yes, Mrs. Reynolds. Your chest pain could have little to do with your heart, as Dr. Pratt suspected, but more to do with your lungs, which control breathing. I want to make sure we have a biopsy done as well."

"Biopsy?"

"I know that word sounds invasive, but what we do is we insert a slender scope, called a bronchoscope, through your nose or mouth, and down your throat to look inside of your airway and lungs so that we can take a small sample."

"But, why?"

"Mrs. Reynolds, this procedure doesn't take long at all, and it's not as bad as it sounds."

"What are you checking for?" she asked, looking confused.

"I'm just checking you out so that I can narrow things down."

"But, you're not sure of what I could have?"

He responded, "No, ma'am. Not yet. Based upon your symptoms, we're just taking steps to rule some things out."

"I see." Her eyes shifted into sad mode and she simply laid her head back. "I'm ready." She looked at the doctor again. "Hey, but aren't you a heart surgeon?"

"Yes, I am. But, cardiothoracic surgery involves diseases that affect organs inside of the thorax, or the chest. And that includes the lungs."

"I see." She managed a surprising wink at Makkai. "From what I hear about you, you can work miracles. I read that article about you winning an award. It was in the *L.A. Sentinel* recently."

Well, I'll be. She was charmed him, too. By the great Dr. Worthy.

Mrs. Reynolds looked a lot like my mother. She was light-skinned and thin and quiet, but I could tell she was strong. I reached under her arm and grabbed her right elbow as she scooted up for her exam.

After Makkai stopped blushing, he stepped to her and attentively looked into her left ear with the penlight. He then checked her with his stethoscope, listening to her heart. If I didn't watch myself, I was going to start catching feelings for Dr. Feelgood, too. I knew he deserved that nickname, bless the heart of whoever gave it to him. If I could sing like Aretha Franklin, I'd have been serenading the world about his prowess myself. *That man can sure make me feel real. That man takes care of my pains and ills.*

He spoke to Mrs. Reynolds with his hand on her shoulder. "You'll be just fine."

"You promise?"

"You're in good hands."

"Yes, Dr. Worthy, I know that."

He smiled, looking at her and then looking at me as he exited the room with his slow and suave Denzel walk.

Damn that Makkai.

Chapter 21

Some say what happened to me when I was fifteen could be considered a good thing. But, I definitely consider it a curse.

See, I used to hang out with my little sister Fonda all the time. So much that we'd play the same games together. Which meant sometimes, like when we were younger, she'd play with my army men, and sometimes, I'd play dolls with her. She'd play with my race cars and I'd help her bake on her electric oven. Well, one Saturday morning, after being gone for two days straight, Dad caught her and me practicing one of Fonda's dance routines in the living room to an old Supremes track. He didn't say a word but gave me a look of distain as he walked by in slow motion. Later that day, my play uncles ended up coming over to take me outside to play baseball.

I stood there in the tight, stonewashed Levis jeans I was growing out of, and a big white tee shirt, with the wooden bat in my hands, ready to swing.

My Uncle Milton said, "Boy, dat dere pussy is the best thang in the world. I'm tellin' ya somethin fa real."

Uncle Leroy high-fived him. "Once you get a chance to stick your dick into that wet, tight tunnel, you'll be chasing it morning, noon and night." Needless to say I swung the bat about two seconds before the baseball reached me.

"What's wrong dere, boy? You ain't even smelt dat yet?" Uncle Milton asked.

I looked down at my weather-beaten tennis shoes. "No."

"You haven't tasted it then, huh?" Uncle Leroy inquired. He surprised me more than anything.

"No."

Uncle Leroy continued, "You will. We promise, you will."

The next evening, my dad told me to go for a ride with him. We drove all the way to St. Petersburg and pulled up to an old, small frame house. We turned into a long, winding driveway. Dad parked his Caddy behind a silver Ford Mustang. As we got out, a small brown, wide-eyed poodle ran up to him, wagging his tail and barking. Dad patted him on the top of his head, as the dog continued to run circles around him. We walked up to the side door. Dad took out a single key from his pants pocket and opened it, walking right in.

"Roosevelt, is that you?" a woman spoke from somewhere.

He responded with his Barry White voice, speaking loudly in her direction. "Yes, it's me." He crossed the threshold taking small, slow steps. "Her name is Erskalene," he told me without looking back at me. "Don't let the dog in," he told me.

I made sure to close the screen door in the poodle's little sad face.

"Oh, little Makkai is with you? Great. Roosevelt, your Aunt Ethel called here looking for you. I don't know how she got this number, but I am listed."

"Oh, she did. That's strange."

The house smelled of the corned beef and cabbage that simmered on the stove, and the faint fragrance of Egyptian musk circulated through the air. Erskalene came into the kitchen, wearing only her scarlet panties and a sheer top. She had to be in her forties, well into her forties. Clearly her large, wide breasts hung flat like pancakes, outlined by deep stretch marks. Her tummy bulged and her waist was as wide as her hips. She had suffered from Noassitol disease, as she had no butt whatsoever. But, she did have the shapeliest, longest legs I'd ever seen, and Dad was definitely a leg man. I was able to check her out intently because by the time she handed us plates full of cabbage and corn bread, and we devoured them and asked for seconds, Erskalene was standing in front of me, blocking my view of "M.A.S.H" as I sat on the sofa. She bent down on her knees. Dad sat on the burnt-orange reclining chair across the room. She leaned her majorly endowed chest toward my face, surely which had been her best asset years earlier, and I looked at my father with eyes that begged him to make her stop.

"Son, tonight you're going to become a man."

My eyes spoke louder than my words. "Dad, she is your friend."

"Tonight, she's your best friend. Enjoy yourself and learn."

She handed me a tinted shot glass filled with some brown liquor. I sniffed it and looked at my dad again. He swigged his glass, and I followed suit. Next thing I knew, in between my coughing fit, Erskalene had my zipper down and my young hardness deep in her mouth. My eyes shut by themselves. The feeling was like heaven. I had jacked off before to a few magazines I found under the driver's seat of my dad's car, but this nut was coming fast, in spite of the fact that my own father was watching. I squirted in her mouth, and she looked up at me smiling. She didn't miss a drop. She pointed her tongue along my swollen tip, wiped her mouth, and then leaned up to put her tittie in my mouth. I licked it like I was licking a Popsicle.

"Pretty good," she said, glancing over at my dad.

"Lay on your back, Ersk," he instructed her.

She obeyed him, pulling down her lace panties and lying next to me with her curvy legs spread eagle.

She played with herself, inserting a finger at the same time, until her entire hand was swallowed by her own hairy opening.

His voice was monotone and no nonsense. "Kiss her pussy, son."

"Dad." My word was tainted with a question mark.

"Roosevelt, maybe you should leave the room. I can show him."

His firmness was evident. "Will you let me handle my own son, please?" He cut his eyes from her to me. "You, my son, are going to be a man tonight. Playing girlie cheerleader routines with your sister. Now eat that pussy. And eat it right."

I leaned up and put my mouth between her legs. She had a wild, unshaven middle, and it smelled like sweat. I kissed it with closed lips.

"Open your mouth and give her the tongue so you can taste it."

I parted my lips and stuck out the tip of my stiff tongue, squinting my eyes. The tanginess was odd. I backed away. The *P* word was staring me in the face.

"Move over, son. I'll show you how to do it. And you watch closely. No son of mine is going to be guessing about how to please a woman. You will not ruin the Worthy reputation by acting like you're afraid."

He yanked me up and then bent down with his knees to the floor. He scooted her hips toward him and parted her lips with one hand. She reached over and took a hit off a homemade cigarette, replaced it, and then leaned back.

"You don't just go right to it, you approach it. You tease it, you enjoy it, you marinate it, you watch her movements, you feel her wetness, you pay attention to her breathing, to her moans, to her ass tightening, to her legs straightening, to each muscle contracting, to her eyes rolling back in her head. Like this."

And Roosevelt Worthy stuck out his long tongue, and licked and teased and worked his mouth and his razor-stubbled chin and his cheeks and his dark brown, aged, professional fingers all around Erskalene's vagina until she contracted her legs and burst out with a scream that sounded like she had been stabbed. She bucked wildly and her breasts started flopping. He held tight to her ass cheek and had one hand on her stomach. She screamed again and called out his name. It was as if I wasn't there.

"Get you a good nut, baby. That's my baby Ersk," he said. "Girl cums so hard." He looked over at me as he stood up. "And you gotta talk to em. Tell em they're the best, that they cum just for you. Make em feel relaxed and free to pump that cum right into your face as though if they peed on you, you'd sop that up, too."

Erskalene breathed short, quickened breaths and tried to sit up.

Dad directed us again. "Now, it's his turn."

I traded places with him, realizing that I had the biggest, stiffest hard-on ever. It didn't even look like my dick. It was twice as big as usual, and it was ready to blow again.

He looked down at it. "That's my boy," he said, walking back to his seated view while I leaned on my knees with my pants to my ankles.

She grabbed the book of Lucky Strike matches from the abalone ashtray, fired things up and took another hit.

I stared at her soft, long thighs and then her womanly hips and then flicked my tongue up and down her southern lips.

"One thing I did that you didn't see is I found that pearl. That clit. Ignore that, and you're worse than gay, because to a woman, it's like a dick is to us. And the best and quickest way to make a woman cum out of control is to suck it, and move your head up and down. You got it. Suck it. Don't lick around it, don't kiss it. Just purse your lips like this. Look at me." And I did, all eyes and all ears. "And curl your tongue so that the clit fits in the circular space of your tongue, and under your upper teeth, and flick that tongue while you suck at the same time. Don't be lazy. And then, stick three middle fingers inside with your fingertips upward toward an area where every woman has a spot, and it'll be just a matter of time. It's called going to work."

I remembered everything he said, always was good at remembering, and did it all to the tiniest detail. Before I knew it, her opening seemed to be getting slipperier and juicier. And then, she let out a long groan and lifted her hips toward me, pushing herself deeper into my face. I could barely breathe from my nose, but I moved my face upward and then back downward, when it needed to, inhaling deeply.

"There you go. That's how you do it. Now talk to her."

"You like how I'm getting you off, don't you?"

"Uh huh." Her eyes were closed.

"Am I making you feel good?"

"Yes," she purred as she jerked her head to the side.

"Don't ask her that. If you have to ask, you're not doing your job."

I talked some more, trying to get it right. "I want you to cum in my face while I write your name with my tongue."

My dad was silent.

Her eyes opened. "Okay."

I started with the *E* and before I could get to the *K*, she exploded in my mouth, squeezing her thighs so tight around my head that I thought I was going to pass out.

Without even being told, I leaned up, spread her legs even more and entered her wetness, burying my length inside of her. She was wide and deep enough to take it, but it still gripped me like no other feeling I'd ever felt. I pulled and pushed rapidly, in and out, over and over, on and on.

"Move one of her legs up over your shoulder, and scoot her on her side."

I did.

"Move fast and don't cum no matter what. Not until she cums first."

She made a revving sound as I sped up, and her eyes rolled back and she grunted. She looked up at me and actually had subtle tears flowing from her eyes.

I shot my juice inside of her and gyrated up against her body, grabbing her breasts as I gave her my last drop. At that moment, I liked her. I liked her a lot.

"That's my boy. That'll get you hooked. Good pussy is only as good as the man who can treat it right. And make sure to avoid the booty sex. That hole ain't good for nothing but an exit. That's what gets folks in trouble." He glared at my wide-eyed expression. "And never, never, ever say I love you if you don't, even if they say it first. That'll make em start acting stupid and crazy. I mean it. And lastly, don't bring more than one woman into your bed at a time. You'll surely hear about it later. It can only spell trouble. It's just not worth it." My expression did not change. "Yeah, you're hooked all right. Now you know how to make em feel good."

I'd hoped she did feel good. Not just physically but where she needed it most, emotionally. Not sure my dad knew how to give that. And now the chip off the old block was introduced to the feel good techniques, missing the mark at making her feel good emotionally as well, I'm sure.

I still smelled her musky scent and salty sweat, even the entire way as we drove home slowly. It seemed like the drive took forever. We only stopped for gas and some fried chicken and lemonade. This time, there was no radio, and no talking at all. That is, until we pulled into the driveway.

He put his royal blue Cadillac in park. "I hope you understand why I did that, boy."

"Yes, sir." My head was throbbing.

"I did it to keep you from being funny, you know, girlie. You worried me the other day. Always around your mom and sister. You'll thank me one day."

"Yes, sir."

A minor smile arrived. "Where'd you learn that spell your name routine?"

"Sir?"

"You snuck and watched a porno movie from the garage, huh?"

"Yes, sir."

Pleasure lived in his eyes, which was rare.

We went inside of the nighttime-filled house through the back door, and my first stop was the bathroom, where I immediately turned the lock. I peed with the force of a fire hydrant. I held my dick in my hand and it looked like it was blushing with a cockiness that beamed with the pride of its virgin experience. If only my upper head agreed.

I wanted to hop in the shower so darn fast that it would have been just fine if I could have left on all my clothes. I turned on the shower and heard my mother knocking on the door.

"Makkai, what are you doing?" She was loud and spoke quickly.

"I'm about to take a shower," I yelled over the sound of the pounding water.

"Where have you been?"

"With Dad."

"Roosevelt, where did you take that boy until this time of morning?" Her voice grew fainter. "Where have you been?"

"Nothing. We were just out." He closed the bedroom door after my mom, and they went to bed.

Not long after that, Mom packed up a very pregnant Fonda and me, rented a U-Haul trailer, took some cash out of Dad's wallet and hit the road, headed to the West Coast. Her only stop before we hit the main highway was an attorney's office to file for a divorce. Dad moved Erskalene in two days later, before we even arrived in Los Angeles.

Fonda and the baby died a few months later of complications from giving birth. Mom never got over losing her only girl and her only grandchild, and I never got over losing my other half, my best friend, my playmate, my baby sister. Mom didn't want Dad at the funeral but he came anyway. He always did what she didn't want him to do. Like be faithful.

"Hello," I answered after snatching my phone from the coffee table in an instant, awakened from my daydreaming state, in my family room without a family.

"Dr. Worthy?"

"Yes."

"The results are in for your patient, Mrs. Reynolds."

"Oh, yes."

"She has high levels of organic acids, creatinine and nitrogen, and the urinalysis indicates high levels of urea and sodium. And both the biopsy and CT scan indicate a high density of micro-vessels."

My attention was focused. "So we'll need to get the cancer specialist to see her right away. Ask Dr. Lois Taylor to see her and do an oncology referral, please. I'll be in tomorrow morning. Call me again if you need me."

"Yes, Doctor."

"Thanks, Nurse."

Just an example of the realities of my life and my career . . . trying to save people, when life goes on all around me. Even when they place their trust in me, I know, above all else, that faith in God is the only thing that gets us through. No matter what else is going on.

Chapter 22

Salina

I met this man outside of a south bay Target store last summer. He seemed a little bit shy, or at least I thought he was just from the fact that he'd smile and stare me down but wouldn't open his mouth. But it was like he had x-ray vision. Like he could see the shade of my crimson thong underneath my perfectly broken-in pair of form-fitting jeans. I kept catching him checking me out from behind as I'd looked back at him. He was a butt man for sure.

When I was about to approach my Nissan, he got in this huge new platinum Mercedes and began backing out. He had to slam on his brakes to keep from actually hitting me with his rear bumper. His car jerked to a halt. I jumped back, looking like I'd lost all cool. My heart dropped straight to my knees. And then I blushed with embarrassment once he got out to check on me. I wondered if he did that back up thing on purpose. Probably so. Suddenly, my heart returned to my chest. He smiled, flexing a single muscle at the right side of his mouth. My heart again dropped to my knees. The next night, we were in a La Quinta hotel down the street backing things up for real. Together.

That's how I met Makkai. It was all about sex from the very beginning.

That summer we did get out and at least see a movie or two. We even went to eat a few meals in public if and when my husband was out of town. But, we tried to be cool because he knew my situation and I knew his. He wasn't ready to commit to anyone, and I was already committed to someone.

But, here's how my husband found out about the very talented, screw-your-wife doctor. This is what prompted the choking.

"That was the best we've ever had together," Makkai said as he rolled off me.

I lay back wearing only my bra, breasts spilling out over the black lace cups, as I was coming out of a rapid panting pattern. "Yes, it was."

"It's like you cum just for me."

"I do. Lord knows I don't get this type of treatment at home."

"Okay, now, I don't wanna know."

I rolled to my right side to face him. "Why are you so closed down to hearing about my life?"

He stared up at the ceiling, left hand behind his head. "Not about your life, but about your wifely duties."

"How do you deal with it? I don't think I could if I knew you belonged to someone else."

"I try not to think about it. That's why I don't want to hear about it." He barely blinked.

"So you're just fine knowing someone else's dick is inside of me other than yours."

"See, that's what I don't want to envision. But, if you think about it, whether you're dealing with a married person or not, any woman a man sleeps with could have had someone up inside of her that morning. Maybe knowing is better than not knowing. But, either way, I just protect myself."

I pointed down to that now loose-fitting rubber glove he still wore. "That condom only keeps you from getting someone pregnant or getting AIDS, not from bonding to someone you know."

"Bonding, the *B* word. That takes a concentrated effort. Hormonally it can happen, but you've got to know what you want, what you can do, and what you can't do."

I rolled on my back, sharing the view of the ceiling with him. "So how many other women do you sleep with?"

In an instant, he stood up and made a beeline to the bathroom. "Now see, those are the kind of questions that worry me. You're either wanting more or you're getting jealous, now which one is it?"

I spoke to his back, and the view of his tight, muscular behind. "I'm . . . I'm just trying to get inside the head of a player to see how he does his thing, that's all."

"Seems to me you're a player, too, Salina. I do it the same way you do. I enjoy being with you." He closed the bathroom door.

"And I enjoy being with you."

He yelled for volume. "You just keep things tight at home and make sure . . ."

I reached for my chiming cell. "Hello. Yes, baby, I know. What? You're where? What are you doing outside? I'm not with anyone." Makkai stepped out of the bathroom with shock in his eyes. He tiptoed over to me. My voice grew louder. My hands were dizzy like my big-ass head. "No, I'm not going to tell you my room number. Tom, you need to go home. I just needed a little time to myself. Fine then." I pushed the off button. "Fuck, my husband is outside somewhere." I stood up, fumbling around for my things.

Makkai opened the bathroom door and just stood there naked. "How in the hell did he find out where you were?"

I frantically grabbed an array of balled up clothes as I spoke. "I don't know. You've gotta go."

"No, you do. You leave first."

I wiggled my way into my cropped pants. "And then he'll see me and burst in here."

"No, you sneak out and he won't know what room you were in. Believe me, he's watching every man who comes out of here at this point. He's not some psycho, is he?"

I hurriedly pulled my curly hair up into a banana clip. "He's no passive man, I know that much."

Makkai stood behind the closed door with his lengthy penis deflated. He waved his hand for me to proceed as he held tight to the doorknob. "Shit. Go, Salina. No, wait." He pointed toward the window. "Peek out of the window first. Do you see him?"

I quickly tiptoed back toward the window as if my footsteps would be heard and peeled the heavy, diamond-patterned drape back slightly. But, all I saw was a faraway parking lot full of cars. We were on the third floor of a fairly big hotel. "No."

He motioned for me to head toward the door again. "Get out of here." He turned the knob slowly and tucked himself between the door and the wall.

"I'm gone. Fuck," was all I could say as I slipped on my dark sunglasses and tossed my cloth bag over my shoulder as he shut the door on my heels, locking and bolting it with force.

Problem was, Makkai and I sat up talking after our marathon fuckfest session until five in the dang morning. Didn't realize how much time had slipped by. For the first time, I'd actually spent the night.

By the time I hopped in my car, my husband appeared from out of nowhere and stood at the hood of my car, wearing all white, looking like he was on a mission.

"Who were you with?"

"Tom, go home."

His blue eyes were glassy and he gave me an empty look like nobody was home in the big bald head of his. He yelled through the windshield. "You go home. I'm not leaving until I see every damn car parked here drive away."

I made sure to press the door lock button and then rolled down the passenger window, yelling toward the front of my ride. The thought of distracting him by changing the subject snapped into my consciousness. "Tom, you pissed me the fuck off yesterday when you commented about me having gotten my tubes tied years ago, like you regretted not being able to be a father. I needed time to myself. I'm telling you, I was alone all night."

He walked around toward the driver's side window. "I was pissed at your comment that I was shooting blanks, but damn, you just disappear and shit? I'm not having that."

"Tom, let's go. We can work on this. Maybe try to find a way to reverse my procedure. I just never knew it bothered you. Why don't you just talk about things instead of spilling them out when you're angry?"

"Salina. Get home." He walked away with Hulk-like steps, still looking around for any suspicious, unknown person who could be the answer to his surefire detective work.

I yelled toward his back after starting my car. "How did you find me?"

"I'll see you at home," he said firmly and loudly, without looking at me as I backed out.

An hour later, I felt some semblance of security in the fact that once he got home and climbed in the shower, and I stepped in behind him, he seemed eerily calm and quiet. He got out first. We got dressed for the day, and he headed out to work, while I headed out to run errands.

To me, he seemed cool with everything. It was like he'd convinced himself that maybe he was imagining things. But, then he sent me a text message just as I pulled up to the bank parking lot.

Meet me at your lover's place of business at the hospital in twenty minutes or else.

Oh fuck. And that's when I jetted over to Makkai's office from Torrance in record-breaking speed, only to find my husband's Lexus truck parked behind Makkai's Benz. And the rest is history.

That husband of mine scrolled through my cell while I was finishing up my shower. He redialed the last few outgoing numbers until he hit the jackpot.

Chapter 23

Georgia

"Mommy, where's Makkai?" Treasure asked a month or so later.

Yes, my daughters still ask about Makkai every now and then. Especially Treasure. They don't see him around anymore, ever since he got pissed at me for showing up at his door. And you'd think he'd at least check on me, since he thinks I'm expecting his child. I call him every now and then. Never at work, though. Usually on his cell but he doesn't answer. Even his mother won't pick up the phone when I call her.

I told my oldest, "I don't know. He's probably working. He'll be back around soon."

Or at least that's what I'd hoped. I'd hoped he'd come to his senses and at least offer to take me to the doctor or something. He's so tripped out by swearing that he always wore a glove that he can't get past the fact that he's the only man I've been with in a while.

Treasure said, "Mom, someone's at the door."

"Thanks, Boo. Isn't it time for you to go to bed? Go get your little sister and brush your teeth. I'll be in there in a minute," I said, headed to the front door.

"Yes, Mommy."

I looked through the peephole and opened the door. "Hey, how's it going?" I asked, greeting Stardust with an embrace. She stood, hugging a grocery bag. She looked sexy and yummy, in her jeans and peasant top, with a hot purse hanging from her shoulder. She always smelled like sugar cookie lotion.

Now, I didn't say I hadn't been with a woman recently.

"Good. You look pretty. Did you get your hair done?" she asked. Women seem to notice shit like that.

"I did. I got it done this morning. You look nice yourself. I love that teal bag. Where'd you get it?"

She stepped inside as I closed the door. "A lady at the club comes in once a week and sells them from the trunk of her car. You like it?" Obviously she meant the strip club where she works, or should I say, performs.

"Oh, yeah. That's sweet."

"I'll have to get you one then." She put the grocery bag on the dining room table and her leather purse on the chair. It had a big round, silver buckle and it looked extra roomy.

"That's nice of you. How much are they?"

"Don't worry about it."

"No, really. How much. I'll give you the money."

She put her soft hand on my forearm. "Georgia, really. I've got you."

"I don't know what to say."

"Just allow yourself to be given to, that's all." Her smile was warm.

"Well, thanks. That's really nice of you."

Love came up to me, talking to me from behind. "Mommy, can you read us a story?"

I turned around. "Now, it's past your bedtime. That TV program you were watching took up your story time."

"Hi, cutie," Stardust said to her.

"Hello," Love said, turning around with hurt written all over her face as she walked away.

"I can read them a story."

I shook my head. "Oh, no. They need to know that nine o'clock means lights out."

"Oh, Georgia, then why don't you go ahead and read them a quick one. I'll be okay."

"Are you sure?"

"I'll be right here." She pointed to my crushed velvet sofa. "I brought some Moose Head beer. I'll just be sucking on a bottle and flipping through the stations."

I handed her the remote. "Okay, well, I'll be right back." I headed toward the girls' room.

"The beers and I will be waiting," I heard her say as I walked.

Damn, that lady is fine.

"Okay there, little ladies, what do you want to read?"

One spoke and then the other. "The Barney book. The Good Night book."

"We'll read both. Now get under the covers."

I later kissed and hugged the girls good night just before they dozed, and closed the door, heading back to my guest.

By the time eleven-thirty rolled around, the living room was dark and my bedroom door was locked. Flickering toffee-scented candle-light was all that illuminated my room. And the mirrored reflection of us, together, in my bed, lying side-by-side, looked sensual and beautiful.

I'd gotten used to the feel and touch of someone who looked like me. At first, it bothered me to see two heads with long hair, face-to-face, or two pelvic areas grinding without a penis, or two torsos rubbing against each other with four breasts hanging. Her skin matched mine in color, kind of a Hershey tone, and our legs were thick. Almost heavy. Hers are much longer than mine. Our shapes matched, hair color, nail color, *C*-shaped rear ends, tiny waists, wide hips, etc. It was like I was lying with myself. But, I couldn't have done to myself what Stardust did to me.

"What is that?" I asked as I felt the front of her body up against the back of mine. We spooned and grinded, but a hardness approached my wetness and pulled out and then back in a little bit more. It felt stiff and narrow and long and cool, and it felt damn good.

"Reach back and feel it, baby."

My right hand traveled over my right butt cheek and then in between. The immediate touch answered the question. It was the danggonned beer bottle.

"Turn on over to your back, Georgia. You've got a head-to-toe tongue bath coming." She pulled the green bottle out as I gave her a look like she was creative, yet stone nuts. "Lie back and relax."

I scooted to the middle of the bed and spread my legs. She positioned herself to face my middle and spread me apart with her left hand, inserting the glass beer bottle with her right. And all the while she licked my point and kissed my point, and slobbered on my point, and played with my point until the thrust of the bottle and the feel of her wet mouth sent me into ecstasy. I closed my eyes and imagined how Makkai would be reacting if he were me and she was sucking his dick like she was sucking on my clit, or how fast he would cum if he were watching us.

Then, a rush hit my butt muscles. I grinded along with her movement, and my heartbeat flopped at light speed. Before I knew it I was forcing myself to not yell out her name. What if the girls knew that Mom was letting a lady lick her up and down? That would not be a good thing. She kept at it, even after I spewed my throb her way, torturing me on the heels of a fading orgasm until another one hit and then subsided. She put the *M* in multiple. My toes curled and flexed. She looked up at me and came up to kiss me on the mouth. Her lips were soft and wet, and her breath smelled like me. She smiled.

She stood up only to bend over so that her ass was in the air. I stood up and got behind her, watching my mirrored image grind along-side her plump backside. It was the motion a man would make if he had been preparing to enter her. But, I had nothing but my mound to grind her with.

"Next time, I'll bring my strap-on," she promised me.

"You'll have to show me that. I wouldn't begin to know how."

"You'll get it. If it's been done to you enough, you'll surely know how to give it."

"If you say so." I prepared to bend down and tongue tickle her from behind, when I felt a warm rush from my inner thigh down the inside of my leg. I stuck my middle finger inside of me at the same time as she moaned in anticipation of my lips. I was bleeding.

Chapter 24

Monday

"Oh damn."

Makkai pulled out of me, and his eyes bugged the size of ice cubes. He looked like he had seen a ghost, or at least the ghost of a condom. The invisible condom. It was gone.

"What?"

"Where is it?" he asked.

"What?"

"The condom is gone." He looked in between my legs and all under the percale bedsheets.

I probed my insides and felt it. "It's inside of me. I thought it was mighty wet, but I thought it was me."

"Well, it wasn't. It was me." He was breathing hard.

"Calm down."

He stood up and talked with his hands. "Monday, I came inside of you."

I reached over beside the bed and nursed a warm glass of straight Hennessey. "And? I don't know why you wear those so tough anyway. It's not like I can get pregnant."

"How do you know? And that's not the only reason."

"I guarantee you. I don't have anything."

"How do you know I don't?"

"You're a doctor."

"And doctors can get HIV and other diseases, too, Monday. Don't just lie there, get that condom out of you." He stepped into his black boxers and snatched his pants from the wicker chair.

"Makkai, calm down."

"Get it out of you."

"I will." I lay back on the massive hotel bed.

"When was your last period?"

"I haven't had a period in months. My mother went through menopause at forty-five. I'm just about there." I said, finally stepping away from the bed toward the bathroom. But, not before I finished off my drink.

"I've gotta go anyway."

"Why do we always come to this hotel, Makkai? When are you going to invite me over?" I spoke loudly as I ran warm water and soap on a white washcloth.

"Soon. When are you gonna invite me over?"

I bent down and inserted my middle fingers to remove the filled condom and tossed it into the trash. "Soon."

"I'll call you later," he said tensely, disappearing before I came back out.

I lay back down after Makkai left, as naked as I was the day I came into the world. This man felt good inside of me, but so had a lot of other men in my life. He was right. Sleeping with him would mean that a woman should protect herself mentally and physically, because he got around. But, so did I. And he was good. But, so was I. It just seemed that once we'd done it with a condom for a while and even got tested, that eventually we would just see what it felt like bare. Well, I guess I did just see what it felt like bare. It did feel pretty intense. I knew something was different.

As much as I don't give a damn about having my own man and settling down, there was something that seemed very comfortable when I was with Makkai. It was like we were connected in a way, kinda like soul mates, but it was something perhaps even more than that. I just couldn't put my finger on it. And on top of that, for some reason, deep down I really didn't seem to like him very much. Just liked the way he made me feel. And, he was very, very generous.

Since Makkai had paid for the whole night at the Los Angeles Hilton, I decided to stay. I mean, why waste his money? I got dressed and headed out to get my dog, Soul, came back and used the fifty Makkai gave me to order room service. I laid up and watched *Casino* and *Scarface*. Loved me some DeNiro and Pacino. By midnight I still hadn't really showered to completely wash Makkai off of me. I could still smell his manly aroma. I just laid back, enjoying the pillow-top mattress. My dog was curled up at the foot of the bed, knocked out, in the lap of luxury.

"Hello." I spoke into my cell.

"Hey. What do you say you come on by?" His voice dragged.

"No thanks." I turned from my back to my side. "I'm in bed already."

His tone was dirty. "Just where I want to be with you. Look, I'll make it worth your while"

I yawned. "No thanks, Paul. I'm in for the night."

His tone dropped. "If you say so."

"Maybe tomorrow."

"Maybe. Good night."

I'm perfectly content staying right here. Kinda hard to get with that old geezer now, no matter what he was willing to hand over today. Especially after Makkai Worthy put a hurtin' on me but good.

Chapter 25

Mary Jane

"Mary Jane, you are one fine lady."

I broke down after at least four phone calls per day and tons of good morning emails over the past two months. Carlos talked me into meeting him for dinner at Dem Bones. The rib joint tripped me out because it was the most ghetto rib joint I'd ever seen, yet it was in a white neighborhood. The bench tables were covered by red and white gingham tablecloths. The floor was scattered with sawdust. It kinda looked westerny. And the smoky, mesquite-smelling place was packed. B.B. King songs served as background music.

"Thanks, Carlos."

"May I take your order?" The waitress stood by with pencil and pad.

Carlos said to me, "I like the red-hot ones, but if you don't do hot, they've got a few types of sauces. Just get what you want and enjoy yourself."

I spoke while still eyeing the menu. "I'll try the teriyaki honey pork ribs, with baked beans and potato salad," I told the young girl.

"And you, sir?" she asked Carlos.

"The same sides, just give me the hottest ones you've got."

"Yes, sir." She took the menus. "That'll be the fire engine red hots."

"Sounds appropriate. And to drink, give me a Dos Equis. Do you want anything to drink?" Carlos asked me.

"Just lemonade please."

The waitress smiled and scribbled quickly. "Okay."

"Thanks," we said in unison.

As she stepped away, he gave my face his full attention as he spoke. His trimmed moustache outlined his lips perfectly. "Wow, I can't believe I'm actually here with you. You finally gave in and made time for me. I was about to show up at your job on all fours with my tongue to my chest."

I crossed my arms. "There you go again."

"Now, I didn't mean that in a sexual way. I'm sorry."

"It's okay."

"So, how's work anyway?" He took off his jean jacket, exposing his muscular shoulders and arms under a black tee.

"I love my job. Work is fine."

"That's saying a lot. I work with a bunch of knuckleheads."

"Where's your office located?" I asked, glancing between his face and his hunky chest.

"In Long Beach."

"And how many hospitals do you service?"

The waitress set down our drinks as he replied,

"All of the Kaisers, and Cedars, and a couple in the Valley."

"At least you get to be out and about."

"That's the cool part of it for sure. So, what do you like best about your job?"

I put the straw in my glass of lemonade. "Just helping people. Seeing them get well."

"And you work with cool folks. Like wild-ass Makkai, huh?"

"Yeah, he's cool."

"You two are friends?"

I took a sip, eyeing him. "We work together."

He swigged his cold brewski from the bottle and swallowed.
"Knowing him, it's more than that."

"Like I said, he's cool."

He talked as though he were a tattletale. "That boy was a hoe
from way back when we were in college. Sometimes, he'd get lovin'
three times a day, by three different women. They loved Makkai.
He was very popular. And good-looking."

"Yes, he is. Both of you are."

"Well, thank you."

I swirled the straw around the crushed ice. "I'm sure you had
your share of ladies, too."

He gulped another mouthful. "Like I said, I was internationally
known as the man with twelve inches."

There he goes again. He just can't stop. "Sounds painful."

"Not if you relax."

"Okay. You say so." So fine yet so darn cocky.

"So many women try to scoot. Like I said, you've just gotta
relax."

I simply eyed him. "Carlos, why are we talking about your penis
again?"

"I'm sorry. I do need to stop that."

"Is there any other part of you that you'd like to tell me about,
like about your mind and heart and things like that?"

"Okay, I got you. I have an eight-year-old son who lives with his
mother in Miami. I see him once a month. I make sure to do that. I
talk to my mother and father on the phone every day. They live in
Miami, too, and my mom is very close with my son's mom. I was on
the honor roll throughout most of my academic experience at
USC. I have a dog named Bullet. He's a Labrador. I like oldies but
goodies, but can get down with some rap, too. Love to rent those
black exploitation films, like . . ."

"Like what?"

"I was gonna say."

"Like Dolomite, huh?"

"You said it."

How did I know? Saved by the huge platters of ribs, we ate and talked and laughed long after we finished eating every bite, along with two slices of blueberry white chocolate pound cake. The waitress started looking at us funny like we were hogging the table. And we were.

Carlos asked, "What do you want to do now?"

"I don't know. What did you have in mind?"

"I thought we could go dancing at La Marina near the beach on Culver. It's a tiny spot but they play great music."

"I'll follow you."

We arrived, and he was right. The dance floor was as big as my living room, but the jams were so right. We ordered more drinks and sat at a little corner table, watching the many different ages and races of folks as they crowded onto the dance floor when the DJ played "*Jungle Love*" by Morris Day and the Time. Carlos sprang to his feet and grabbed my hand. I followed him, bouncing and shaking my booty to the beat while we walked.

I must admit that I was intrigued by the way Carlos grooved. He did seem to keep his eyes on my legs, but he had this move he made as he did this side-to-side kind of grinding thing, bending his knees and pumping the air. I backed it up on him, and he subtly rubbed up against me with his hands in the air. Yes, it did feel like he was happy to see me. It was obvious that he had one heck of a banana in his pocket. The syncopated movements definitely served as foreplay. I noticed a few ladies checking him out. He had one heck of an energy about him. Or maybe it was the vodka and cranberry we sipped on all night long, all hugged up in between dances. He continued to tell jokes, making me laugh most of the night.

He was lighthearted. I'll say that much.

And did I say fine?

I think that with Carlos, so many women have oooohed and aaaahed over his looks, and his member, for so many years that they've got him convinced that's where his value lies. I'd promised myself I'd never get to know. I considered that I was just out with him as a little distraction. Makkai had been pretty quiet after he pushed me aside with his fraternizing fears. We did seem to be working opposite shifts around that time anyway.

Before I knew it, Carlos followed me to my place and was inside of my apartment, backing me up as he supposedly kissed me good-bye. But, the door was behind us. He closed it by touch with his foot.

"Where are you taking me?" I asked, as his arms were around my waist and our bodies were pressed together, face-to-face.

"Just to the couch."

He smooched me like he was starving, even though I could taste his combination of vodka and ribs and I know he could taste mine. I felt his teeth as he swirled his tongue about, stopping to kiss my neck as we sat down and he laid me on my back. He unbuttoned my blouse and exposed my breasts, also managing to bite my hardened nipples. I felt him rub against me, lying upon my thigh. And inside his pants, spanning almost the width of my thigh, was definitely a penis that I'm sure would have given any woman stretch marks around her mouth if she'd even attempted to give him head, not to mention a hysterectomy if she'd let him inside of her, even momentarily.

"Do you mind?" He spoke within an inch of my mouth.

"What?"

"If I take off your panties," he said, with one hand under my white ruffled skirt.

"What are you going to do?"

"I just want to taste you."

Ten minutes later, Carlos was tasting me all right, and licking me, and moving his head up and down so fast he looked like one of those bobble-head dolls in the rear window of my grandfather's car. It was like he was having a conniption fit. And, I felt his dang-gonned teeth again for some reason.

His gigantic eyes looked like they could have exploded. "Wow, what happened to your clit? It is the biggest one I've ever seen."

That makes two of us with big ones, I thought. I smiled nervously. I didn't know what to say in response. I know some men think it to themselves. But, they just don't blurt it out like that. Considering how many women I'm sure Carlos has been with, I guess he'd be the clitoris expert.

I closed my eyes and tried to focus upon the sensation, but every time he almost had me on the road to the Big-O, he'd readjust himself and ruin it. Plus, I felt his dang upper front teeth again. Maybe if he'd stuck his tongue inside of me or licked me while sticking a finger somewhere, I might have felt something, but he wasn't using his hands at all. Where were they?

I looked down and he was unzipped. He had one hand on himself, stroking his exposed wand that looked like a dang tree trunk. I wondered if I'd lived such a sheltered life that I hadn't seen large ones like that before. Maybe that was commonplace to some women, I don't know. But, I doubt I could handle that if he stuck it in even half-way.

He stopped for a minute as he inhaled me, then he looked up at the ceiling, making a squinted face, stroking and choking himself to death with increased speed. He placed his thumb over the tip of it, thank goodness, perhaps to keep from shooting all over my mocha suede sofa. It didn't look like much liquid, considering it was from such a long shaft. As light-skinned as he was, his private part was a very dark, Tootsie Roll brown. He then stood up, and it was pointed straight out into the ozone. This time my eyes could have exploded.

"Where's your bathroom," he asked, cupping himself with one hand.

I lifted my hips to pull up my panties and readjust my skirt. "Down the hall on the left." I tried not to look at him, or it, another second longer.

"I'll be right back." He scooped up his clothes and went down the hall.

I stared around the dimly lit room, almost wondering how I'd gotten there, let alone how I let him in. I barely remembered driving home. There I was lying with this man's saliva down there, and I really didn't even know who he was.

I could have crashed right there on my back, lying on my couch with my legs hanging off, spread wide open. I was exhausted just from watching him try to please me.

He looked around. "So, where's your room?" he asked, coming out of the bathroom fully dressed.

"Oh, Carlos, I'm going right to sleep," I replied with an exaggerated yawn.

"That's fine."

I left no doubt. "Alone." I stood up and readjusted myself.

He played it off. "Oh, okay. I see. Well, all right then. No problem. I had a good time." He fiddled around like he was feeling through his pockets for his keys.

I flashed a smile, guiding him toward my front door. "I did, too."

"I'll see you later, right?"

He gave me a peck on the cheek, which was great because I wasn't about to open my mouth again, not that night anyway. He scratched his scalp, stepped out and down the hall, looking back at me as if this were a first for him being sent home. His ego screamed in pain. I continued to smile and closed the door.

Before I could even set my alarm clock, my phone rang.

"I really did have a great time. I want to see you again," Carlos told me.

I was buttoning up my silk zebra pajamas. "Okay." Did I just agree?

"There's this golf tournament in Palm Springs soon. I wanted to know if you'd like to go with me. It would be great to have you on my arm."

"Sounds interesting. Let me know a little more about the date and I'll see."

"I will. Again, I had a great time." He mentioned nothing about the one-sided orgasm fest.

My head was ready to hit the pillow. "Thanks for dinner. Good night, Carlos." Dang I miss Makkai's touch.

"Good night, Miss Cherry."

"Nite."

I hung up and reached over to turn off the light. That was utterly draining.

Chapter 26

Georgia

"What's up?" Makkai asked as I answered my cell phone.
"What do you mean, what's up?" A while back, I would have raced to answer his call; now I wished I hadn't answered it at all. I mean it wasn't like he was calling because he wanted us to be like we were or even more.

"I haven't heard from you for a while."

Please. I was so not feeling him. "I haven't heard from you even longer."

"Georgia. How are you?"

"What difference does it make? It's not your baby anyway, as you said."

"Hold up now, Georgia. In my mind, I did try to give you the benefit of the doubt. But, there are ways to find out."

I tried to keep it down as I sat at a crowded bar of a nearby restaurant. "Relax yourself, Makkai. I had a visitor already."

"A visitor? You had a visitor? So what are you telling me?" I heard the volume of his car radio dissipate.

I responded, "Duh, I'm done with my, you know. I already had it. It was just late"

"I got that part, but are you telling me that you really weren't pregnant? Didn't you use one of those home pregnancy tests or something before?"

"Maybe." A man sat two seats away from me, flashing his teeth. I turned for privacy.

"Maybe? And?"

"Like I said, it doesn't matter now. You're off the hook."

"Georgia, you know what? Okay, fine." The sound of his forced exhale assaulted the phone. "So how are the girls?"

Oh, please, how fake. "Don't ask, Makkai."

"Why are you so mad at me?"

"Actually, because I'm out, and about to have dinner. You've called at a bad time."

"When would be a good time to call?"

"Why? Since I'm not pregnant, now you want to start screwing again or something?"

"I didn't say that."

"Good, because that will never happen again. I've given up on you men."

"I got it, Georgia."

"Makkai, if you cared about me, you would have been calling from the moment I told you, just to make sure I was okay. You were around more when I was pregnant with Rydell's baby than when you thought it was your own."

"I needed time to get my feelings in check. And I didn't believe you were pregnant anyway. At least not by me." I heard the sound of him setting his car alarm.

"Well, congratulations, you were right. And if I have my way, I'll never have another drop of sperm anywhere near me ever again."

"Georgia, I don't want to be your enemy."

"Surely you don't, now. Goodbye, Makkai Un-Worthy."

My boss, Tucker Hill, had connected with this girl he met online while he was chatting via email, acting like he was me, using my photo and everything. It was time to meet. The Joint, a popular chicken wing house, was the spot.

"Wow, you're even cuter than your picture," said lovely, yellow, thirty-something Whitney.

"Thanks. So are you," I replied.

She smelled like fresh air amongst the smell of fried foods and alcohol.

"I told you I was thick. I actually started losing weight, and my girlfriend told me to gain it back."

"I can appreciate that. You've got it in all the right places," I said, looking her up and down and stopping at the middle.

She took a seat at the bar next to me, looking down at my baby-oiled legs extending from my shorts. "So, how long have you lived in L.A.?"

"All my life," I told her amid the sound of the many voices nearby.

"I just moved here from Detroit. Actually, my kids are still there with my husband. We're separated. But, a friend of mine, this dude, hooked me up here with a place and a job, so I'm getting settled in."

"Sounds like a nice friend. So what do you hope to find online?"

"Just a woman who I can kick it with, you know, shop with and rent a movie. I have to have me a woman. It's just something I crave."

"So, does your family know?"

"No, not even my friends. I have female friends, and I have a few girls who I can let my hair down with, you know?"

"So you do like dudes, too?" I asked her.

"Oh, I love men."

"Me, too. Although I must admit that lately they've been getting on my last nerve. You could say I did something stupid, though. I'm probably madder at myself for trying to test this dude, only to find out that he really didn't care like I wanted him to. It sort of backfired on me. But, at least now I know. I read too much into it I guess."

"We all do things like that. We're all just looking for someone to care."

"I just think women understand so much more than men. But, we can't live without em, or so they say. But, I think I'm willing to try," I confessed.

"I'm probably going to file for divorce, but I need to get my kids here first."

"That's smart. I have two girls and wouldn't be able to breathe if their father pulled some crap like trying to take em from me." The guy sitting behind her was grinning all up in my face.

"I know." She leaned in closer. "You know what, I was going to ask you, do you want to eat here or go to this spot I know about."

"I'm down."

"Do you want to follow me?" she asked.

"Okay."

"Let's do it."

The spot was a little gentlemen's club called Sixty-Nine. It was tiny, but the scenery was unlike anything I'd ever witnessed. The ladies were tall and toned and pretty and attentive and limber, bending over to the front to touch their toes. We ordered chicken strips and tangerine wine coolers.

As we took a seat along the main stage, most of the hot and bothered men glanced at us as though we must have been stone freaks. Whatever.

I grabbed my cell. "Mind if I invite my friend to stop by? He's my ex-boss, but he's cool."

"Sure."

One dancer came out and stopped right in front of the both of us wearing a grape thong, shaking her moneymaker. Her name was Tricks, and she was limber enough, from what I could see, to put her own mouth on her own stuff.

"Damn, look at that," Whitney said with one hand in between her own legs.

I stared with my mouth wide open. My lower muscles were jerking.

After a few dancers did their things, in no time Tucker arrived walking all fast, looking impressed at the sight of our new friend. She didn't even seem to notice him. He took a seat with a bulge in his pants. His nature had risen already.

He was average in every way, height, looks. Everything about him was simply average, except for his wallet. He always took care of the bill. He bought us all we could eat and drink. I stuck to coolers, but Whitney had a Long Island, or two.

Before long, I scooted my chair over next to Whitney, whispering in her ear with more tongue than words. "What do you say we go to my place?"

"Sounds good to me," she replied, kissing me on my chin, and then my cheek, and then my eyelid, and then over to my ear, giving me some sort of smooth blowing sensation.

"Okay, it's time to go," I told Tucker, grabbing Whitney by the hand and walking fast to our cars.

She staggered out into the light of day as I guided her. Since she was obviously not holding her liquor well, Tucker drove behind us as I drove her mint green Altima.

"Whitney, now, you need to stop that," I told her as I tried to keep my hands on the steering wheel and eyes on the road.

She leaned over to my lap and started kissing my bare thighs. I squirmed and asked, "Do you want me to wreck your car?"

"Just let me put my head down on your lap. I'm dizzy."

I hugged her hip with my right arm, driving with my left hand while she put her head in my lap. She didn't say a word, but just kept licking my thighs. I think I disobeyed every speed limit by twenty miles per hour. I just had to get this woman to my house.

We all ended up in my bedroom, naked, with Tucker on his back and his dick in my mouth while she watched.

I put one hand on her leg as she sat on the bed. Tucker grabbed a condom from his wallet.

She sliced her eyes at him. "Oh, no, I'm not getting with you like that. I don't think so. I want to be alone with Georgia." She wasn't too buzzed to know that much.

"Okay," he said as I rose up from him. He lay back without opening the condom packet, still excited, and watched me lean her back, as I kicked off my flip-flops and climbed on top of her.

Before she could take her pants off, stubborn Tucker pulled me back on top to finish him, and as I did, she approached his nipples and started sucking and flicking them while he watched us both, rolling his eyes back in his head within no time. He released his pulsation just as I backed away, happy to leave him to himself.

I finally approached her as she was on her knees. As soon as I slid her aqua G-string over to the side, Tucker started to approach her exposed rear end, burying his face deep into her backside. She poked herself out even farther, while I adjusted myself under her, lying to the side. She immediately found my mouth with hers, kissing me with her eyes wide open, watching my every expression. Her tongue was wide and strong. She sucked my tongue like she was trying to get something out of it. Her big, doe-like eyes were sexy, and kind of a brownish green. Her skin was vanilla and her short hair was curly, which smelled like citrus. She moaned while Tucker did his thing. Yeah, she liked the guys, too.

She jerked a couple of times like she was gearing up, and then asked, "Will you rub yourself against me?"

He backed away, hard once again, as Whitney and I banged coochies for about fifteen minutes. She grabbed my tits and played with my nipples while rubbing her V-shaven pubic area all up against me and eyeballing every inch of me. She was getting off fast as she banged me harder and harder, pressing against my flesh, tossing her head back and sucking her thumb.

She focused on my face and gave me this sensual stare. "You're so pretty," she said as her jaw tightened. Her hips collapsed and she squeezed every ounce of her excitement out of her, sliding her fingers deep into her own slippery walls.

Tucker, the little fucker, stood over us with his mouth wide open, getting a grip on himself.

All I could do was look at Whitney's hot ass.

She looked over at me while she came down from her panting moment. "Next time, I still want you to Cook4Me. Alone."

"You know it."

"I've gotta get home," she told us as she arose from the bed, searching for her lace bra.

"Me, too," said Tucker while he zipped up. Boyfriend had to get home to his little family. He also slipped me five, one hundred dollar bills. "I have another one set for this weekend," he said close to my ear.

"Just let me know," I told him while my nipples were still hard from watching her sashay away as they both walked out.

Before hitting the refrigerator for some ice water, I checked my voice mail.

First off, I know we've shared your girlfriend, Stardust. She told me she knew you, even though you will deny it as usual, and besides, knowing what a freak you are, it wasn't hard to put two and two together. Secondly, I saw your hoeish ass today at the club, Georgia. You are scandalous. Third, and lastly, don't give me a reason to take my daughters away from the sick-ass environment you have them in. You will not twist their minds while you act like a dude around them. You're a damn pussy hound. I see you earned your last name, Manley. Fuck with me, okay?

Oh, please, get a life. Where was he while the ladies were shaking their butts today in the club? Probably sitting in the back shellacking himself at the sight of me and Whitney getting lap dances. Oh, hell, now he's really gonna spread some gossip. But, he can't take my kids away just because I like the girls. I'm not worried. Dammit. I can't believe I left my car at that damn club.

I dialed frantically. "Tucker, come back and get me please."

I grabbed my teal purse that my honey Stardust bought me and ran out the door. I missed her.

Chapter 27

Salina

The night before my husband's hearing, which had been re-scheduled way too many times due to him changing attorneys over and over again, Makkai and I spent the night together. Makkai had been subpoenaed, so he had to make sure to be there more than I did. I really wouldn't have been missed, I'm sure. But, the bottom line was, Tom Woodard was my spouse, and until we divorced, I suppose I did have certain obligations. After all, he was trying to kill Makkai because of me.

"Did I tell you my husband is such a punk, that he shaves his private area?"

"His private area?"

"He shaves his Christmas balls and his chest." I had to crack up on that one.

"Salina, that is way more information than I need."

"Okay, but really, have you ever heard of a man mowing his lawn like he's some little bitch? He might fit in just fine in that jail-house."

"Salina, why is it that you don't sound like the dutiful wife? Why did you stay with him if you feel like that? You should have just left him."

"We were trying to work it out. I wasn't going to leave him. But, hell, it's never too late."

"Then do it and stop talking about it."

"Maybe I will, hell." This man is trying to call my bluff. Please. "Anyway, why do we always have to come to this hotel? How come I can't come to your house?"

"For obvious reasons. Why are you complaining? It's a luxury hotel."

"No one is coming after you now, Makkai. No need to hide out. He's locked up."

"You are still married, and you still have a jealous husband."

"Yes, I do, don't I? Well, he's got a new woman now, so I don't think he's too worried about me."

"Don't be so sure. You pissed him off. Don't ever underestimate a jealous man or a man scorned. She could just be a distraction to keep him from feeling the hurt."

"Screw him. I know the best way to get over one is to get into another one." I reached for his belt buckle, undoing it. "So what do you say you help me get over that prisoner?"

I glanced toward his zipper, pulling it down, falling to my knees while he sat on the bed.

"Salina, aren't you hungry? Let's eat dinner first."

"That's just what I want to do, Papi. Feed me." I reached in and took it into my cave of a mouth.

"Salina."

"You love the way I do this and you know it. That's why you can't leave me alone and I know it. Now tell me I'm wrong." I kept my grip on his wide shaft and inserted him in and out of my mouth, making sure to keep it juicy, taking him all the way back, deep into my throat. My wide mouth had always been able to accommodate the good doctor, and he knew it. No gagging, no teeth, and no one handed action.

All he could say was, "We've got to get some sleep before tomorrow morning."

Knowing he'd surrender, I simply watched him as he slowly lay back on the king bed and closed his eyes. His words turned into sounds of pleasure. I then pulled his pants all the way down to his ankles, and he grinded along with my technique. I licked his underside and slid my hand up and down his length.

"Salina, you are the best."

He pumped himself deeper down my throat, and I felt him strengthen. A pulsating burst expelled his fluid into my mouth within seconds. He looked down at me, and I looked up at him, and he watched me swallow every last drop of him.

"Take it all."

I gulped and licked the side of his shaft. "Yummy, baby. Dr. Worthy tastes so good."

"Now come up and kiss me." The boy was a freak. He stuck his tongue all inside my mouth and sucked my tongue the way I'd sucked him. "Now sit on my face," he said with authority.

Makkai had a way of seeming as though he was the only man who had mastered the secret of what it took to make me cum in a split second as well. As soon as he centered his mouth, it was on. And as I lowered my full lips onto his face, he immediately found my spot.

His hands squeezed my backside. I looked down at him go to work. He made it look succulent, the way he was pulling on my meat and licking my wetness. It sounded like he was enjoying a feast. It felt like he was writing graffiti down there. "Damn, that feels good. You like this plump pussy, don't you? Spell my name like you did last time."

"Uh, huh."

"There it is, *S, A, L, I, N, A*. Do the *S* again."

"Uh, huh." He did just as he was told. That tongue had a life of its own. "I'm looking at the best, prettiest pussy I've ever had." He spoke all up against me. I could feel his hot breath. And I believed him. That sentence sent me to Latin mania.

"*Eso se siente tan bueno, el bebé*, so good, like, like, ooooh, Papi, you do me like you love me." I jerked and hit the wall with my fist, flinging my hair wildly while propelling my rush from every muscle of my body down to my swollen opening and to my pink tip.

He spoke from underneath me. All I could see were his fine brown eyes. "I can feel it throbbing. Yeah, that's it. Let it go for daddy."

It felt like I released enough fluid to fill up a shot glass. I pushed forward and then back, looking down at his wet face.

He smiled. "That's my crazy ass-girl. You're the best I've ever had."

The next morning at the courthouse, Makkai and I actually sat on opposite sides of the room. Didn't want to be too tacky, even though we were devouring each other's asses the night before.

"Please rise," the bailiff said as the older, conservative-looking judge came in.

"First case," the judge said as he took a seat, as well as everyone else, and he began stating the names of the first defendants.

Tom ended up being third, which was good. I hadn't seen him in weeks. When they called his name, the side door opened near the jury box, and out he came. Unshaven and looking a tad bit less muscular from not lifting weights regularly or eating my home cooked Latin meals, he wore his prison blues, and his hands were shackled behind him. His ankles were chained as well. He looked kind of rugged and tough and handsome, almost thuggish. In an odd way I found it to be kind of sexy, even though he was very pale. Obviously he'd missed the sun he used to get while running every day. It was sad in a way to see him like that. My husband was in custody because of me.

He took slow steps as the guard assisted him in sitting down. He never looked over at me, or at Makkai for that matter, even though I tried to garner eye contact from him. Instead, he smiled at a dark-skinned woman seated in the front row as she talked to an attorney who leaned over her.

She smiled back at him, and I'll be damn if she didn't wink and then blow him a subtle-ass kiss. My mouth opened involuntarily. I guess Miss Ghetto Queen herself decided to play this thing out and act like she really gave a damn.

"Please advise the defendant to not communicate visually or otherwise with those in the courtroom," the judge told my husband's attorney.

"Yes, Your Honor." The middle-aged black attorney went over and spoke to Tom. And then Tom stood.

The judge spoke. "Mr. Tom Woodard, you have been charged with one felony count of attempt to inflict bodily harm and one count of making a terrorist threat to a Dr. Makkai Worthy. Is Dr. Worthy in the courtroom?"

Makkai stood. "Yes, I am, Your Honor."

The judge nodded. "You may be seated. Attorney Martin, how does Mr. Woodard plead?"

"We have worked out a plea bargain with the district attorney, Your Honor."

"And what is that?"

"Mr. Woodard will plead guilty to a misdemeanor, and the sentence will be time served, plus any other restrictions the court wishes to institute."

"Is this correct, Ms. Pitt?"

The young blond lady D.A. replied, "Yes, Your Honor. We agreed that the defendant be released to the custody of his family."

The judge asked, "Is his family here?"

"Yes, Your Honor," I said as I stood up like a Girl Scout, tall and at full attention.

"Yes, Your Honor," Ghetto Queen said as she stood up, chewing gum.

"Ma'am, you will remove the gum from your mouth before addressing the court."

"Yes, Your Honor," she said, balling up the wad into a tissue.
I shook my head.

"Who are you?" the judge asked me.

"I'm his wife. Salina Alonzo Woodard."

"And you?"

"I'm his girlfriend. Shanaynay Jackson."

The judge looked over at the bailiff with question marked eyes. "Well, whoever he is released to, we need to get a signed agreement from Dr. Worthy, stipulating that this plea is acceptable to him. And I am placing an automatic restraint order, instructing that the defendant stay at least three hundred yards away from the plaintiff for one year, and no contact for three years. Mr. Woodard, do you understand that?"

"Yes, Your Honor."

"Who are you to be released to?"

"Ms. Jackson, Your Honor."

Ain't that a blip? Ghetto Queen turned back toward me with a snarling smirk, as we both took our seats in slow unison.

"Well, I guess that settles that. Now, let me make it clear that if you violate this order, you'll be right back in here. Your fine is twenty-five hundred dollars and one hundred hours of community service, along with ninety days of anger management counseling. And I suggest that you work out your little situation here. Next case."

Makkai stepped up to the bailiff and talked to the D.A., signing the paperwork, and shaking hands while Tom was escorted back through the prisoner door. He still never even looked my way.

Ghetto Queen eyed me as she walked out, after keeping an eye on my husband until he turned the corner and was out of sight. I stepped out right behind her, within two inches of her back. I'm sure she could feel the heat of my breath on her furry neck.

"You'd better be glad we're in court and that there are police all round. The nerve you showed today could have gotten you in big trouble. And by the way." I looked down at her lower body. "You don't have enough ass to keep a freak like Tom."

"Sounds like you just made a terrorist threat to me. All you need to do is get home so you don't miss the delivery of the divorce papers. And here . . . this is my address. Feel free to come by anytime. I'm not scared of you, shorty. But, you might want to use this address when you send all of Tom's things to his new home."

I took the card without even realizing it. "Where's this, in the alley where you prostitute?" I dropped it at her claws.

She barked. "Very funny. We used to screw at my apartment while you thought you were the slick one, out there screwing that doctor. And we've talked on the phone every night since his arrest for hours, just laughing about your pathetic ass. Now, if you'll excuse me, I need to go and make arrangements for my man's, oh, I'm sorry, my future husband's, release." She started to walk away on all fours. "Oh, and by the way, you know what I heard? I heard that you're a hoe who wishes she were black. I heard that this has happened to you before because of your love of big black dick. But, this time, spicy lady, you really fucked up. And you even had the nerve to arrive with the very man whom Tom was trying to defend your honor from. I saw you two when he parked his Porsche. I'm willing to bet he doesn't want you full-time either. The way I see it, Tom can't go anywhere but up from here." She managed to muzzle herself for one quick second and then just had to get in one more jab. "And the reason Tom knew you were at that hotel that night, was because we were both just leaving ourselves when he saw your tired-ass Maxima. Small world, huh?"

That Nigga-ass white man. "You can both go to hell. *Cállese*," I said with flushed cheeks, pressing my index finger to my lips for her to cease her chatter. I turned away with a forceful pivot, walking outside, exhaling into the fresh air, looking back at the courthouse where my husband was. "Dammit, Tom. You were slicker than me," I said to the wind.

"Are you okay?" Makkai asked as if he really could give a damn, walking at breakneck speed.

"No. I can't believe you agreed to that deal." I stayed one step behind him.

"You should be happy."

"You punked out. And slow down," I demanded while putting on my amber shades.

He fooled with his Sidekick. "No, you keep up. And calm down. Let me get you back to your car before you snap and end up locked up yourself. You need to take some time and think about your life, Salina."

"Not that you'd possibly care enough to play a role in where my life is going?"

"Salina, this is what it is. I'm not interested in settling down. We got in some mess, and we should be happy that it turned out as well as it did." He dangled his keys as he walked.

"Well, it looks to me like you need to work on your life, too. Don't come at me like I'm the one who's fucked up. You're so caught up in the sexuality of women that you seem to forget that we have feelings, and a heart, and that we bond. What happened to you in your lifetime to make you such a damn Casanova, Makkai?"

"Good question, Salina. Good question." He got in the car, snatched on his DG sunglasses, and started the car without even opening my door. As soon as I sat in the passenger seat, he took off, burning rubber.

Chapter 28

Salina

"Baby, what is going on out there?" my mama asked while I lie alone in a bed made for two, feeling as though depression is setting in. "Tom called today saying you wouldn't bail him out of jail and he's staying somewhere else. Are you okay?"

My voice moved slowly. "Mama, Tom is staying with his mistress. Did he tell you that?"

"When did this happen? Why didn't you tell us, baby?"

"Because I started all of this, or at least I thought I started all of this, and now my marriage is over."

"Salina, what happened? I thought maybe it was over disagreements about wanting kids, but Tom said he went after some doctor who you were seeing. You didn't do that, did you? You weren't seeing someone else, right?"

"He's one to talk. And did you ask him why he's out there going after people, inflicting bodily harm on strangers?"

"Salina, I asked him a lot of questions. In particular, your dad asked him. Here. Hold on." They did their usual handoff routine.

"*Bambina? Que pasa?* Have you two lost your minds out there? Did Tom lay a hand on you?"

I lay flat on my back, looking straight up. "No, Papa."

"Then what happened? Why do you sound like that? Were you sleeping?"

"Papa, we're just having marital problems. The way it looks, it's over."

"You don't end a marriage, Salina. We told you years ago that unless a man is abusive to you or has some financial dealings, you work it out. And even then sometimes you stay together because of your vows. You work through it. It takes work, but you live up to your marriage. Now, I want you to call him and you two get some counseling, or some type of therapy. Together."

"Papa, you also told me that if infidelity was involved, that you don't negotiate through that."

"I told you not to fool around. That's what I said. But, if it happens, and it does sometimes when a couple is together for years and years, you try your best to stay together. Sounds to me like you two haven't even talked about it."

"He doesn't want to talk."

"Why do you think he called here then? Men are complicated, Salina. He wants us to talk some sense into you, I'm sure. It's not over."

"Papa, don't let him fool you. Tom is living with a young woman who has no class whatsoever. He's right where he needs to be."

"Don't be so sure. You call that man on his new cell number he gave us and talk about it."

"I don't want to. I've met someone else just like he has."

"And who is that?"

"He's a doctor."

"Not the one Tom went after."

"Yes, Papa."

"Salina, any man who would fool around with a married woman is not husband material, I'm telling you. He has no respect for the sanctity of marriage."

"You don't even know him, Papa."

"You are right about that. But, you need to really think about this one and figure out what need you're trying to fulfill by straying from your marriage. Because from what Tom tells me, that's exactly what happened."

"Papa, Tom was straying right along with me."

"How do you know?"

"His new girlfriend showed up in the courtroom to claim him. She called me at my own home and gave me the gory details, play-by-play, not leaving me much to guess about."

I heard him sigh. "Salina, a woman like that will say anything to hurt you. I mean think about it, she's out there dating a married man without any regard for his family. And I still can't believe you didn't tell us what you were going through. We would have taken the first flight out from Daytona Beach, and been there right beside you. Were Tom's parents there in the courtroom?"

"No."

"See, you're both letting the embarrassment weigh more than the strength that family can bring. When was the court date?"

"It just happened yesterday."

"Then how can you say it's over already?"

"Because, I honestly feel nothing for him any longer."

"I don't believe you. I know my baby girl. I can hear it in your voice. You can't fool me. If you're married and in love, you don't fall out of love that fast."

I rolled over on my side and pulled the covers over my shoulders. "Well, I have. You act like I'm not thinking clearly. The point is, I want to be with someone else. Or maybe I just want to be single. But, the way his skank, excuse me, new woman treated me at that courtroom, and the way he refused to even look at me, I never want to see him again in my life."

"Like your mother said, you are angry, but the heat of all that will cool down soon enough. Here, talk to your mother and I'll check on you later. And, baby girl, think about what I said."

"Yes, Papa. Goodbye." The muffle of the handoff was obvious.

"Baby, your dad is right. Fight for your marriage. Fight for your husband. He still loves you. This much I know."

"Mom, I'm done."

"Think about it, Salina. Just take some time."

"Mama, I want Makkai. I want to be single so I can see him on a more regular basis."

"Whoever he is, it may look like that's where you want to be, but close one door first before opening another, Salina. What's the rush?"

"I have closed it. I'm done with Tom. Can't you see that? She can have him."

"Salina, what are you going to do about money? Tom was the sole breadwinner."

"Mama, I'm not worried about that. And just so you know, I have some money saved up. I'll probably go back to finding a clerk job at the courts one day. I'm fine."

"You don't want to look up and your money runs out."

"I think he'll be giving up the cash soon enough once I get through with him."

"Salina, don't. Please. Look, I'm going to let you go but I'll check on you later. You take care of yourself now. I'm worried about you. And maybe you should think about going to see a doctor if this all gets too heavy to handle. We love you."

She doesn't friggin' believe me. I'm fine without Tom.

"I will, Mamma. I love you both, too. Good night."

"Good night."

Again, I lay flay on my back, this time on top of the covers in my huge purple bed, wearing the sexy nightgown Tom bought me on Valentine's Day last year. Looking down at my ankle I spied the two purple hearts I had tattooed when we first got engaged to represent us, together. Purple was our color. Around the room, Tom's jazz artwork hung everywhere. I perused the walls that surrounded me, and portraits of us together, traveling and posing, seemed to bear witness to my every single move. I still had our smiling, framed wedding photo staring at me from across the room. I jumped up, taking weighted steps, and slammed it flat against the dresser. I walked back to the bed, got back under the lilac woven sheets, and again picked up the phone.

"Makkai, can I meet you somewhere? I need to see you."

"Salina, I can't. Not tonight."

"Why?"

His tone was so damn bland. "I have something to do."

"How about tomorrow?"

"I'll call you. They're paging me, I've gotta go. Goodbye."

I don't think he even waited for me to respond before he clicked over. What was going on with him? As was the usual, sleep simply took me out of my misery.

Chapter 29

Georgia

"Hold on a second, Georgia."

About four weeks or so after our last conversation, Makkai and I finally talked briefly. He kept leaving me on hold, clicking over to answer phone call after phone call.

"Okay, I'm back. Sorry. So what were you saying?"

About ten minutes into the conversation, I realized Makkai was definitely starting to see things my way. I wasn't surprised because it was obvious he could only think with his lower head. Negro talked a lot of trash, acting like he was damn near gonna file a restraining order on me if I showed up at his house again. Please. Plus, he treated me like a fool when I told him I was pregnant. But, see, I knew this time he couldn't resist. No man could resist this. No man in his right mind and no man who is one hundred percent straight, and even some gay men. This is every man's fantasy.

"I'll see you tonight," he said just before he hung up.

"I can't wait."

That night, I peeked out of the window just in time to see Stardust's off-white PT Cruiser pull up. She pressed the button to her remote key lock.

I spoke into my cell. "I'm coming down to meet you. Don't move." I had giddy sprinkled all in between my speedy words. Disconnecting from Star's call, I ran toward the open door of the Playa Del Rey hotel room in fifth gear, shutting it behind me, hurriedly making my way downstairs.

She grinned as I approached her.

Our hugged greeting lingered. I spoke into her ear. "Makkai is so excited, girl. This is all he's been talking about since he got here about an hour ago."

Stardust didn't know that all I did was email him a photo of her while he and I were on the phone, and he was down for the count. Telling him she was a stripper didn't hurt either.

Holding hands, we headed toward the hotel room. As usual, I was dwarfed by Star's five-ten frame as I led her to the elevator door. "Is that backpack all you have?"

"Yes," Star said, lifting her gold pack over her shoulder.

"You're spending the night right?"

"Maybe," she replied as she blushed. She looked at me like she suddenly had a case of the shys, glancing around as we exited the elevator and onto the outside walkway, looking down the hall toward the third floor room.

"Girl, you look like an innocent schoolgirl. You need something to drink. What's with the frigid face?"

Star continued down the hall next to me without saying a word. She seemed reserved about doing this, but she'd almost begged me at the last minute since I was giving her my wounded routine about how she needed to try this. Damn, now I'm starting to feel a little bad. Not.

She was surprisingly dressed like she was suddenly on her way to church, all-stylish in her snow-white stretch-knit pantsuit. Her pretty toes, two of them ringed out, looked like they'd been freshly painted with a loud red polish. She normally wore French. Star showed off her perfect feet in three inch, copper sandals. Her toes wiggled as she walked, as well as her ample bottom.

I stood behind her for a second to check her out just before I slipped the key card to room number three sixty nine through the slot. If I'd had a dick, it would have been at full attention. I knew what was between her legs and I couldn't wait to share it with him. Share it my way that is. Funny how it's cool to share a man with a woman I choose, but I'll be damn if he can run around hiding and hitting every girl just because.

The green light flashed, the lock clicked, and I turned the knob and pushed the door open for her to proceed.

I'd sprayed a little Red Door perfume in the room so it smelled luscious. And manly-luscious Makkai Worthy stood from the end of the huge bed, placed the remote on the green and gold comforter and greeted her with a handshake.

Star hesitated, looking him in his face without blinking.

I looked her up and down. "Isn't she just as fine as I told you?"

He replied, "Uh huh. Even finer than her picture."

He pulled her near for a hug. She suddenly seemed even taller, rising up onto her tiptoes to extend a full-frontal embrace and a pat on his back. Now she was looking right around the area of his pectorals. His black dress shirt was unbuttoned to reveal a white wifebeater.

"Nice to meet you," she said.

I swore I saw at least one of his nipples harden as he replied, "And you as well, Stardust."

She placed her backpack near the foot of the bed. I pulled a bottle of chilled champagne, or nerve killer, from the mini refrigerator.

"Have you eaten?" Makkai asked us both.

"Not yet," Star replied.

I shook my head no.

"Let me take you both to dinner," he suggested. "Because you know you should never drink on an empty stomach."

"Oh, you don't have to do that," Star said, shaking her head.

"Believe me, he's planned all of this," I informed her while putting the bottle back in the fridge next to the other two bottles. I moved in close to squeeze Makkai firmly around his waist, standing right next to him. It felt so good to be near him again. It was as if my jealousy drama had flown right on out of my mind, and his.

He hugged me back tightly, looking down at my face. "Did you tell her that you've been getting ready for this all day? Hotel, clothes, everything."

I looked up at him and rubbed the side of his clean-shaven chin with the tips of my long fingernails. "I did."

Star smirked at him and then looked at me. "Yes, she did."

I reminded him, "Baby, this is for you. I know you have a birthday coming up and we just want you to enjoy yourself." I whispered close to his ear. "Stardust is my gift to you." I walked back to the refrigerator to make sure the three champagne glasses were chilling in the tiny freezer.

"My birthday is not for a while but, that's very nice of you. Very nice of you both." Makkai grinned subtly.

He then checked out Star's more than adequate ass as she stepped along the light green carpet to the dresser mirror to freshen up her clear lip gloss. She was rarely made up. But, today she had a sheer-looking, golden shimmer of a glow to her face.

"Let's go," Makkai said, with urgency, breaking his stare and shaking his head in amazement of her rump as she and I walked out of the door. His ass-loving preference was showing.

He motioned for us to proceed first, walking behind both of his birthday gifts. She and I walked hand in hand.

I let her get in the front seat of Makkai's spaceship so she could sit next to him. I hopped in the back behind him. Before we knew it, we were at the Olive Garden on Sepulveda Boulevard, deep into pasta and shrimp and fancy drinks. The ménage à trois was about to be down and dirty, just like me.

Chapter 30

Georgia

A few hours later, three-the-hard-way were back in the room all aglow, laughing and chatting more than before.

"That was a good drink," Star said, looking bright-eyed and bushy-tailed.

"How many Venetian Sunsets did you have, Star?" I asked.

"More than I should have, that's for sure." She giggled as she spoke.

I gave my glance to Makkai, who stood tall and composed. "The designated driver here seemed to abstain."

"I had to look out for you ladies."

"But, it's your birthday," I told him.

"You must think my birthday is this month. It's not until August."

"Whatever."

"You say so. I'm not complaining."

"Oh my. That's one big-ass Jacuzzi there," said Star, jerking her head back as her eyes met the oversized, emerald-green ceramic tub. She looked at it like it had not been there before.

"Thanks for reminding me. We need to get this thing going," I said, turning the long, golden faucets to release the full force of soothing, hot water. I handed Star a box of bath beads.

She poured a tiny bit of the ocean blue Calgon crystals into the water and swirled her hand along to do a temperature test. "It's just right."

Makkai popped the cork on one of the chilled magnum bottles of Cristal and poured a tall glass for Star.

"I will if you will. Take a sip, that is," she told him as she took the glass from him.

"I will." He immediately poured one for himself.

"Good." She held up the glass and looked impressed. "Nothing but the best I see."

"Absolutely." He handed me a glass as well. "For you."

"Well, just a sip or two," I joked.

"Yeah, right," he said unbelievingly. "Cheers." Makkai raised his crystal flute.

I said, "To you and your birthday celebration, whenever your birthday is. And many more."

"Here, here," Star added, as we all raised our glasses and sipped in unison.

Makkai took two long gulps and his glass was empty. He poured himself another one.

Star sloshed the bubbly around in her mouth and said with a frown, "I need to brush my teeth from all of that garlic." She placed her glass on top of the tiny white linoleum bar. "And Georgia, you brought real glasses too. That's some good advance planning there."

She reached into her backpack, removing her tiny cosmetic bag containing her toothbrush. She left the door open to the bathroom as she swirled Aqua Fresh along her tongue and teeth with her finger, finishing up the job with her blue toothbrush.

"Me too," I said as I entered the bathroom just as Star exited. I slapped her butt and she giggled. It bounced just as she put her own hands on it, as if to stop the rolling motion herself.

Star grabbed her glass again and plopped down on the bed after another big gulp of champagne made its way down her throat. "Now this is some good-ass champagne." She sucked her tongue.

Makkai inserted a CD into the portable boom box and began to play *"Freak Me Baby"* by Silk. He said, "It's about to get even freakier once Georgia shows you her new outfit."

I exited the bathroom, lit a ton of candles, turned off the lights, and grabbed my pearl white underwire bra and G-string set from my overnight bag. "This is for later."

"That's new, huh?" Star asked.

"It's for Makkai. I showed him earlier."

Makkai remarked, "Yeah, but I didn't get to see it on you."

"You will," I promised him.

No longer shy, Star said to Makkai, "I dare you to strip down to your birthday suit."

Makkai didn't even blink. "You haven't said nothin' but a word." Within three seconds, he was butt naked, sporting nothing but a grand smile. He was at full attention, pointing at both of us as we sat on the bed. Star crossed her leg over mine. I hugged her as we took in his perfect frame.

The words, *"I wanna get freaky with you,"* flowed through the speakers.

"I want to see what's under there," Makkai told Star with an inquisitive voice, glancing down just below her waistline. He finished off his second glass of champagne and poured even more.

She still seemed amazed by the sight of his private part.

"Now if you need help, just let me know," he volunteered.

"No, I can do it," she replied while smiling but still staring. Her eyes looked stuck.

"Show him what you've got, baby," I encouraged her.

She broke her stare to look down as she pulled off her white pants and revealed her leopard, bikini-cut panties, and then she took off her lemon colored tube top. She was braless and her tits were perky and firm and round.

She did a half-turn as her full, red-boned cheeks bounced in vibration to her step.

"Now those are some cheekz, there. I've got two shapely, big-boned, Coke-bottle ladies up in this room."

Star joked, "We've got dick for days and ass for weeks."

"Make it a week for your tail alone," he joked.

She turned back around chuckling, and this time her brown-skinned titties bounced, tipped off by tiny, dusty rose nipples that looked like bugs on a headlight. They looked extra suckable tonight.

Makkai started to moonwalk. "Well, it's my turn to get fresh breath, and when I come out of that bathroom, I want to see some mutual admiration up in here."

Star told him, "Oh we know how to do that."

"I'll bet you do."

"Hey, girl, the Jacuzzi is ready. Wanna try it?" I asked.

"I'm game," she replied without a second thought.

She removed her panties and I stripped down bare body. I poured myself into the tub to bask in the luxury of the eighty-degree water. Star sat on the edge.

"Hey," Makkai said, reentering the room, grabbing his glass and turning on the jets as he stepped in next to me while Star watched from the side. He placed his glass on the tile ledge. His sights were on her clean-shaven pussy. His chin dropped, which only made her open her chocolate legs farther.

With eyes frozen, Makkai said with a moan. "That's so pretty! And you've got a little mole on the side." Her baldness stared back at him.

"I call it her chocolate chip. I keep trying to lick it off but it won't go away. I'll just have to keep trying," I told him as I leaned over and put my mouth to her southern lips.

Makkai watched while Star closed her big brown eyes and moaned. I moved my head up and down and side-to-side as the sounds of lubricating Star's vagina took over the room.

Makkai swigged another long sip, leaned back, securing him-self farther into the water, with his knees protruding outward through the bubbles. He had a major up-and-down grip on his hard-on.

Star leaned her head back and started to damn near growl. She jumped and flinched and flexed her legs and wiggled her hips. I had a firm grip on her swollen muscle, with just enough tongue-time just below. I took Makkai's hand and placed it on her right breast. He squeezed it and rubbed it and she suddenly looked down at his hand on her skin. She moaned louder and grinded deeper into my face. I reached over under the water and took Makkai's penis into my hand. He groaned deeply while I stroked his shaft. He continued to grip her breasts and I continued to eat her out, keeping one eye on him. Makkai exhaled and inhaled rapidly, over and over again, struggling to catch his breath.

"Work him, Georgia," Star told me as he squeezed her nipple with his thumb and forefinger. It's as if he knew what she liked.

She grunted and squeezed her legs around my head. He grunted and pumped his dick faster inside of my hand, and they both made an undignified, similar sound of passion-satisfied, as he spilled his liquid through his tip, and she secreted her liquid into my ready-to-receive mouth.

Star looked at him, and he looked at her, and I pulled back and wiped my mouth with my hand.

"You're good," they both said to me at the same time.

I smiled pleasingly and wiped my forehead. "I don't know about you two but I'm headed for that enormous bed. It's hot in here." I got out, found a towel and patted myself down.

"I'm right behind you," Star told me.

Makkai stepped out behind us, finishing off the other half of his glass of bubbly.

I stretched out on top of the white cotton sheets, propping a down pillow behind my head. Star lay next to me, still wet, eyeing every inch of my body while sniffing her way down within an inch of my brown skin. She briefly kissed my navel and touched my thighs with exploring fingertips. She then lay on top of me, lying just so our nipples brushed against each other. She looked me dead in the eyes and kissed me.

"I love you," she said with passion.

I was never going to get a chance to wear that bra and panty set now. It was on.

Makkai gave an inquiring look, but still stood over us with a full erection, eyeballing the happenings while towel drying his heated self with a scissor-like, back-and-forth motion across his back. He reached into the refrigerator to open a second bottle and filled his glass to the rim. He gulped two swallows in two seconds flat. He popped his tongue, "*Ahhhh.*"

Star kissed my smoky eyelids, mascara coated lashes, my earlobes, and then she traced a trail up and down my neck. She moaned and started to grind. I moaned and started to grind back. Makkai moaned and assumed the jack-off position.

I bent my knees upward and inward in a missionary position. Star lay on her belly, and moved down to the exact spot of my entry and adjusted her position for comfort. She pulled my lower lips apart to expose my pinkness and licked with a flat tongue, spitting and licking over and over. She buried her face and went to work. My clit throbbed. Her middle finger probed my deepness. She looked up at me with big half-drunken eyes.

My ass flexed. I closed my eyes. The thought of Makkai watching us in action was burning my desire fast. Star's tongue-tickling was fueling an early explosion. I felt a rush and then heard deep, full-on grunting sounds, followed by a scream of pleasure. It was as if Makkai had his penis inside my woman. My eyes popped open.

"What the fuck are you doing?" My heartbeat was as loud as my words.

Makkai stood behind Star with her generous ass meeting his groin. "What?" he asked, still half-pumping.

"Star, don't let him do that. Don't let him fuck you. You don't let guys fuck you."

I forcefully pushed her face away from my middle as she looked up at me.

"Ouch." She squinted her eyes.

I scooted back and sat up. "Makkai pull out. Get out of her."

Star had the nerve to look amazed. "Georgia, what is wrong with you?"

"Get the fuck out of her Makkai. You were only supposed to fuck me. I told you that."

"You did not." He pulled out with major reluctance. She tried to hide the sounds of a sigh that signaled the sensation of his exit. I wanted to slap her.

Instead, I pointed to within an inch of her nose. "Well, you knew. Why did you let him inside of you?"

She sat up with nipples as hard as steel. "Georgia it felt good."

"Felt good? You told me you don't even like dick."

"Georgia calm down."

"No, you calm down." The volume of my voice was as strong as my anger.

"Baby, I was pleasing you. I thought him inside of me would please you too."

"You weren't thinking of pleasing me when you let him inside of my pussy. That is my pussy, Star. I can't believe you let him do that. We talked about you only sucking him off, that's it."

With his deflated member hanging soft and low, Makkai made his way to his pile of clothes and stepped into his sweatpants. "You know what, I'm just going to get dressed and head out."

I crossed my arms. "You do that."

Star leaned toward me. "Baby, I love you. I would never want to hurt you." She looked back at him, and then at me, and then back at him again. "Makkai, we can finish. Georgia, I can watch him fuck you if you want. Makkai don't leave. Besides, you've had too much to drink to be driving so soon."

"Yes, Makkai leave." I cut my eyes and stayed focused on her. "Star, you lied to me. You got caught up and you broke the rules."

Star spoke as though confused, "Why is it that you're the only one who gets to enjoy the dick, Georgia?"

"Because you told me you don't enjoy it. You said it disgusted you before. And now you say it felt good. Screw you, Star."

Makkai cleared his throat but I still ignored him.

Star's arms reached my way. "Come here."

I retreated. "Get your hands off me."

"Georgia, stop." Her eyes were begging me.

"Star, you really were feeling him, huh? Acting all giddy and shit. Fuck it. Just put on your clothes and let's go." I jumped to my feet and wrapped a half-damp towel around me.

"Georgia, you're ruining this night we planned for Makkai."

I looked over at him as he put on his watch. "You're not gone yet?" I turned my back and heard his keys dangle. I saw a torn black package from a Magnum-ribbed on the floor lying next to an open box. "And take your condoms with you."

Makkai's voice jabbed my earlobes. "You can have them. Put it on your strap-on. Goodbye."

I heard the door slam. "I can't believe you, Star."

She walked up behind me, rubbing her still-naked self against my butt. "Georgia, I'm sorry." She damn near purred.

I jerked. "Get you damn hands off of me."

She turned me to face her. Her arms took over my waist. I found myself crying on her chest while she held me like I was a child. She soothed my forehead with her hand and brushed my hair back. She looked down at me and rubbed away my single falling tear.

My eyes burned as I shut them. I squeezed her tight. "I love you too, Star."

Chapter 31

Don't say I love you. No anal sex. No threesomes.

My weakness . . . women. I should have known better as soon as Georgia sent me that email, forwarding sexy Stardust's photo. I should have known then there was going to be trouble.

Okay, so I broke one of the three cardinal rules. Or should I say I broke one of my father's cardinal rules. I guess he was right for once . . . more than two in the bed is nothing but trouble. Jealous women will be jealous women no matter if they're straight or gay. That's the last time I bring more than one woman into my bedroom. I am done.

I know that much in spite of the hangover beast that was repeatedly banging me upside the head with a billy club. All I could feel was the intermittent pain and throbbing of what champagne can do to me, even Cristal. The oddness lived in my system. In lieu of that, my black Aviator lenses shielded my blood-stung eyes from the world.

"Excuse me, Dr. Worthy, there's a call for you. Line two," the young swing-shift bed nurse told me as I stood near her desk at the beginning of my shift. I removed my shades and began to pick up the receiver.

I asked the nurse, "Who is it?" I popped four Ibuprofen and swigged from a bottle of Evian.

"Beats me. Some man," she said as she walked away.

"Dr. Worthy here."

"Hey, son. How are you?"

"Dad?"

"Your one and only."

Just stop the world and let me off. "Hey, Dad. I'm fine. What's up with you?"

"What do you mean what's up? Does there have to be something up for me to call my son?"

I flipped open a chart. "You know what? I have a patient to check on in a few minutes. I'm going to have to go."

"Aren't you even gonna offer to call me back?"

"I'm just really busy."

"I was never too busy to call my father when he was alive."

"Dad, I think I stay in touch just fine."

"You do, huh? I know you're a big-time doctor and all, and I'm real proud of you for that; but you just never know if this could be our last conversation, and too many years have gone by for you to sound like you do."

He always gave me the what-if-I-die guilt trip.

"I'm not trying to sound distant, but I'm at work, Dad."

"I get that."

"And by the way, it takes two to stay in touch. I haven't heard from you in years."

"Well, I made the move to call you this time. It's not like I have your cell number. I have to call the main number at that hospital to have them find my own son."

"I sent all of that to you, including my home number, when I mailed a birthday card a few months ago, and the Christmas card before that. And to be honest with you, I enclosed a one-thousand-dollar check that you never even called to thank me for. But, I did notice that you cashed it."

"Oh, I thought you didn't have any time to talk. How long have you wanted to say that? Looks like you sure have time to get on my case. I've never asked you for money. And that's not why I'm calling now."

"Really though, I've got to get going. I'll try to call you back."

"Son, what I need you to do is head this way for the Worthy family reunion here in Wildwood in August. Actually, it'll be in Orlando. Everyone will be here. Your cousins put a lot of work into this, and they asked me to get in touch with you. Everyone's proud of you and would like to see you. Will you take some time and come on out?"

"I'll try, Dad. Send me the information. Do you have access to email?"

"Boy, even after all these years, you know me better than that. Nothing beats picking up the phone and talking. All of that email stuff just keeps people from talking spontaneously. Whatever happened to the good-old days?"

"Well, ask someone to send me the info to *Mworthy@aol.com.*" He was silent. "Dad, did you get that?"

"Hold on, now."

"I have to go. *Mworthy@aol.com.* I'll get back to you. Now, goodbye."

"Oh, okay, fine. I love you, Mr. Doctor, son. Never forget that."

"I love you, too, Dad. Goodbye."

The nurse on duty walked over as I hung up the phone. "What's wrong with you? I haven't seen you frown like that since we had our last flat-lined patient."

"Just a voice that gets to me. Family stuff."

"Who?" Nurse Mary Jane asked.

"My dad."

"Your dad? I've never heard you talk about him. Where does he live?" She flipped through the patients' files, taking some out, replacing others.

"In Florida. He was telling me about our family reunion coming up."

"Are you going?"

"I'm thinking about it. If I can work it in, I probably will."

She looked up at me. "Take it from someone whose parents are dead. No matter what, make time for family at any cost. The blood-lines you share are what life is all about."

"I've got my mom here. She's who I make time for because she made time for me." I signed a prescription and initialed a lab slip.

"I don't know what the issues are, but life is short. Better to for-give a living parent than wish you'd forgiven them once they pass away." She resumed her filing.

I watched her work. "Okay, Nurse. You know you need to trans-fer into the psychology department, right?"

"Just life experiences, not schooling."

I smiled her way. "I hear you. So wise to be so young. Hey, what are you doing later on?" I asked, almost wondering if I already knew the answer.

"Nothing."

"Got time a little later on for a man whose frown you helped chase away?"

"I suppose so."

I couldn't believe she replied like that so easily. Especially after my speech about my fears that people at work will know about us. And here I was standing like I could suddenly give a damn. "See you around midnight?"

She whispered discreetly, "I'll be home." This time, she ended up being the one looking around to make sure no one was within earshot.

Another nurse walked up and handed me a chart. "Dr. Worthy, your valvuloplasty patient in 2508 is refusing to take his meds. He's telling me you told him he didn't have to."

"I'll go take care of it," Mary Jane offered.

The nurse added, "Doctor, you also have a family waiting for you to go over the CT scan results. They're in the ER waiting room."

"Give me ten minutes."

Nurse Mary Jane asked, "Do you want me to see about the pa-tient with the meds?"

"No, I've got it. But, thanks."

"No problem."

Damn, that woman must be trying to get me to let my guard down. And she's doing a good job. It didn't help that I caught a glimpse of her from the back as she walked away, making that baby blue and pink nurses uniform look like a sexy jumpsuit. Her figure eight was definitely showing.

As Mary Jane turned the corner I heard, "Hi, Dr. Feelgood," in a drawn-out tone. It was Dr. Lois Taylor walking side-by-side with another female doctor.

"Dr. Worthy," I responded.

They both giggled like children and talked amongst themselves, turning their backs as I headed toward my patient's room. Grown women can be so damn silly, especially when one is the head of three departments. But, hell, I guess being that I think with my dick most times makes me one to talk. My bad.

Chapter 32

Mary Jane

Makkai will be by soon. I walked around, straightening and cleaning up my small, earth-toned apartment, cleaning glass tables, vacuuming, scrubbing sinks and toilets, selecting just the right lavender incense, just the right amount of light, just the right scented candles, just the right sexy black skirt and top combination.

It has been a long time since we've seen each other outside of work. I really miss getting ready for him. Can't believe I agreed to let him come over. Oh, well. Makkai is simply irresistible. I'd never anticipated a man's arrival like I anticipate his, ever. I never would have thought I'd let a man come by so late simply to accommodate his schedule. But, for some reason, I don't care what time it is.

Overall, I realized that spending time with Makkai is nice, and easygoing, and pretty much drama free, unlike with some men. For the most part, he doesn't disagree with me when we talk, he doesn't toss his one-sided opinions my way and judge me for mine, he doesn't criticize me or tell me what I need to do, he asks about my brothers and my niece as if he really cares, and he makes me laugh. That's worth its weight in gold. I accept this arrangement, and he hasn't given me the impression that anything other than spending time at my house every now and then is part of the deal. He doesn't ask me who I hang with, and I don't ask him. He hasn't given me the impression that I'm his girlfriend, and I haven't given him the impression that I want to be. Though I do want to settle down and have kids. I'll reassess this situation if and when I meet someone whose my Mr. Right. But, for now, I'm enjoying a man who can make me feel good in every way, whether I'm in his arms, or just sitting next to him, or when he's inside of me. This is new for me and I'm going to enjoy it.

His hands were full.

"Thanks, you didn't have to," I told Makkai as he walked in with a round vase full of short stemmed, baby pink roses. He hadn't done that before.

"I wanted to. That's for the little pep talk you gave me earlier today. I really appreciated it." He placed them on the mantel over my fireplace.

"Anyone would have done the same thing if they noticed the look on your face."

"Most probably wouldn't have noticed, that's just the point."

"Well, thanks. They are absolutely beautiful." I gave him a soft peck on the lips.

He looked around. "Your place looks great as usual. I love the candles burning in the fireplace."

"I got that from *O* magazine."

"That Oprah knows everything, doesn't she?"

"Yes, she does. Listen, can I get you anything?"

"What do you have?"

"Your usual, rum and Coke, or do you want to try something new?"

"Like what?"

"I have this butterscotch apple martini I can make?"

"What are you having?"

"I'm down for trying something new."

"Then I'll join you. Make it two," he said, taking a seat on the sofa, pointing the remote toward the TV screen.

I spoke from the kitchen. "Okay. And watch whatever you'd like. I know you don't watch much TV, but I'm sure your "*Law and Order*" show is on some channel." I took down my martini glasses and squeezed butterscotch onto the insides in a swirling motion.

"Oh, you're right. It's on right now."

I gave a quick chuckle. "So did you ever get the guy to take his meds?"

"Sure did. I had to promise him he'd get a date with you, though."

"Yeah, right."

"No, really. I told him you offered to come in but I decided to see to him myself."

"No you didn't." I poured the chilled apple martini blend to the rim.

"He said he'd take the pills if you brought them to him next time. Said you were a fox."

"That guy did not say that."

"He did. Can you blame him?"

"Please, people don't even notice me. My name should just be Jane instead of Mary Jane. I should just replace the Mary with Plain. Plain Jane Cherry."

"I'll tell you, you're gorgeous inside and out, and it doesn't hurt that you've got the best shape I've ever seen. I don't know what mirror you're looking in."

He took the drink I carefully handed him along with a paper napkin. "Here you go, charmer."

"Thanks. Looks good."

"Okay, so, enough with your exaggerated compliments. You're going to get some anyway, so you don't need to go there." I tilted my head and winked.

"Believe me, woman, my compliments are real."

"Well, thanks." I headed back to the kitchen to get my drink.

"So, how are your brothers and little Yardley?"

"They're fine. I got an email from my oldest brother just yesterday. He said Yardley is growing so fast. They're going to mail some pictures once they go to this photo place in the mall this week-end."

"I know you'll have that one framed and placed right up there on your mantel."

"Yes, I will. I love that little one."

He gave a chuckle and stared at the TV.

"So, have you thought any more about your dad?"

"I've tried not to."

I glanced at his handsome face and wondered if he took those good looks after his dad's side of the family. "I can see that you need to unwind and think of nothing but relaxing. Just sit back and enjoy your drink and some TV."

"As much as I love *"Law and Order,"* I didn't come here to stare at the box." He patted the couch, motioning for me to come and sit next to him. "I've wanted to hug you all day."

I turned off the light in the kitchen, walked over to the sofa, set my drink down and sat next to him as he put his arm around me. "That feels nice." I kissed his chin and then his lips. He found a way to lie back, and he pulled me on top of him. The whole time we were tonguing each other with passion. I could feel his nature rise and rise. He kissed my mouth firmly, and kissed my cheekbones, and made his way to my ears. "That feels so good, too," I told him. They say the ears are wired to trigger a rush in the vagina. I believe it now. My eyes closed.

I heard him say, "You feel good."

My phone rang louder than it had ever rung.

"It's okay if you want to get that."

I never even opened my eyes. "No, I'm okay."

He stopped. "It is pretty late." He leaned upward, helping me to a seated position as I opened my eyes. He took a long sip of his drink.

I leaned over and picked it up. "Hello. Hey, what's up? Yes, I was. No. I forgot about that. I'll let you know tomorrow. Yes. Yes. No, it's okay. Talk to you later. Good night." My short sentences were generic.

"What's wrong?"

"Nothing. I just need to get back to someone later, I mean tomorrow." I took a gulp of my drink myself.

"If you want to call them back, it's cool."

"Makkai, it's fine. I'm fine. I'll call them back tomorrow. Where were we?" I leaned toward him. He was stiff.

"Them?"

"Them."

He shook his head as if to snap out of it. "Sorry to distract you from the call." He downed the martini glass full of tannish green liquid.

"No need. I'll tell you now though, it was Carlos."

"I thought so. Can I have another drink?"

"Sure." I stood up and headed to the kitchen bar. "Are you cool with that?"

"I am. Just as long as he's not calling because he knows I'm here."

"He wouldn't do that."

"You say so."

"Well, I guess you know him better than I do."

"Oh, yes I do."

I placed his second drink on the coffee table next to mine. We each picked up our glasses, drank from them, and then held on to them. I crossed my legs. He crossed his legs.

I said, "He asked me to attend a golf tournament with him. Some sort of weekend in Palm Springs."

"And?"

"I haven't decided. I'll let him know tomorrow. Enough about him." I placed my drink on the table and sat back.

He didn't follow suit. "Well, I know I'm not going now."

"You were going?"

"I was." He downed the remainder of his second drink as well, placing the glass back on the coaster.

"Don't let me stop you from going. I'm not even sure I'm going. And, Makkai, if you bring someone I'll be fine, so don't even trip."

"You're better than I am, then."

"Look, is it that it's Carlos? If I showed up with someone you don't know would it matter?"

"It's not supposed to matter now. That's how Carlos and I deal with each other. We can throw up a red light if we want to."

"Do you want to?"

"I can't."

"But, do you want to?"

"You know there have to be more interesting things to talk about than Carlos."

I put my feet up under me and rested my head on his shoulder. "But, Makkai, tonight I don't want to talk about anything. I just need some TLC. I had a rough day, too, you know."

"You did, huh? Well, let me see what I can do." He looked like he was willing to surrender.

He scooted me down toward the end of the sofa, lifted my skirt, got down on his knees and went to work. This new sensation he introduced me to was something I couldn't believe I'd missed out on my entire life.

He talked to it. "This is the best pussy, the prettiest pussy, the sweetest pussy, I've ever had." He parted my legs, rubbing my thighs as he kissed me, sticking his tongue inside. He then came up to kiss my mouth. With his left hand, he reached down and inserted his middle fingers, which seemed to be hitting upward toward a spot in the direction of my belly, and it was causing a sensation that was indescribable.

With his right hand, he reached back and grabbed my foot, bringing it toward his mouth, and licking my arch and sucking each toe, from the baby toe on over. I closed my eyes, still feeling his left hand inside of me.

He brought his face back downtown, and started doing something to my clit. That and the combination of his fingers moving in and out made my rush pulsate, and I yelled out, "Makkai. *Oooohhhhhhhh. Aaah.*"

Maybe I just felt something special for him, but the brotha was good.

He took a big gulp of my martini, and then gave me a sip from my own glass, picked me up and carried me to my bedroom where I had already pulled back the dark red covers. He set me down on the bed, stepped back and slowly removed his clothes.

His saluting woody was major. I looked at *it. It* looked at me. *It* was hard and ready. I told him in a submissive voice, "I want to take you into my mouth first."

"No, baby, it's your night. It's all for you."

He turned me to my side and lay behind me. I didn't even notice when he put on his condom, but it was on when I reached back to grab him and place him in the exact spot. He pushed himself inside, pressing his groin area against my butt. The sound of our skin meeting, and the feel of his hands around my waist, and the feeling of his tongue in my ear, as if he were licking me down below, was a sensual, beautiful turn-on.

"You're the best, Mary Jane. Are you going to let Carlos get some of this?" Oh no, the trash talker in him came out.

"No, baby. Because you're the best, too."

"Are you sure? I think you want to fuck him."

My voice was shaking. "No. I've got a lover who takes care of me, makes me cum and, and, and makes me . . . Makkai, I'm cuming."

"I feel it grabbing me, baby. Take it all." He went deeper as I reached down to rub my clit, pushing out a bursting rush. I could feel the heat of his dick, even through his condom. Or maybe it was the heat from my own insides. I had never cum that much, and that fast, with him before.

I looked back at him. "I don't know how you do it."

"It's easy with what we have. You're the best." He slapped my butt cheek.

"What do we have?"

"We have chemistry. Now, turn over on your stomach so I can give you some more."

"Makkai, it's your turn."

He took off one condom and put on another. "No, it's time for your third one."

He stood up and leaned me over the foot of the bed as I watched our erotic reflections in my oval dresser mirror. It was like I was starring in a porno movie. After a while, he got a rhythm going, faster and faster, and his muscular cheeks pumped away as he bent his knees. He leaned his head back and closed his eyes, and then pulled out, yanking off his condom while he shot his juices onto my ass while he grunted.

He immediately fell over onto the bed. "Now that is some good pussy," he said, lying upon his back. "Damn, it smells like sex in here."

"You are one hell of a lover," I reaffirmed, heading toward my bathroom.

"You make me want to be."

I yelled to him while I wiped off my back, "Makkai, I won't go with Carlos."

"You can go. You should go. Don't let this get in the way." He came to a stance as I walked back toward the bed.

"I can get you a towel," I said.

"No, I can get it, thanks." He casually headed toward my hallway linen closet.

That night, I found out that pillow talk and the real world are two very, very different things.

Chapter 33

Georgia

"Makkai, what is wrong with you?"

"Georgia, what do you mean, what's wrong?"

"I haven't heard from you in a couple of weeks."

"Heard from me? You kicked me out and cussed me out for the last time. Besides, I thought I'd leave you to your domestic problems. Stardust is your woman?"

I whispered. "She's just a friend."

"Oh yeah, right. Georgia, friends don't trip like that. You two have clit-bonded."

"What does that mean? You knew we'd been together before."

"Not like that. And why the hell you're in denial, I'll never know. Don't be afraid to be who you are, gay, straight or whatever."

I heard a voice in the background. "Georgia, your mom called on your cell to see if you picked up the kids from Rydell yet. Apparently he told her he's been calling you like crazy. What time were you supposed to pick them up?"

"I'm on the phone, Star."

Makkai said with a warning. "Georgia, go pick up those kids."

"They're fine."

A click sounded like the other phone had been picked up. I said, "Get off the phone."

"Who is that?" Makkai asked.

He knew good and damn well who it was.

"Rydell is at the door, Georgia," Star said from the other line.

"Stardust, hang up the damn phone. And why did you answer my cell?"

"It vibrated like twenty times. The question is why are you talking to *him*?"

I just had to go there. "You're the one who bonded to his dick skills, you should know."

Star still downplayed everything. "Believe me, it was not that serious."

I replied, "You'd never know it."

"Georgia, hang up," Star said insistently.

I demanded, "No, you hang up my fucking phone. This is my house. Hang up now."

"I'm going to sit on this end of the phone until you hang up and answer your front door. I know you'd rather that I be on the phone than answer that door." The girl had nerve.

"I don't give a flying fuck."

Makkai said, "Umh, umh, umh. Here we go again. Goodbye."

"Makkai wait," I yelled like my life depended on it.

"Why me?" I heard Makkai ask as he gave me the damn dial tone.

"Why are you still calling him anyway," Star asked.

She got ignored. I slammed down the kitchen phone.

"Don't beat the door down Rydell, I'm coming. And you need to calm your ass down," I said, pointing to my woman as she walked into the living room. I yanked open the front door. "What Rydell?"

Rydell stood with his arms crossed. He was short and reddish-brown and baldheaded, and he looked kind of square, but he absolutely wasn't. I don't know what I ever saw in him.

He asked with a scowl, "What is your problem?"

I stood with hands on hips. "Again, what, Rydell?"

"The girls are in the car."

"I told you I'd pick them up."

"You told me you'd meet me at Starbucks hours ago. And, you're not answering your cell." Star walked from the sofa to the kitchen. Rydell peeked inside. "Who is that?"

"Don't worry about it."

"Georgia, please tell me that's not who I think it is." He peeked into my dimly lit living room.

"Rydell, I can't believe you left those girls in the car. Bring them up."

He pointed. "Is that Stardust?"

"Bring them up here."

"No. I'll take them to your mother's house. This is no type of environment for young girls. Are you all up in here licking on each other, or something? Is she living here? She'd better not be living here, Georgia."

Star spoke demurely as she headed into the bedroom with a glass of lemonade. "Hi Rydell."

I spoke to her and then him. "Please excuse us. Rydell, forget it. I'll go down and get them."

He put up his hand. "No, you can pick them up from your mother's house. If you were so worried, you should have answered your phone."

"Rydell, just let them come up."

"You have fucked up for the last time. You just wait."

"Are you through? I'm not going to fight with you. I'll ask my mom to call me once they're there and I'll go get them. Now what else do you think you can find to argue about?"

"You're not going to live the lesbian lifestyle and expect to have my daughters, too."

"What goes on in my house is none of your business. Do I trip over your little knock-kneed bimbos running all up in your place like it's a revolving door. Just when one leaves, another arrives. At least I show some consistency."

"Oh, so this is a relationship you and Stardust the slut have?"

I took one step toward him. "You know what? You need to watch your mouth. And yes, we are together, okay? Now what? Now leave me the hell alone Rydell. Good bye."

"Just what you needed to say. Goodbye."

Slam.

Door lock.

About face.

Star came to take my hand.

I promised her, "Now it's out. Mom will know too."

Star smiled.

"Or should I say, I'm out?"

A moment later I picked up the cordless phone to call Mom while I sat on the love seat next to Star.

I asked as the phone was answered, "Who's this?"

A reply came without hesitation, "This is your father?"

"Dad? What are you doing there?"

"Hey Georgia, nice to talk to you, too."

My voice shifted into loudness. "Where's Mom?"

"Hold on."

I spoke to Star with a frown. "I can't believe my mom took my dad back."

Star rubbed my back.

"Mom, what is going on?"

"Ask yourself that. Why didn't you meet Rydell so he could drop off the girls? He said he's been calling and calling."

"You took Dad back after all he did to you?"

"Georgia, I am not in the mood for this. You cannot ask me about my private life. You just handle yours."

"Oh, I will. See, now I remember how you talk to me when he's around. You're so different. Mom, I'm on my way because Rydell is dropping the girls off there at any minute."

"Fine."

"And I'll just honk. Please have them ready."

"Fine."

"We'll just honk. Me and my girlfriend, Star."

Click.

Chapter 34

Mary Jane

By the end of the month, dark and handsome Carlos drove his jet black Escalade on bright shiny chrome from the off ramp of the 10 freeway. He left me in charge of his large collection of CDs all the way to the desert. Most of my selections were female artists like Anita Baker and Toni Braxton. I replayed *Seven Whole Days* more than a few times.

"I haven't been able to get you out of my mind since the other night."

"Carlos, that really should not have happened."

"Oh, I'm glad it did happen. You are an amazing woman. You're smart and beautiful and funny and sweet, and very, very sexy. I'm just proud to have you coming out with me to spend some time alone."

"I'm happy I was able to make time to go. But, really, Carlos, I want you to know that I'm here strictly for the rest and relaxation."

"Oh, no, I understand that. I need that myself, too. Don't you wanna get in a round or two while you're here?" He grinned sexily. "Golf, that is."

"Oh, Carlos, you know I don't play golf. I'll leave that to you while I lie out and rest." I flipped through the CD sleeves.

"Sure, and get you a massage or two while I'm out."

"Did you book two rooms, like we talked about?"

"I booked a room with two beds. The Hyatt is completely sold out."

"You're sure there are two beds."

He nodded. "Yes. I made sure."

"Carlos, I just want you to know, I'm not interested in getting intimate with you again. Maybe I was buzzed the other night, I'm not sure, but afterwards, I felt I shouldn't have let that happen."

"Mary Jane, my word is bond. Nothing will happen unless you want it to. I'm honored, like I said, that's all."

I reached back to put the leather CD case in the backseat. "Okay, now, because I'm sure there were a lot of other women who would have been glad to come along and be with you in any way you'd want them to."

"That's why I'm here with you. You're not just any other woman."

"Well, thanks."

He pulled up to the luxury resort and put the truck in park. "Here, I'll get that laptop for you, and we'll let the valet get the rest."

The heat was Africa hot as we proceeded before entering the grand, air-conditioned lobby.

"It feels good in here." I looked up at the fancy ceiling, and crystal chandeliers, and dark gray marble floors, and beautiful tree-lined atrium. "This is a very pretty hotel, Carlos."

"I'm glad you approve. Listen, I'm going to get the key. I'll be right back." He pointed for me to sit on the maple leather sofa as he walked away.

Within no time, we entered our third floor room. He stepped aside and looked proud of himself. "See, I told you. Two beds. I'm a man you can trust."

"That's good to know." I barely heard his self-congratulating sentence. I was too spellbound by the huge room. It was classic, like a little black dress and a strand of pearls. The contemporary, plush, wine and chocolate brown furnishings were like right out of *House and Garden.*

While I looked around this lap of luxury, Carlos put down his suitcase and placed his car keys into his pocket, checked his wallet, and then glanced at the end table clock. "Well, I'm going to head downstairs to meet the guys at the bar and then we're going to take off until later this afternoon, maybe even get in a few rounds. Will you be okay?" He put about five twenties on the walnut dresser.

I separated and peeked through the layers of upholstered, room-darkening, silhouette drapes that matched the brown and tan bed-spreads. The pool-side view beyond the long balcony was heavenly. "I'll be right out here, lounging around that dream pool." The Olympic sized, tile swimming pool was filled with water that looked dark blue, and the rows of chaise lounges and umbrellas and palm trees and sun-tanning bodies seemed to call to me.

"Okay. I'll see your soon-to-be tanned self later then."

I turned to face him as he approached me. I nodded.

"Oh, and here's your key."

"Okay." I took the key card as he reached for a hug. I leaned to-ward him and patted him on his back as I remembered to ask about his hundred-dollar tip. "What's that money for?"

"It's for you. Just in case you need anything, you can use that in-stead of spending your own money."

"I won't need that, but thanks."

"I'll just leave it where it is. No problem."

I flashed a half-smile. "Goodbye, Carlos."

"Later."

Carlos seemed a little different today, almost like a real gentle-man. He actually wasn't so bad, or at least he didn't seem to be. Maybe because we were sitting in the middle of paradise. I guess it was sweet of him to make sure I knew the weekend was on him, and that I didn't need to worry about anything. But, what I didn't want was for him to have any expectations of me whatsoever. I didn't want to owe him a thing.

I proceeded to put my small suitcase on the satin settee and searched inside as I thought about how glad I was to get away. Now, where did I put that green bikini and coconut oil?

The next morning, after having ordered solo room service the night before, I looked over to find that Carlos's bed was just as made up as it was when we first came into the room. I looked over at my cell on the nightstand and didn't have even one missed call.

"Hey there," he said, suddenly walking through the door wearing his designer shades, tucking the key card into his pants pocket.

"Hey." My reply was weak.

"Sorry about that. The boys and I went out after playing eighteen holes, and the time just slipped away from me. Hey, you got a lot darker. At least your face looks browner anyway. Looks good."

"So whose room were you in?" I sat up, leaning back against the mahogany headboard with the cotton sheets up to my neck.

He emptied out his pockets onto the oak desk. "No one's. I mean I hung out in my buddy Nate's room. He's a couple of floors above us."

"I see." I levitated from the bed wearing a long black nightgown, and followed one step with another, headed to the bathroom and leaned in the huge stall to turn on the shower.

"Why are you getting up so early? Come on back to bed," he yelled my way.

I tiptoed with bare feet back near my bed toward my overnight bag and noticed he was unbuttoning his crumpled white shirt. "No, I got enough sleep. You need to get you some. I'll be back after breakfast, and if not, I'll call you on your mobile."

He pulled down his jeans. "Okay, then. Well, hey, there's a banquet this evening and then a party at a club nearby. I can't wait to see you all dressed up and looking like a fox. And don't forget to take this cash with you." He pointed to the nightstand as he stood in his boxers and then crawled into his bed.

I turned my back and headed into the bathroom. "Carlos, I told you thanks but no thanks. Anyway, good night. I mean, good morning." I closed the bathroom door, turned the lock, and proceeded to get undressed.

"It's cool." I heard him say.

"This is Mary Jane. Ain't she fine?" Carlos introduced me to his friend as we stood at the greeter's table later that evening, waiting to be shown to our table. Carlos looked handsome in his dark blue suit. I wore a white skirt suit and bronze high heels.

"Dang, dude, how'd you pull that?" His older, heavyset buddy looked like he was trying to peek around me to see my backside.

I darted my head back, totally insulted. "That? I'm not a that."

"I mean how'd you pull her? Excuse me." His baritone chuckle wore a very slight tinge of embarrassment.

My eyes sliced him in half. "Anyway. Carlos, I'll be at the table waiting for you. I'm starving." I stepped away just as I felt the vibration of my cell phone. I snatched it from my bag to raise it to my ear without looking. "Hello."

"Hey there, Ms. Cherry. What's up?"

"Nothing much. Hold on a second." I eyeballed a route for a quick exit, hurried past the groups of patrons, and strutted into the lobby, taking a seat.

"Hey, Makkai."

"Hey. So, I can only imagine where you are."

"Yes," I replied while finding cozy comfort upon a cranberry suede sofa.

"Cool."

"Is it?" I crossed my newly tanned legs, making sure to pull my fitted skirt down just to below the knee.

"Oh, for sure. Are you having a good time?"

"It's all right. Mainly just resting, you know, laying out and hanging out. Tomorrow I'll get a massage before we come home."

"From a masseuse?"

I pressed my back against the oversized sofa pillows. "Of course."

"So you drove together?"

"Yes."

He sighed deeply. "Hmmm."

"What about you? What have you been up to?"

"I'm just in the middle of my day. It's fairly quiet, but you know how it is. You never know when all hell will break loose here at work."

"Boy, do I know."

"Okay, well, I was just checking on you."

Carlos's voice rang in my opposite ear. "Hey, Mary Jane, I thought you were headed to the table. Dinner is about to be served."

Makkai volunteered. "I'll let you go."

I leaned forward while covering the phone with my hand, turning to give Carlos a look. "Excuse me, I'm on the phone."

He put his hand up. "Oh, I'm sorry. I'll be in here."

I returned to my phone call as he walked away. He looked back at me like he was reading my lips. "Sorry about that."

"No problem. Well, I guess I'll talk to you when you get back."

"Sure. I'll see you on Monday at work if nothing else."

"Right."

"Have a good one."

"I will. And you be good," he said, making it sound almost like a warning.

"I will, Makkai."

After a nice steak dinner, it was party night at The Dancing Machine nightclub down the street. Carlos and his boys, who it appeared all came solo, were cracking each other up while sitting at a bar table near an empty dance floor.

Carlos clowned his buddy. "Man, I had par for the first five holes. You were never even under par, not even once. You were strokin'."

He acted like he told one hell of a joke and then took a minute to give me a glance. "Baby, are you okay?" he asked me.

My elbows rested on the table. "I'm fine. Just a little tired from that heavy meal. I think I'm going back to the room." I assumed a stance and put my purse strap over my shoulder.

His hand took my hand. "Hold up, don't you want to dance?"

"No thanks." I took my hand back.

He released his vocabulary close to my face. "But, we had a great time dancing the last time. Girl, you were really getting down." He flashed a wink.

"No thanks, Carlos. I'll see you later." I began one step.

He gave a light embrace to my upper arm, and then an ex-rated squeeze. "I'll be there soon." My arm frowned.

And then I took another step, all the while searching for the perfect sentence to deliver in return. As I turned his way, my eyes stood in for the absence of words.

"Hey, Mr. Big Stuff, how are you?" asked a short, portly white girl who snuck up behind him.

I was all ears as I ceased my departure.

"I'm fine."

She spoke on as though earshot was limited to just the two of them. "You and your friends really showed us a good time last night."

He shooed her away with his expression while giving her his back. "I'll talk to you in a minute."

"Okay, we're over here at the bar." She pointed toward a giggling group of youthful estrogen.

"Okay." His reply screamed of a prayer for her disappearance.

I crossed my arms, nodding my head in the direction of his fans. "You really should get on over there."

"You know, I guess I should. I don't know what you have an attitude about. I'm not getting any lovin' in my own hotel room."

The previously absent words immediately skidded into my head. "You know, you've got some nerve. That's why I told you to book separate rooms, just so this wouldn't happen."

"So you wanted me to hook you up with a room, take you out of town, take care of everything, and then I get nothing in return?"

"Carlos, you said you were cool with nothing in return. But, I surely didn't ask you to take care of everything."

He blinked a mile a minute. "But, you waited until you were in my truck, three miles from the hotel, to tell me."

I did not blink even once. "I told you about the separate rooms a few days before we left. Anyway, it doesn't matter. Just let me know what you want me to do at this point. I can definitely afford my own room."

He looked back at his friends and spoke low. "No. You stay in that room. I'll see you tomorrow."

"Fine. And I can fly home if need be."

He spoke through clenched teeth. "No, I'll drive you. But, I just want to know why you let me put my face between your legs on our first date, and now you're playing the nun routine."

I uncrossed my arms and pointed my index finger in his face. "That's it. I'll just go ahead and take the next flight out right now. I don't want to deal with your attitude for two hours on the way home."

"If you say so."

"I say so."

He excused me with his hand, accented by, "Good. Get on home to Makkai."

"Goodbye, Carlos."

"Whatever." He turned around and trekked toward his friends, who were eyeing us down like they were watching a soap opera.

I blazed a trail out of sight.

Chapter 35

The day was bright and warm. The afternoon sunlight shone like a welcoming hug. A much needed hug. Things seemed kind of quiet for a minute. Even though I hadn't had a chance to get with one of my real loves for months, I made sure today was the perfect day. There was no excuse. Above all else, it was time to grip it and rip it.

"Hey, Dr. Worthy," one of my USC alumni asked from the lynx in the Valley.

"Call me Makkai on the course." I was decked out in all black from cap to shoes.

"Okay, Makkai. How's it going?"

"It's going," I responded, removing my black bag from the cart and then visually sizing up the hole.

"Where's Carlos?" he asked, still seated in the cart.

"He's out of town."

"Oh, I remember. That Black Golfers' Association weekend, huh? That can get pretty wild."

"I know. I've checked that out before."

"I know he's having a blast. Why didn't you go?"

"Too much going on. Plus I'm about to go out of town, myself."

"Oh, yeah, where?"

"To Florida, for a family reunion." I gave a practice swing to get a better idea of what it would take to go the distance.

"That should be fun. There's usually a whole lot of family drama during those reunions. I know I went to one last year, and a fight broke out between two of my cousins who fought over something that happened when they were twelve." He stepped out of the cart and grabbed his tweed bag.

"I know. That stuff from our childhood can haunt our butts for years. Excuse me a second," I said as my phone vibrated. I looked at the screen and noticed it was from a private number. I let it go. It rang again. I let it go again. It vibrated again with an emergency message and rang yet again.

I firmly pressed the answer button.

"Dr. Worthy here."

"Hey, Makkai, it's Salina." She sounded in first gear.

"Hey, what's up?" I stepped aside. "Was that you with the priority message?"

"What are you doing later on? Can we get together?"

"Aahhh, not today. I'm getting ready to get out of town for a while."

"Makkai, is there someone else?" Her voice dragged.

I glanced over at my golf buddy, who was selecting his club from his bag. "What do you mean? Is this what you wanted to ask me with an emergency page?"

"You're not making time for me like you did before."

I could barely make out what she was saying. My intention was to whisper my reply, but I failed. "I'm just busy, Salina. Like right now, I'm on the golf course, so I'm going to have to call you later."

"Okay, but don't forget." She sounded like she either needed a nap, or had too long of one.

My jaw was tight. "Okay." I released the call, shaking my head. Damn, I wished I hadn't answered that. "Sorry about that." I turned off my phone altogether.

"No problem. Hey, Makkai, I know you have a crazy schedule, but look. I've got this client, I mean, I'm handling a divorce case for her, and she's a nice woman, an attractive and sweet and good woman, who was done so wrong by this wealthy jerk, and it burns my butt. Hey, do you think I could tell her about you and maybe, if you're interested, the two of you could hook up?"

"No thanks. I don't do blind dates."

"That's cool. I just haven't seen you with anyone on the few occasions we do run into each other. You are single, right?"

"Very." I grabbed my iron.

"She's a real catch." He sounded like a salesman.

"So then why did he leave her?"

"It had nothing to do with—oh, I can see you're not buying this." He read my face well.

"Why don't you talk to her?" I asked, stepping up to set my ball.

"Attorney client no-no."

"Well, thanks, but I promise you I have my hands full."

Another alumni friend of ours walked up. "Hey, do the two of you want to play or stand up there running your mouths? We've got time to make up and the folks behind us are about to throw darts."

"Okay, okay," I told him.

He replied, "Play on, player."

"I'm on it." I swung with precision and hit the tiny white ball up and over, and in the distance I could see it hit the green and bounce and roll on over and right up toward the hole, slowly rolling and rolling, inching along in slow motion until it spun with a curve, right into the cup. A grand hole-in-one. I gave the air a fisted pump. "Yeah," I yelled. "Let's pray my life hits a target like that. It sure needs to be." I felt like Tiger himself.

"Do the damn thang, man. You couldn't have a care in the world," said my alumni buddy.

"Oh, but I do. I do," I assured him, still grinning ear to ear.

Chapter 36

"I missed you," she kept saying over and over again later on during the week. I'll bet she did.

"How badly?" I asked Mary Jane as she panted with urgency. She had me flat on my back while she did her straddled, smack it up, flip it, rub it down, erotic grind routine to the sounds of Baby Face's "*Whip Appeal.*" She was giving it to me, but good.

I didn't make time for more golf, but I did stop by to see Mary Jane for the first time since her lovebird weekend with Carlos. I had to make her really work it after the stunt she pulled.

"So you went on ahead and headed out of town anyway, huh?"

Her face was sweaty and her hair was wet. "You said it was okay."

"I know what I said. I think you owe me an apology, though."

"I'm sorry, Makkai." She raised her hips up, braced herself, and started bouncing her ass along my upper thighs, leaning her torso forward to rest her tanned breasts on my chest.

"Sit up and turn around for me."

She stopped her pumping motion and asked, "Turn around?"

"Yes, give me the reverse cowgirl so I can hit it right."

She flashed demure eyes that didn't match her hips. "Makkai."

"Baby, turn around so I can see just how sorry you are."

She lifted her legs over and faced the other way, leaning toward my feet as she held onto my shins.

I stared at her toned back. "I see that tan looks good. You went away with some other brotha and then you bring that dark body back for me to see after he's been showing you off?"

She spoke without looking back. "No. We barely spent any time together."

I stroked her harder. "And you won't ever again, will you?"

"No." She was getting the hang of it, and it felt damn good.

"Mary Jane, don't do that again."

"I won't." She flung her hair back.

"Show me you really missed me. Work it so that you cum for me."

I looked at her ass that was full and wide, working an up and down, side to side motion while it flopped about. The sound was ex-rated.

"Do I need to put my mouth down there?"

She breathed harder. "No."

"Then lean back so I can hit the right spot."

She bent back and readjusted my entry. "Like this?" She balanced herself and threw her hands in the air.

"Yeah. Ride it."

The loud sound of her headboard banging repeatedly against the wall was as if somebody was getting their back broken.

Her words were throaty and sexy. "Oh, baby. That feels good."

"It does?"

"Yes."

"Well, it feels good to me too, Mary Jane. You're gonna make me . . ."

"You're gonna make me, too." As she leaned back even more, she held on by bracing herself with her hands behind her, flat on the bed on each side of me.

"Do it for me, baby. Do it for me hard. Damn, that's it. That's it right there. That's my spot." I grunted, swelled up inside of her, and froze.

"Aaaahhhh, Makkai. Uhhh, yes, yes. Yes."

She slowed down and exhaled as the last drop spewed from my tip and into the condom that engulfed her.

"That's my girl."

She looked back at me. "That's my baby."

"I'm glad you're back."

During the last week before the reunion, I got a call from long lost Monday, whom I hadn't seen in a long while. Not by my own choice, though. I'd been trying to get with her for months but she hadn't returned my calls. However, today, she had the operator page me at the hospital.

"Makkai, where are you?" Her voice was frantic-coated.

"I'm in my office. That's the number you called, isn't it? Where have you been?"

"Can I come and see you?" I heard the sound of traffic.

"Why, what's up?"

"I need to talk to you. I need to tell you something important." The bark of her dog in the background filled my ears.

"Now, Monday, the tone of your voice tells me something is wrong, so what is it you need to tell me?"

"Makkai, I need to see you. I don't want to talk over the phone."

"Where are you?"

"I'm on my way to my doctor's office for another appointment." She took a breath. "I'm pregnant."

Oh, Lord. "What? Monday, I thought you said . . ."

"I know I told you I couldn't get pregnant. But, my body and my words didn't hook up. It had to have been that night the condom broke."

"That was so damn long ago."

"I know."

"And you're just now telling me?"

"I was away for a while. But I'm back now."

"You're back now? And they didn't have phones where you were?"

"Makkai, I'm telling you now."

I turned my back from the nurse who stood nearby. Lowering

my voice as best I could, I battled to figure it out. "Telling me now, after months and months? So you're telling me that the one time the rubber busted, you got pregnant?"

"Yes, I am. And I'm having your baby." She spoke like she was simply telling me what the weather was like.

"And there's no one else?"

"No."

"Now, Monday, we met at a swingers' club. You expect me to believe there's no one else?"

A sound of irritation flavored her every word. "I practice safe sex just like you, Makkai. I've had sex with you far more regularly and frequently than anyone else. You can try to deny the baby's yours if you want. But, I'm telling you, it is yours."

"Monday, I can't believe you didn't pick up the phone way before now. That's just not right."

"Why is it not right? Would you have preferred that I let you know before the third month so that you could've suggested that I get an abortion, Makkai? That is so damn selfish. Maybe that's why I didn't tell you. You don't care about what my body goes through, yet you stick your dick in me and bust a nut, knowing that condoms break and tear and come off. So don't get funky with me. You'd better be glad I'm telling you now. Some women make the call when they're about to deliver, or not at all. So don't try me. I am not in the mood to be scolded. This has been hard on me, so screw you, Makkai. I'll do this on my own."

I breathed a deep, long sigh. Waited, and then asked, "What time is your appointment?"

"It's this afternoon."

"Where?"

"King Drew."

I fought to keep my voice down. "King Drew. You mean the county hospital? Is that where your doctor is?"

"Oh, excuse me. Yes, I'm going to see the OB/GYN at King Drew, Dr. Taksa."

"No, you'll come here. I'll get Dr. Marshall to see you right away. Come to my office. Now."

She exhaled loudly. "Fine." She hung up in my face.

Dammit, I said in my head while heading back to my office.

Right away I made a few calls to arrange things as quickly as possible. A text message from Carlos popped up on my phone.

What up?

Hey.

Man, Palm Springs was a bust. Anyway, guess who I'm seeing?

Look dude, not right now. I'm headed out. Something came up.

What?

Man, Monday claims she's pregnant.

By who? I know not by you.

She says it is. So, I'll get back at you.

Handle your business, dog. Let me know if there's anything I can do.

Out.

Chapter 37

Monday

I had an abortion maybe ten years ago. I got pregnant and then started clotting early on, so the guy I was with talked me into getting it done. I never got over that. And so I'm not doing that this time. I just can't kill a life again. Even if I don't end up raising this child, I'm going to give birth, unless God chooses to take it from me first. I admit that I'm absolutely not the motherly type, though. I've got some things about me I need to straighten out before I let anyone call me Mom. Maybe adoption. Maybe Makkai will agree to it. Maybe not. I really don't give a damn.

"Well, Miss Askins, your own weight is on track for your height, but your blood pressure is a little high. Have you had any pre-natal testing done to check the baby for Down syndrome and neural tube defects? I mean, considering your age? Being that you're over forty," Dr. Marshall asked at Cedars, while sitting on a small stool.

"The blood test?"

"It's called maternal serum."

"Yes, they did that at King," I replied while sitting on an examination table wearing a white gown.

"So if you've been getting treated there, then why are you changing doctors now, if I might ask?"

I used my eyes to point to Makkai. "Ask him."

Makkai stood near the sink with his hands in his pockets. "It was my idea. I want to be close by when she goes into labor, since I'm here more than anywhere else."

"I'll bet," said the doctor.

He continued, "And she has to get the best care. I'm financially responsible one-hundred percent."

I'm sure I flashed a look of shock.

The young female gynecologist asked, "Did you put her on your health insurance? You know you don't need to be married."

"No, we haven't discussed that," said Makkai. "We're not living together."

I added, "We haven't discussed a lot of things, Doctor."

"I'd say now's the time," she said while she wrote. "Okay, so, we'll get your file sent over here from King Drew Medical Center. Just make sure to sign the release document when you make your next appointment." A nurse walked in and stood behind the doctor.

"Okay," I said.

She stood up. "I'll need to examine you now. Nurse Thomas, did you set up an exam tray?"

"It's right here," the nurse replied while wheeling it toward the doctor.

"Can I get you to lie back and scoot forward as close to the edge as you can?"

"Sure."

Makkai actually stepped forward and helped me scoot my butt down by bracing my upper body.

"Have you had an ultrasound yet to determine the gestational age?"

"Yes."

She smiled. "Did you see the baby's image? Did they give you a copy of the image?"

"No."

"Did they tell you the sex of the baby?"

"Yes."

Makkai looked confused. More like dumbfounded. "They did?"

I decided to stop looking at him. "It's a girl." I said to the doctor.

Makkai said, "A girl?"

My lips were as tight as my jaw.

The doctor put on her clear, thin gloves and began the vaginal exam. "So, let's see here. What due date were you given?"

"They said eight more weeks from now."

Makkai cleared his throat as if he had doubt.

She had her fingers inside of me and was looking at the wall behind me. "I'm not so sure about that. Your cervix is pretty thin. Are you sure this is your first pregnancy?"

"Yes." Why was I lying to her?

"I'd like to see you back in one week and we'll know more. But, it looks like you might be back here sooner if this baby has her way, and we don't want that. Have you had any pain or pressure at all, or any spotting?"

"No."

"And your last period was when?"

I felt Makkai looking at me. "I don't know. Maybe eight months ago. My periods have been sporadic for years. I didn't think I was still ovulating."

She removed her hand, taking off each glove. "Well, then, this little one might just be considered a little miracle. It's extremely difficult for women in their forties to conceive. Especially after one's cycle starts to become irregular."

This time I did eyeball Makkai, who looked both a little excited and a little like, why would he be the lucky one to impregnate a woman with half-dried-up eggs.

"Do you remember when was the last time you had sex?"

I replied quickly, "It was about six months ago."

Makkai replied quickly, "It was less than that, wasn't it?"

"Six months," I reiterated to her.

"Let's take a look at the ultrasound. You can stretch out your legs," she said as she extended the padded table.

She put a generous amount of cold, conducting gel on my belly, and we all looked over at the monitor. She rubbed the small disk with her hand to warm it up, and then placed it on my belly, moving it up and down and side to side.

She said, "It looks like your uterus is fairly small to be that far along, and the fetus is very tiny, so it's difficult to determine. I'd say you're not as far along as they thought. I'd say about twenty-four to twenty-seven weeks, so roughly five months, but I wouldn't say six. The average pregnancy term is thirty-eight to forty-two weeks, so you might be more than halfway there. And yes, it is a girl. But as I said, she is very small."

Makkai spoke, while eyeing the image, but his eyes spoke louder. "I can make out her eyes, and her nose and mouth. And look at her legs." He asked, "How do you determine gestation, by measuring the diameter of her head?"

"Yes, the side-to-side diameter of the head, and the length of the longest bone, and a couple of other factors, including measuring the size of the uterus. We can still be off by about a week or so but it looks like she'll probably be, maybe six pounds full term. It's just hard to determine an accurate gestation period this way, without knowing the last cycle date." She wiped off the excess gel and pulled my gown closed. "Did you want this?" she asked after tearing off the printed image of my daughter.

I pointed at Makkai with my head again. "He can have it."

He took it, eyeing it with great focus. "Thanks." His face looked different. Different from the way I'd ever seen him look before. Less like a renowned doctor, and more like a man who just might be moved by seeing his very own daughter for the first time.

The doctor sat down again while making notes in a manila folder. "Well, I'd say that's about it. I've ordered a Doppler sonography so that we can check the health of the baby and take a closer look at your cervix, and I'll request the previous ultrasound from

King Drew, just to see if we can use that for dating purposes." She spoke while looking up at me. "Since it was taken earlier on, it'll give us a better idea of the gestational age. The best time to guess, because that's all we're really doing when we don't know without a menstrual date, is usually between eight and eighteen weeks, but you're past that. Let's see, we can do the sonography when you come back next week. I'll be able to determine a better due date then. The nurse will give you an appointment time when you check out. But, please call me if you need me sooner." She handed me a business card from her white coat pocket.

"Even if I'm out of town, I'll be available via cell if you need me," Makkai told me.

I spoke up, again without looking at him. "I'll be fine on my own."

He didn't reply.

The doctor broke the silence. "Okay, then, any questions?"

"No," I said.

Makkai told her, "I have one. Is the baby healthy?"

"From what I can see, she looks fine."

He looked back down at the ultrasound photo. "I'm just glad everything's okay."

She told him, "But that's why we're doing the Doppler sonography, Dr. Worthy. And Ms. Askins, I want you to stay off your feet as much as you can until I see you again."

"I will. And why wouldn't she be fine, Makkai?" I asked him with frustration in my eyes.

"No reason." This time he answered without looking up.

Men.

Chapter 38

Okay, that's it. I've had it. That's enough. I've had enough of all of my women telling their stories from the female perspective. This is my story and this is something I need to finish off myself. And so if you don't mind . . . I'll take it from here.

Let's see, where should I pick up? Oh yeah, after the pre-natal exam, Monday took her time getting dressed, while I paid the front office clerk for the last-minute doctor's visit. In complete silence, after she made her appointment and signed the paperwork, she simply walked ahead of me as we headed down the hallway. She then popped into the restroom, without saying a word to me, leaving me standing there.

My cell vibrated so I stepped down the hall a bit to catch it. Oh damn. "Hello."

"You asshole."

Here we go again with the blocked number expert. "What, Salina?"

"First off, I heard you got some woman pregnant?" She was breathing a mile a minute, blasting 50 Cent in the background.

I kept an eye on the ladies bathroom door. "And how did you hear that?"

"I called you to get answers, not the other way around. So is it true?"

"I'm about to hang up, Salina. I am not down for this. Find a man who will love you and try your best to be true to him."

"Why wasn't I good enough, Makkai?"

"Salina, it was what it was. You married a man who you continued to stay with, and you saw me on the side. And you know what? Honestly, I agreed to lesser charges for your husband because I thought the quicker he got out, the quicker you two could work things out. But, whether you two do that or not, I am out of your life, and I don't want you calling me. Now, is that clear?"

"Oh, please, like you're not gonna be the one calling me within a week to get your dick sucked anyway, trying your best to play tricks with my coochie. I've heard this before. Like when you denied me so tough when you were getting your ass choked and then called the next afternoon."

"I mean it. Now, I don't want to be a jerk, but it's over." I kept my words firm and low.

"I know you. Whoever this chick is, you'll try to talk her into getting rid of it so this baby doesn't ruin your career. You are so selfish. Anyway, why in the hell didn't you wear a condom with her? Oh just forget it. I already know you'll be in my bed before my next period is over. And rest assured that I'll be ready when it does happen. You're not a one-woman man, Makkai."

"Salina, I know you're mad, and I understand that you're hurting. But, I can't help you get over your husband."

"Well, then maybe Carlos can."

No she didn't. "Oh. I've got it. Okay, whatever, Salina. Goodbye." Women.

"Call Carlos," I spoke into my phone one second later, still keeping an eye out for Monday. A moment later, his voice mail came on. "Hey, Carlos, your ass can't hold water. And now I know who it was you were about to tell me you're seeing. Look, do something for me, man. Scratch the idea of ever contacting me again in life. I mean it. Don't even think about calling me. Not my home, not my cell, not my job, and don't text or email me. Forget that you ever knew me, brotha. Good riddance." That fool's trying to be like me. He can have it.

I stood outside of the restroom as Monday exited, she was moving extra slow like she was struggling to walk, big time. We took the elevator down to the lobby and exited the front doors.

A young resident walked by and nodded. "How's it going, Dr. Worthy?"

"I can't complain." I lied.

Monday definitely looked pregnant from the front, but not at all from the back. She really was all baby. And damn her, she was still sexy. But, obviously, she was still mad.

Finally, she had something to say. "Makkai, if you could just get over me being in my forties, you'd sound a whole lot more like a father who's expecting a healthy child, than one who's expecting something to be wrong. I'm only seven years older than you, you know. I'd say you waited a long time to have a child yourself. And maybe it's about time." Woman sure knew how to fuss.

I walked side-by-side with her. "It's all in God's time."

"Yeah, blah, blah, blah." Her eyes were red, and she was heated.

"You act like I've had time to get used to this. You just told me a few hours ago. Now, that is what I think is unbelievable."

"Whatever. Have a good time in Florida. We'll be fine, my daughter and me."

"Hold up, Monday. Really though, are you going to be okay?" I asked, trying to get her to look me in the eyes.

She looked everywhere but at me. "Blah, blah, bah."

I reached out to hug her. "I'll call you. And call me if you . . ."

She turned her body and turned up her nose. "Like I said. We'll be fine."

I just looked at her as she walked away toward the parking lot. "Okay, stubborn."

"Blah, blah, blah," she said without looking back.

I turned around and headed back toward the hospital front doors.

What the hell was that?

* * *

While I was barely inside of the elevator, I glanced down at the display on my phone and it was her already. I suppose she just had to continue with her cranky, hormone-filled attitude.

"Yes, Monday."

"Five thousand, Makkai."

"Five thousand for what?" I asked her loudly, repeating what she said in case my ears were deceiving me, or in case the elevator had caused a bad connection.

"For baby furniture." In that short amount of time, she sounded a little more upbeat but feisty and unreasonable nonetheless. And the connection was just fine.

"What kind of baby furniture is that?"

"That's not a lot of money. And it's surely not like you can't afford it."

I ended up saying, "We'll talk about it."

"Sure."

She hung up as I stepped out of the elevator. I talked out loud as if it would begin to make some type of sense. "Okay, so all of a sudden Monday is mad because I won't give her five thousand dollars to buy baby furniture."

My cell rang again. "Hello. Yes, this is Makkai. Hey, how are you? Yes, I'm still at work. Uh huh. I thank you for returning my call. Oh, so you can make it. Good. I'll pick you up on Monday night at seven-thirty, is that cool? Good, just leave your address on my voice mail if that's okay. I'll be returning from out of town that Sunday. So let's just write it in pen. It'll be great to spend my thirty-eighth birthday with you. Yes, it'll be a great first date. See you then."

Chapter 39

By the time I headed home, barely pulling out of the parking lot at nearly one in the morning, a voice blasted through my earpiece. Why in the heck did I not even glance at the caller ID only to see that it was blocked?

"Makkai, I can't believe that I'm going through this shit in my life."

I turned down my sounds.

"I thought you got what I was said before. What is it, Salina?"

"You men aren't worth a damn."

"We men? Salina, I am really in no mood to hear about this right now." My voice was dragging.

"Well, you need to be. First, you screw me knowing I'm married, and then when my husband finds out, you fucking deny me like I don't even exist. And then you continue to screw me with no regard for my feelings. You sign the papers to release my husband from jail so he can go back to his ghetto-chick. And then you move on and continue to screw your harem only to get one of them pregnant. Funny you always taped up that dick when you were with me."

She was dancing on top of my last nerve. "I'm about to hang up."

"Of course you are, Makkai. You don't have time or feelings for me. You ran all through my pussy but you can't take the time to hear me speak my mind. Wouldn't you at least do that for a friend who you weren't fucking? Shouldn't I get some kind of respect?

That's just plain old unkind of you. God is going to get you back for this, that's for sure. This is not how you're supposed to treat people, Makkai."

I was one second away from pressing the end button. "What do you want me to say, Salina? You started demanding my time and then to get back at me, you started dating my friend."

"Oh please. You acted like you didn't even care, and he surely acted like it didn't matter either. It was almost like it was some kind of bet or something. And then his ass had the nerve to tell me he can't see me anymore because he has some things he needs to deal with. See, you two play games and damn near run trains with no intention of bonding or concern for anyone, and then you both run off, back to your playboy lives at the first sign of commitment."

"Salina, let's not forget you're still married."

"Yes, I'm still married. But, we're separated and I'm filing soon. So don't give me that, *you're a marred woman* sermon. I am single and my husband has someone of his own. But you, Tom, and Carlos don't want me. Like I said, you're all alike. You know what? I'm tired of this. Nobody understands. My own mom doesn't know what it's like to be single, and feel hurt and lonely and used. She's had my dad since she was fifteen. Hell, why is it that I can't find a man who will treat me right?"

"You may have had that in your husband."

"Yeah, so maybe I did. But, you're to blame as well for dating a married woman. You're no more than a damn gigolo."

"If you say so. Look, Salina, you must admit that you have to take some of the blame for the fact that we dated. It was your choice to be unfaithful. But, yes, I take responsibility too. I accept my part."

"Oh, so now you want to talk about responsibility? You seem to forget that my husband was fooling around on me, and you were fooling around with another man's wife. I tell you . . . black men, and white men too, can kiss my ass. I'm sticking to my own race from now on."

"It's not the race of men, Salina."

"You know what, Makkai? Fuck this. No one is going to get me. I'm about to fix this shit. I have a little something in my nightstand and I'll solve this for everyone."

"What are you going to do?"

"Don't you worry about it."

"Salina."

"I won't be your problem anymore."

Click.

Knock, knock, knock.

My heart echoed the quickness of the sound of my knuckles upon her front door in Torrance. Maybe she was bluffing. But, maybe she was desperate enough to make good on her threat. I hoped I was doing the right thing.

Without a verbal inquiry as to who I was, she immediately pulled the door open and eyed me from head to toe. The darkness of the room behind her framed her stature. The dim stove light shone in the background. I stood before her in a leather jacket, jeans, a baseball cap and Air Jordan's, feeling as though she could see the tinges of worry in my eyes beneath her porch light. Worry because I was knocking on her husband's door, worry that she was okay, and concern that I might need to bolt. Glad I was wearing the right shoes.

"Salina, what is going on with you? Why are you talking so much crazy shit? You aren't doing anything to yourself." She wore a sheer black shirt and booty hugging jean shorts. She was barefoot.

"You don't care about me so why ask? Why are you here? How did you know where I live?"

"I sometimes followed you home to make sure you made it safely."

Her eyes showed surprise.

I stepped inside and walked past her, proceeding to sit on her black leather love seat.

She closed the door and stood over me, pacing back and forth while using her hands to add extras to her loud words. "Don't come over here trying to play saint. I'm not buying it."

"What's wrong with you? Have you been drinking?"

"No." She moved close to me.

My sight took her image by the hand. I forced myself to get a good look at her. "What did you do to yourself?"

"Nothing."

"Then why are your eyes so red?"

"I've been crying, okay, deciding if I should put myself out of my misery."

"So you think the answer is to shoot yourself?"

"I'm not going to shoot myself. I'm going to take some sleeping pills. That's all."

"That's all? Suicide is suicide."

"Who would give a damn?" She gave me an inquiring, but hopeful look.

"Your parents would. Have you ever thought about them?"

"My parents are too busy telling me what I should do than to take the time to understand what I really want."

"You have your whole life ahead of you."

"No, you have your whole life ahead of you. You have a baby on the way, a career that is your calling, all the money you can spend, looks, and you're in control of your life. I am nothing more to you than a fuck."

"You were a wife, so that means a lot. And, you are more to me than a fuck. And more to your husband I'm sure."

"But, I destroyed that by . . . by fooling around on him. I'm a mess." She shook her head.

"You are not."

"I am. I haven't heard you say that you even give a damn."

"If I didn't give a damn, would I be here?"

"You don't care. You just don't want people to blame you if you're the last person I talk to. Makkai, why don't you love me?"

I looked up at her face.

I did not speak.

I couldn't.

She kneeled down and put her hands on my knees. I sat forward, mentally preparing to stand, but I didn't. Suddenly, she placed her head in my lap, laying her right ear upon my zipper. She stayed still for a long, slow minute. Her chest was against my knee. My hand made its way to the top of her head. Automatically, I ran my fingers through her hair.

She looked up at me and sequestered my eyes. I could smell her stale breath. It seemed alcohol-free. "Makkai, do you know how much I care about you?"

"I know."

"You never took the time to get to know me outside of the bedroom."

"I know that."

"And?"

"And I thought that's how you wanted it, too."

"Makkai, I love you. Why don't you love me? I just have to know."

When all else fails, answer a question with a question. "You love me?"

"Yes."

Again. "You're sure?"

"Makkai, I know what I feel."

I glanced down at her pretty face. "Salina, all I want you to do is think about what you're doing. It will get better. You're thinking about ending it all over Carlos and me. Please. I mean, I know he didn't mean to hurt you any more than I did. None of us did."

"See how you guys stick together. Makkai, Carlos is not your boy anymore so you don't need to protect him." She placed her head down on my lap once more.

"I'm not trying to."

"Makkai."

"What?"

"Please stay with me."

I squirmed and removed my hand from her hair. "I can't. I have to get back home and wake up early in the morning to play golf."

"Please."

"I can't."

In a flash, I felt her head rubbing against my groin, and in an instant she managed to maneuver both hands to unbelt and unzip my jeans, and within one fell swoop, like magic, she had my dick, which was not cooperating with me, standing at full attention in her hot mouth. Before I knew it, I was at the point of no return. And that is not a good place to be.

Something in me told me to stand her up, back her up, and spread her legs. Before I could, she pulled off her shorts and panties and laid flat on her back. She gave me her bedroom eyes in the living room.

"Fuck me," she demanded as usual.

"No." My penis jumped as if to ask if I was nuts.

"Fuck me, dammit. Don't talk back to me."

"Salina."

"Stick it in, now."

I did. I stood up and mounted her, grabbing her tattooed ankle, pulling it back so I could go deep at an angle.

"Grab a handful of soft ass."

I did.

"Now, slap me hard. Not my ass, my face."

"Slap it?"

"My face. Slap my face."

I did.

"Pull my hair. Pull it back and wrap it around your hand."

I did.

"Now really ram it in. Make it come through my back."

Still wearing my cap and jacket, I did.

"Squeeze my arms and pull them back."

I did. Her sheer sleeve ripped near her wrist.

She pushed my chest and said, "Pull out." She rolled over on her stomach and stuck her hips high into the air. Her heart shaped, hairy middle view was all lips, begging me to join her again. And so . . . I did.

"Grab my wrists from behind." I tried to grip her wrists but her right hand slipped from her grip. Before I knew it, I scratched her forearm with my fingernail."

"Ouch. Dammit, Makkai, stop. What are you doing?" She froze.

"What am I doing?" I froze.

"Stop I said."

"Okay." I stood up and reached down to pull up my jeans that were riding around my ankles, and then I zipped and buckled them.

Her volume turned to shouting level. "Help. Help please. Somebody help me." She grabbed her cordless and pressed three buttons. "Please help me, I've just been raped."

While she disconnected the call, I stood by the door with angry eyes and shook my head. "What in the heck was that about?"

She pulled up her shorts and looked down at the scratch on her arm. She peered into the mirror over her fireplace. "My head hurts from you grabbing my hair, and my face is red."

"Oh Salina, please."

"Just get out of here and wait outside for the police."

"Oh, I'll wait, all right. What I can't wait for is to tell them how bogus this is."

"Me too. And don't even think about leaving. See, I knew your sorry ass, pussy-lovin' self would come. I promised you one day you'd pay for what you do to women. This, high and mighty Dr. Feelgood, is your payback. It's a motha, ain't it?"

Chapter 40

After three in the morning I took a ride in the backseat. I had no choice but to lean forward. "I didn't do it," I said to the policemen as my hands were cuffed behind me. I spoke during the long patrol car ride to the station. For the first time in my life, I was on my way to get fingerprinted and booked. "What have I been charged with?"

The policeman in the driver seat spoke. "We told you, battery and forcible rape, Mr. Worthy. You have already been given your rights."

"I know that. But, you didn't tell me what I was being charged with."

"I suggest you wait for your attorney before you say anything else."

I just know they didn't tell me. But, I'm not about to be a Rodney King example. I stared out of the backseat window, looking around at the world, wondering how this happened, and how I didn't see this coming. Here I was headed to the same place Salina's own husband had been held. Only my crime is that I showed up to show concern for a woman who was in distress. Correction, my real true crime is that I allowed myself to be seduced by Salina Woodard. I just got played.

*   *   *

The walls were baron. The mattress to the twin bunk where I sat was as thin as a pancake. No pillow, no covers, no sheet. The room was cold. The invasive search was dehumanizing. The company I was keeping was questionable.

"So, you didn't do it, right?" a young, thin, unshaven man said, standing over me as I sat. I broke eye contact and assumed the thinker position.

I didn't look up. "No, I didn't."

"Me neither. That lady I robbed asked for it."

"I didn't rob anyone."

"What did you do?"

"Nothing. I've been set up."

"Some woman, I'll bet."

"For sure."

"Hey man, I always say, never trust a big butt and a smile."

I looked up and nodded. "You can say that again."

"First time I'll bet, huh?"

"And my last."

"That's what I said three years ago. But, hey, life happens. Hope you get out soon."

"Oh, I will."

"Good. Cause you don't want to be up in here more than one night. You might lose your virginity if you know what I mean." I stared at the floor. "Anyway, dog, good luck." He walked back toward the door, pulling up his sagging pants and peering through the bars.

"Good luck to you too."

All I could do was replay the evening back in my head. Over and over again it rewound and played and paused and fast forwarded and ended and began. I needed to be able to recall every dang second.

A guard approached the bars. "Your phone call, Mr. Worthy. Who will it be?"

I stood up. "My mother."

"Okay, just one minute."

I yelled his way. "Hey, can I get out right away?"

"I don't think so. You have to see the judge in the morning."

Even though it was already late, it's going to be a long night.

The next morning, after meeting with the defense attorney Mom contacted from the Cochran group, saw the judge and I pled not guilty. My bail was set and posted. I couldn't wait to get back into some fresh clothes and get the heck out of there.

As Mom drove me to the place where my car was towed, I leaned back in the passenger seat of the baby-blue Thunderbird she drove. She made small talk and then looked out of the window in silence. If she were anyone else, I have no doubt they would have felt a little embarrassed, but knowing my mother, she was simply worried. She turned up the talk radio station for two seconds, and then turned it off.

"I'm not going to preach, Makkai, or ask you any questions. I trust and believe in you. All I'll say is, you need to leave all of these women alone. That's just a curse. You've got to break this one."

"Mom, I deserve anything you feel like saying. I just appreciate you for stepping up." I put my hand on her shoulder.

"Anything for you, you know that. But, I will say this as well. You do so much good and I don't want you to be defined by one bad situation. Don't let the shame identify your destiny. What you need to do is get closer to God. You need stability, Makkai. You need a foundation. You've been drifting. But, know that once you seek to know God better, He will meet you right where you are."

"I feel that with all my heart, Mom."

"And also know that crazy woman isn't going to get away with this."

"I have faith. The preliminary hearing is in a few days so we'll see."

"Thinking positively is key, Makkai. But, also, hold tight to that faith you say you have. It's easy to lose. But, I'll tell you one thing, if you keep the faith, the faith will keep you."

"Thanks."

"You can trust Him to catch you." Mom held my hand as she drove.

"I do."

Later that afternoon, as soon as I walked into my office, Dr. Lois Taylor greeted me, standing with the hospital administrator, Dr. Pointer.

Dr. Taylor spoke as I put the key in my office door. "Dr. Worthy, the chief of your department is out of town, but I'd like to know, can we see you for a minute? Just down the hall here in the small conference room."

"Sure. I'll be right there."

I tossed my things onto the desk and headed a few doors down, sitting across from Dr. Taylor and the older administrator, who had been part of the decision to hire me years ago.

I spoke first. "Good afternoon."

"Dr. Worthy, you're out on bail?"

"Yes. My hearing is this Friday morning."

Dr. Taylor did all the talking. "Will you please help us understand what's going on with you? We received word that you have been charged with a felony. And to top it off, the most serious charge is rape. How are we supposed to allow you to treat patients at Cedars Sinai when you have been accused of such a crime? Not to mention that this comes on the heels of the woman's husband who came to your office trying to kill you, Dr. Worthy."

I gave them both even glances. "Doctor Taylor. Dr. Pointer. I understand all of that. But, with all due respect, these charges are false. I was set up. I understand your concern and I'm willing to accept your decision."

"Our decision is to place you on administrative leave, with pay, until this all comes to a close. We pray that you are not found guilty. That would be a big loss to this hospital. If you say you're innocent, I will give you the benefit of the doubt. But, we think you may need to clean some things up, as far as the decisions you've been making. Because obviously, those decisions are affecting your career. You have had an untarnished career thus far. This will only get bigger and more damaging for you if you don't nip this in the bud now. You need to take care of your business. In the meantime, I have to let the medical board know what occurred. This is strictly business, Dr. Worthy."

"Yes, Dr. Taylor."

Dr. Pointer nodded in agreement.

"We'll be in touch after this case is resolved. Until then, please leave this hospital, Dr. Worthy." She stood and then he stood.

I stood. "Yes. I understand completely. Thanks." I headed back to my office and then left the hospital.

I sat at home hours later, drunk with thoughts.

Okay.

So here I am.

I'm at home.

I'm in my large house all alone.

I have absolutely nothing to do.

Work is my life.

Life is my work.

But, I cannot do what I love to do.

I dare not call anyone.

Especially a woman.

Not now.

And not anytime soon.

I need to figure this out.

Figure out how I can get my life back.

Less the drama.

My voice mailbox was full.

Makkai, this is Mary Jane. I just heard. I'm here if you need me. Please call me. Everything will be fine. Pray on it, and believe that the truth will set you free. Take care, Makkai. Goodbye.

Hey Makkai, it's Lois Taylor. I just want you to know how difficult that was for me this afternoon to chastise you and suspend you like that. I had to do what I had to do. But, I hope you know that I do believe in you. I will see you later. I'll check on you again.

Hey, son. I see you're not picking up the phone. I made dinner if you want to come over. It's that Vodka Pasta you love so much. This isn't the end of the world, Makkai. God is faithful, so release your faith. If it's in God's plan, then His will shall be done through this. Always know that we love you. Goodbye. Call me.

Makkai, this is Attorney Cross. Call me as soon as possible. Let's meet first thing tomorrow. We've got a lot of work to do.

Chapter 41

"Defense, please call your first witness."

A judge, bailiff, stenographer, attorney, plaintiff, defendant, a few unknown faces were sprinkled here and there . . . all of the usual suspects inside of the average looking superior courtroom in downtown Los Angeles. I'd asked Mom not to come, but she came anyway, sitting right behind me.

There I sat, next to my attorney while wearing my fifteen hundred dollar Versace suit, looking like a million dollars but not worth anything more than the opinion of this judge.

"We call Mr. Carlos Jenkins."

Attorney Cross had told me what the deal was with Carlos. Carlos stepped up and pledged to tell the truth, whole truth and nothing but the truth. He looked over and stared at Salina. She cut her eyes. He looked at me and nodded. I was not allowed to reply back in any way, so I nodded with my eyes. He nodded back with his.

"Mr. Jenkins, please tell us what happened the afternoon in question."

"I talked to her that afternoon."

"Her who?"

"Her." He pointed at Salina who sat all alone on the other side in the front row. She was without her parents, without her husband, and without a friend.

My sharp and sophisticated attorney spoke. "Let the record show that the witness has pointed to the plaintiff, Mrs. Salina Alonzo Woodard."

"Mr. Jenkins, please tell us what Mrs. Woodard said to you over the phone that day."

"She said she was going to get him back that night."

"Get who back?"

Carlos looked at me. "The defendant. Makkai Worthy."

"And did she indicate how she was going to do that?"

"Yes."

"How?"

"She was going to tell him that since Mr. Worthy and I, along with other men, have done her so wrong, that she was going to threaten to end it all and then make these allegations."

"Allegations of what?"

"Of rape."

Attorney Cross put his hand to his chin and regrouped. "What did you understand her to mean by the term rape?"

"That was her word. Not mine."

"No more questions, Your Honor," he told the judge.

The judge spoke to the D.A. "Ms. Chen. Your witness."

She stood with confidence. "Thank you, Your Honor. Mr. Jenkins, are you trying to get her back for rejecting your offer of a committed relationship? You wanted her to be your girlfriend, didn't you?"

"I did suggest that, but she didn't want it."

"Then what did she want?"

"All that was on her mind was getting back at Makkai. As long as she could have him on a regular basis, she was fine, but once he no longer made time for her and got someone pregnant, she constantly talked about the fact that when her husband had gone after Makkai, he denied her. She said she wanted to get him back for acting like he didn't know her."

The young, short skirt wearing Asian lawyer looked perplexed. "Why would she tell you all of this, Mr. Jenkins?"

"She thought Makkai Worthy and I were enemies. And, she thought I'd do anything for her. Because I told her I would."

"Why?"

"Because I wanted to end my old ways and be with her. But, obviously I picked the wrong girl."

Sarcasm owned her words. "Sorry about that Mr. Jenkins. But, what do you think set her off? What could have possibly set her off to make up something as serious as this?"

"Me telling her that Makkai Worthy got some woman pregnant."

"No more questions for this witness, Your Honor." She shook her head like she was getting nowhere, or like this was just plain old ridiculous.

The prosecution called the two police officers who were at the scene. And then they called Salina herself.

She stood up and adjusted her classic black blazer. Her knee length skirt was feminine and frilly. Her pearls were large and bright white. Her hair was pulled back into a curly ponytail. Her checks were rosy. Her lips were red. She looked credible, and she looked ready. She took slow steps and smiled at everyone along the way. She put her hand up and swore to not lie. She swore to not lie. She took her seat after she swore not to lie.

Ms. Chen started off. "Mrs. Alonzo Woodard, what happened the night in question that prompted you to call the police?"

Salina's voice actually had a slight Spanish accent today. "Makkai Worthy came to my home to try and get back with me. He was jealous about me dating his best friend. He'd ended that friendship because Carlos was seeing me. And then he came by my home, uninvited, and forced himself on me."

"What did he do?"

She simulated a motion of pulling on her own arm. "He grabbed me and scratched my arms, tore my clothes, jerked me around by my hair, and slapped me in the face. And then, when I lay still, about to pass out, he entered me and started yelling for me to come back to him."

"Did anyone hear this happening?"

She clicked her tongue. "I don't know."

"Mrs. Alonzo Woodard, did you try to get back at him for the incident regarding your husband at the hospital?"

"No. I was over that. I even started dating him again."

"So you did not want to have sex with him that night?"

"No."

"Did you tell him no?"

"Yes. Over and over again."

I leaned in toward my attorney, but he put his hand on my forearm. I sat back.

"So you didn't want to have sex?"

"No. I was seeing Carlos Jenkins."

"No more questions." Ms. Chen took her seat, giving me a look I can't explain.

"Your witness Mr. Cross."

"Thank you, Your Honor. Mrs. Woodard, so you're saying you only sleep with one person at a time.

Ms. Chen spoke up. "Objection."

"Sustained. The defense's comment will be stricken from the record. Mr. Cross, you are being warned that opinionated questions like that will not be tolerated."

"Yes, Your Honor. Mrs. Woodard, were you trying to get even?"

"No."

"Were you setting up Mr. Worthy because he got another woman pregnant?"

"No."

"I see. Let me ask you this. Do you have a prescription for any drugs used in the treatment of psychotic hallucinations?"

"No." Salina looked at her attorney with question-marked eyes.

Ms. Chen jumped to her feet and spoke. "Do not answer any further, Mrs. Alonzo Woodard. Objection, Your Honor."

My attorney continued, "Your Honor, I have a notarized letter here from Mrs. Woodard's own husband stating that she receives regular medications from Mexico. Packages that contain Haldol and Zypreza. And he attached a letter from a Dr. Barber in Century City. He's a psychiatrist. He diagnosed Mrs. Woodard with chronic schizophrenia nearly ten years ago. His diagnosis indicated that Mrs. Woodard has disordered thinking, similar to a split personality."

"I do not."

The judge spoke firmly. "Mrs. Woodard, you will remain silent until you are asked to respond to a question."

Ms. Chen used her hands as she spoke. "Your Honor, this evidence was not disclosed. And besides, just because someone might have a mental illness does not mean they cannot be raped. No means no."

My attorney replied, "While that might be true . . ."

Salina suddenly lost her accent and spewed words, pointing as she spoke. "While that might be true, Ms. Chen is the only one who gets this. I've been dealing with the fact that I can't have children and he simply runs off and shoots his juice in someone else. And I heard she's an old broad. See, all men are the fucking same. That foolish Dr. Barber, my tattletale, violent husband, this not-so-good doctor, Makkai, that sorry-ass attorney, and you, too, chauvinistic Mr. Judge. *Olvídese todo usted.*"

Ms. Chen pleaded, "Mrs. Woodard, please stop talking."

The judge banged his gavel. "Mrs. Woodard, I will hold you in contempt of court."

"I don't care. I've already gotten him just like I warned him I would." She squeezed her eyes at me as voices in the courtroom geared up.

The judge hit the gavel repeatedly. "Order in the court. Bailiff, please place Mrs. Woodard into custody." He turned back to Salina. "I have asked you to remain quiet and you insist on disobeying my order. I'm holding you in contempt. Take her into custody now."

Salina frowned intently and stood up. "Carlos, are you going to let them do this to me? I thought you were different and yet you still come in here telling them everything I told you. Screw you too, Carlos. I was falling in love with you."

The defense and prosecution attorneys approached the bench as Salina, now totally speaking in Spanish, was led out.

Ms. Chen spoke up. "Your Honor. Obviously she is stressed from the incident in question, but we think her accusations of battery did occur. We're willing to settle for a misdemeanor charge of battery and will drop the forcible rape charges if the defense agrees."

"Ms. Chen. Are you deaf? Did you just hear Mrs. Woodard admit to setting this man up? The order of the court after his preliminary hearing is that there was not enough evidence to hold this case over for trial. I'm making note that these charges be dismissed. Both charges, Ms. Chen." He looked over at me. "Have a nice day. Mr. Worthy, you are free to go." I stood and nodded. "And Mrs. Woodard will remain in custody on contempt charges as well as being charged with filing a false police report." He hit his gavel while shaking his head and exited the courtroom as everyone stood up.

Mr. Cross approached me with a handshake. "Mr. Worthy, you know you can fire back and sue her for slander and negative infliction of emotional distress." We headed through the swinging doors toward the first row.

"Mr. Cross, I'm just glad to know she broke down at just the right time. You kept those letters to yourself, huh?"

"I should have entered them as evidence and made a full disclosure, but hey sometimes you take a risk in situations like this. Instability in witnesses is an attorney's dream. I'm just surprised they called her to the stand."

"Surprised and happy," I said as my mom approached.

"I'll be right back," he said. "Hello, and thanks, Mr. Jenkins." He and Carlos shook hands.

"Hey there. No problem." Carlos replied as the attorney walked away.

Carlos touched my back as I hugged my mom. "Hey man. Hey Mrs. Cotton."

"Hello, Carlos. Thanks so much, honey." Mom hugged him and rocked him back and forth.

"Yes, thanks." I shook his hand, too . . . the brotha handshake with a shoulder tap.

"No thanks required. The truth is what it is. And, through all the years, you've been my boy. I couldn't let you go out like that."

"I see that. I appreciate it."

"Though it looks like you didn't even need me with a sharp attorney like that."

"No, we did. It all helped."

"Good. Well, I'll talk to you later, partner. Gotta get to work."

"For sure."

I hugged my mom again, feeling the weight lifted from my shoulders. "As soon as Mr. Cross tells us I can go, let's get out of here. I've got to return some calls."

That night, I sat back on my lounger, sipping on cognac, with "*Family Affair,*" by Sly and the Family Stone, dancing through the surround sound stereo speakers. I had made a point of scheduling the security company to come by to fix my driveway gate so that an access code would once again be needed to get in. I'd even changed the code again just for peace of mind.

Through my sliding glass door I had a full view of my side yard. Everywhere I looked I saw greenery and shrubbery and flowers and bushes and orange trees, and in between each of those, blue skies and cottony white clouds were threaded here and there.

Here I was, not even forty yet, living the life, making a good amount of money, healthy and strong, with all that I could have imagined when I was young. The very field that greeted me back in the day every morning in Wildwood contained maybe three leafless, fruitless trees that took up barely one one-hundredth of the yard space. Dirt covered the earth and bits of broken rocks crunched beneath the soles of my young feet. I'd dreamed of owning land with lush green trees. I'd forgotten about that dream until today. Today I had dozens and dozens that surrounded my property. Something so simple suddenly meant so much.

How in the heck did I manage to scoot by that rape charge crap? That could have meant the end of my career. My mother always said that you can't get changed until you draw near. And that you will never have a testimony without a test. That God will put you through certain situations so that you seek Him out and desire to get to know Him better. I'd hoped that my situations were done. He knew, and I knew, that I needed to slow down.

Speaking of slowing down, I needed a little escape, and some new scenery, so the upcoming reunion was right on time. For the moment, I wanted to listen to my Stevie CD next, but as I pressed the remote to change CDs the radio came on and *Jesus Is My Help* seeped from the speakers and absorbed my soul. *I tell you where my help cometh. It cometh from the Lord.*

I closed my eyes and tuned out the final ring of my home phone. I heard my own voice in the background.

Can't answer the phone right now. Leave a message.

Makkai Worthy. It's Lois Taylor. I got your message. Congratulations. See you at work when you get back from your weekend away. It hasn't been the same without you. Glad everything worked out well. Okay. Goodbye.

And right there is where I rested all night long. A restful, uninterrupted eight hours of sleep. I could have sworn that for the first time in a while, I actually woke up with a smile on my face.

Chapter 42

Back to life. The day of my flight to Florida had arrived. I knew this was going to be interesting. First of all, there was a whole group of my dad's offspring who wouldn't come just because they've been brainwashed to hate him due to what their mothers have had to say about him, branding him a dog for life. And he is, but they'll never get a chance to experience the other members of this family, their lineage and their blood, who are pretty cool. It seems as though my sister and I were the only kids of his who actually got to live with him, if that can be considered a good thing. He married my mom, and then married a woman who couldn't have kids, the one who took my virginity, or should I say the one my dad gave it to, Erskalene. I was off the plane and inside of my dad's house in no time. An oldies radio station played *"Back Down Memory Lane,"* by Minnie Riperton.

"Come on in, Makkai. It's good to see you. We have a room all ready for you, so just make yourself at home." Erskalene pointed down the hall.

The small house seemed even smaller now. The wallpaper with the small palm trees Mom had in the living room was replaced by dark blue paint, and the beige furniture with the plastic slipcovers was now powder blue. The shag rugs were pulled up, exposing the run-down strips of hardwood, covered by small circular throw rugs here and there. Near the living room window where the cane and bamboo rocking chair was that my mother used to sit in while she'd wait for my dad to come home, now served as the spot for two re-cliners, each mixed with fifty shades of blue. Blue was Dad's favorite color.

I said to myself, *Make myself at home? This was my home. And that was my room.* "No, I'm staying at the Marriott next door to where the reunion is. But, thanks."

Dad spoke up, walking with his cane at a slow pace, coming from the bathroom. He now stood with an arched back. He had less hair on his head and fewer teeth in his mouth. And he looked a whole lot shorter than he used to.

"Son, now you know you can stay right here. Just because you have money doesn't mean you have to blow it. This is precious time, having you here. You need to spend time with your old pops. I'm not getting any younger you know. This could be the last time you see me."

There he goes again. "Dad, you're not going anywhere. You're going to outlive us all."

"That would be a lot of outliving," Erskalene joked. "Did your dad tell you that his ten-year-old son is coming?" she asked me. Which I thought was strange being that she'd been living with my dad for over twenty years.

"He couldn't make it after all," Dad told her, almost sounding relieved.

Neither Erskalene nor I replied to his statement.

Dad took a seat in one of the reclining chairs. He began sorting through some old cassette tapes.

Erskalene, who before had the skin of someone half her age, now looked nearly twice her age. I watched her walk into the kitchen to check on a pot full of black-eyed peas and ham hocks. The soulful aroma was everywhere. She'd lost a lot of weight, and her hair was now totally gray. She came back in, tying her orange robe at her waist.

"It's good to see you," I told her. I found myself touching her hand as I spoke.

She didn't look me in the eyes. Not even once. She took her place in her recliner next to Dad and crossed her legs at the ankle. "You, too, Makkai. You, too."

The reunion in the grand ballroom of the beautiful Adam's Mark Hotel was packed. The room was all abuzz. I saw many, many faces I knew, but hadn't seen in years. And, I saw faces I didn't know at all. I saw my aunts, and cousins, and nieces, and nephews, and tons of elders of the family. Everyone was dressed up, looking good. I went dressy casual with a black shirt and black pinstriped pants.

As my dad and I sat at a rounded table for ten, one of my cousins brought over an elderly lady who used a walker. Dad smiled brightly in his midnight blue three-piece suit, looking pretty dapper for an old man.

He stood up to greet her, bracing himself with his cane. I stood as well. "Son, this is my Aunt Ethel. She's one hundred and five years old." Pride took over his face.

I told her, "What an honor to meet you." The elegant-looking woman had on all white, including a white dress and hat with big snowy white flowers. I reached out my hand, and she pulled me to her for a hug.

"Call me Auntie, chile. Is yo name Roosevelt, too?"

"No, my name is Makkai," I said as we parted our embrace.

She looked at my dad. "Oh, Roosevelt, didn't I jus' meet two a yo boys name fa you?"

"You probably did, Aunt Ethel. There are quite a few juniors," he replied.

I just had to know. "Dad, how many sons named Roosevelt do you have?"

"I think about six. I don't know. A few of them are here. You'll meet them."

Aunt Ethel asked, "Chile, is you da baby son?"

"No, I don't think so," I told her.

Dad spoke up. "No, Aunt Ethel, he's not."

She scratched the back of her neck. "Roosevelt, yo mom told me bout chu but I thought chu'd a stopped all dat Don Juan stuff long, long time ago, boy."

"I did eventually."

She patted my hand. "Good. I don't mean no harm but chile, don't chu take afta yo dad, cause he addicted to da ladies. Dat wife a his must be a good woman, I'll say dat ret now."

"She is," Dad said.

Aunt Ethel spoke to me while clutching her large white leather bag. "Well, it's nice ta meet chu finally. If it hadn't happen' dis time, it sholey wudn't gone happen on da nex one."

"Nice to meet you too. You're pretty sharp to be over one hundred years old. You'll be around."

"Chile, dat's one thang bout dis family. Da womens live long lives but da mens die young jus' from chasing us arounds."

"Don't I know that," Dad said.

She pointed to me as she turned to walk away. "He look mo likes you den any yo' tribe," she commented to my dad.

Dad missed the comment as he focused on looking past his aunt, who was headed back toward her table. Dad's eyes bugged. "Come on, Makkai, I want to introduce you to my twin daughters."

"Twins. Where did the twin gene come from?"

"Their mom's side." We took a few slow steps to another table.

"Oh, Lawd," I said, as two tall, stacked women stood up, wearing matching tan outfits and high heels.

I whispered, "Dad, please don't tell me those are my sisters?"

"Yes, Makkai. This is Rita and Renee. Rita and Renee, this is your brother Makkai."

"Damn, Dad. *I* can't take this," I said toward his ear.

Rita said, "Nice to meet you, big brother." Big was a word that I did not feel like. They were both at least two inches taller than me. And fine as hell. Long hair, long legs, long nails, and short-ass dresses.

"Nice to meet you, too."

Dad bragged, "They played basketball when they were in college in Arizona."

"I guess they did, looking at their height," I commented.

Renee said, "Our mom is six-foot-three inches."

I asked in jest, "Dad, you were climbing some trees back then, huh?" The girls laughed.

"Height didn't matter any more than age." He actually seemed to be bragging.

"Hey there, Makkai," an old man said, now standing next to Dad.

"Hello," I replied simply.

He said, "Hey there, Roosevelt. That boy has grown into quite a young man."

"Yes, he has."

Familiarity grabbed hold of my brain as my eyes expanded. "Uncle Leroy?" I asked with anticipation of his reply.

"Yes. Of course it's me. Has two decades made me look that much different?"

Actually, they had. Uncle Leroy was always built like a running back. Before, he was stocky and muscular, and had a broad face. Today, he was thin and his face was very slender. And his skin had gotten lighter and it sagged with age. Years of not seeing him made it so much more noticeable. But, oh, now, that's a man I will never forget.

I said, "No, no. How are you doing, Uncle Leroy? It's good to see you." I stepped up and gave him a strong hug. He had on a sharp gold suit.

We backed up, and then he spoke. "You, too. I hear you're not married yet."

"No, not yet."

"But, you ended up being a big-time M.D., huh? Being a doctor takes a lot more effort than playing baseball, that's for sure."

Dad looked proud. "The boy has always been smart."

"I am a heart surgeon. But, how are you?" I asked him again.

"Good. I'm divorced now. I was married for fifteen years, but I'm living the single life and loving it. And I am dating, believe it or not. I even got me a page on *Match.com*."

"No way."

"Oh, yes. You've gotta get with the times." He slowly sipped copper liquid from a large shot glass.

"Will you teach my dad here about computers, please?"

Dad shook his head. "No thanks, I'm doing just fine without all that."

"And where's Uncle Milton?" I asked.

Dad said matter-of-factly, "Son, Uncle Milton died a few years ago."

"What? Dad, I didn't know. You didn't tell me." My face was blank.

"I thought I did. I thought I left you a message at that hospital. It was sudden, and his wife had the services in her hometown of Rochdale, New York. Anyway, that didn't make any sense to me. She was a strange one," said Dad.

Uncle Leroy spoke. "We've all been all over the place. None of us have been all that close through the years, Makkai. I can understand how you didn't get word of his passing."

"Wow." I was in shock.

"Hey, but we're all here," Uncle Leroy said with a smile, obviously trying to liven up the mood.

My smile was slight. "Yes, and that's a blessing."

Chapter 43

The rest of the evening pretty much went the same way. I met strangers who were my own siblings and reconnected with long lost family. I wished my sister Fonda could have been there. So many people said they wished they'd met her. And some of them asked about Mom, too.

Later, I took Dad home early because his bad knee was swelling up. Plus he'd had one too many whisky sours. Erskalene stayed at the reunion and danced the night away with my aunts and uncles. I heard they'd always treated her like family from day one.

"Dad."

"Yeah, boy." He sat in his chair and leaned back, closing his eyes and rubbing his belly. "Those ribs were meaty and tender and sweet like a woman. I need a cigarette."

That man always has sex on the brain. And he does not smoke. At least that's one vice he hasn't taken up.

"Dad, I'm gonna step outside for a minute. It's a beautiful evening. I'll be right back."

"You say so. I'll be sitting right here picking my teeth."

He grabbed a beat up toothpick and went to town, sucking back in whatever he found in between. That brought back a memory. My country dad.

Heading back through the front door to the mock baseball field, I simply stood and glanced and took in the view that now seemed less vass and less inviting. It was still grassless, but now there was a wooden shed smack dab in the middle, and an old broken down car near where my first base used to be. It seemed smaller and hard to imagine as the same place.

I turned back toward the house after only a few minutes. Those three chipped, burgundy painted steps were familiar. The front door was still a dark wood, but it was weather beaten and dingy. The same dull brass door knocker was there before me.

I grabbed the doorknob and stepped back inside where it all happened. Where it was still happening, after all these years. Roosevelt Worthy and his main woman. His main woman who had to deal with being number one, as opposed to being the only one. Same thing, different woman.

With tiny eyeglasses perched toward the tip of his nose, Dad sat in his comfy recliner, rummaging through an old beat-up shoebox, searching through some old pictures. He now had a forty-ounce can of Old English on the small round end table, and some pork rinds. He continued to peruse the photos as if I'd never walked in.

I took ownership of Erskalene's chair and leaned back as well, raising the footrest.

He handed me a wallet-sized picture. "This is my grandfather. He only had one daughter, Aunt Ethel, who you met, who is your Uncle Leroy and Uncle Milton's mother, and one son, my father, Theodore Worthy. Here's his picture. My dad was married to my mom for sixty years."

During the handoff of the photo, I noticed Dad's hands looked nearly the same as when I was a teenager, just with more wrinkles. "That's a long time." My dad was the spitting image of his dad.

He sipped his beer and gave a small burp. He then crunched into a rind. He spoke with his mouth full. "How's your mother, son?"

"She's fine. I think she might finally be ready to retire."

"She should. She deserves it." I handed him the photo back. He stared straightforward and leaned back. "Son, I really did love your mother. I just didn't know how to deal with a woman who couldn't share me."

"Most women wouldn't put up with that, Dad. Especially when you're married."

"I know."

"Why did you marry Mom if you needed other women?"

"I didn't want anyone else to have her, and she wanted to be a wife. Had to make an honest woman out of her."

"And what about Erskalene? Why did you marry her?"

"Because I knew she'd be the type of woman who would share me. She's one of a kind."

"That's gotta be a terrible way for her to live, Dad. For her to know that when you're not home, you're in someone else's bed."

"She's open to it. It's just the way she is."

"And how would you deal with it if you had to share her?"

He spoke casually. "I have, son. Erskalene has had a younger lover since I've known her. I'm telling you she's pretty open. You of all people should know that."

On that note, I fought the battle to hold in a long overdue breath as long as I could, but felt that if I didn't follow up on that comment then and there, I never would again. "Dad, speaking of that time, why did you stay in the room when that happened? I can maybe see you setting me up with a hooker or something, or maybe even with someone you knew, but someone you loved enough to marry, and then you joined in. Why?"

"That's the only way I knew. My dad showed me, too." He put the top on the box of pictures.

"I thought your dad was married for sixty years."

"He was." He paused and took another sip. "Son, I did the best I could to keep you straight. And I'm sure having those Worthy skills hasn't hurt your love life any." His toothless grin was almost devilish.

"I'm not so sure, Dad."

"Well, son, what do you want me to say?"

"After all these years, I suppose there's nothing to say. But, I'll tell you one thing. I don't know how many other sons you've done that to, but I'll never bring my son into my bedroom, no matter how feminine I think he is."

"I never touched you, Makkai." He looked like he was fishing for credit.

"Oh, but you did in a way. You touched my youth with an experience that stunned me, yet kept me focused on sex."

Silence.

I flashed a smile to lighten up the mood of a old man. He grinned back at me.

"Dad, anybody pregnant right now? You're shooting blanks finally, right?" I smiled just short of a laugh.

"I don't know. I hope so."

"Ever heard of a rubber, Dad?" Again, I smiled, but harder.

"I've used one a few times if they insisted. Most don't."

"If they insisted? What about you doing it for your health and for the fact that you've contributed enough to the population explosion."

"I'm from the old school. All of that safe sex stuff happened not so long ago. Anyway, it's too late for that now." He swigged a long sip, leaning his head back.

"It's never too late."

He swallowed audibly. "Son, go find yourself a good woman and settle down. Do what I couldn't do and, to be honest with you, still fight to do. Stay true and satisfy one woman."

"You know what? As I look at you and look at how you've lived, I'm actually sorry you went through what you went through, with being obsessed with the need to have so many women."

"I've had a grand life. No regrets. But, I am sorry to you for what happened. Believe it or not, I did what I thought was necessary."

"Enough said."

He handed me the box. "Here, look through these and take the pictures you want. There's nothing like music and photos in life. I'm going to put in this old Joe Tex cassette." He leaned over and pushed a few buttons to an old, old stereo. It actually had an eight-track deck.

"I hear you." I lifted the top and filtered through the black-and-whites, Polaroids, the faded ones, and the newer ones. I grinned at the sight of the stacks of memories, unorganized and disheveled, yet and still, saved and obviously cherished. "You need a photo album, like yesterday." My eyes found a small manila envelope, turned toward the back, flashing a California return address. My eyes widened, my hand reached toward it hovering over it for a moment, until my apprehensive fingers grazed against the right corner, taking hold and lifting it up for a better view. "Hey, what's this, Dad?"

Dad sat back and tapped his feet to the beat. He looked over for a split second. "That's just a group of some photos an old friend sent me." He waved his hand toward me.

My squinted sight revealed seven tiny letters, written in purple cursive ink that set off bell after bell in my spinning head. A facial muscle jittered. My bottom lip quivered. My eyes blinked rapidly. My words sounded off in slow motion. "This envelope says Asskins."

"That's Laurie Askins. We called her Asskins because, son, this woman had the biggest behind I had ever seen in my life." He used his hands to describe the roundness, cupping his hand around as he spoke.

I opened the flap and looked in to find one particular photo. Removing it, inch by inch, bit by bit, it revealed a sight for sore eyes. Two females standing, looking at me, hugging each other, smiling at me, ringing more bells with each feature, each curve, and each smirk. Each image filled my head as though I were the photographer and they were frozen in time, as if I were there and they were now, but they weren't and I didn't know them, or at least I didn't know them then.

The tune *"I Gotcha"* by Joe Tex served as background to his words. "It was sweet and plump and had its own zip code. She says she had my child, but Laurie herself died years ago. Woman was shot to death. She sent me those photos years ago from when her daughter, supposedly our daughter, graduated from high school. She didn't tell her a thing about me. She even gave the girl her last name, Askins."

My eyes forgot about my father. My eyes felt dry and my throat felt drier. I could feel my heart muscle pound in overdrive. The vision sent my heart to my belly. I squinted my sight as I devoured the photograph and examined the younger female, taking her into my sights as though my eyes had hands and I could snatch her from the seventies and ask her myself. "What's the girl's name?"

"What does it say on the back there?" He didn't even know his own child's name.

With a slow flick of the wrist, I turned over the Polaroid and read the faded cursive name. I waited for a few hurried breaths to pass. I swallowed. "It says . . . it says Laurinda. It says Laurinda Askins." The name rang a bell.

"That's it. She's a cutie. Doesn't look a thing like me, though."

Still, with no eyes left for my father, I turned the photo back over. How could I be about to form my lips to ask this? How could this world be so small? "So, this Laurinda is my sister?"

"Yes, son. I guess she's your half sister."

Bullet ridden thoughts fired away in my head like a machine gun that I wanted to aim his way. My left hand rose to rub my ear and then to my forehead. My two middle fingers massaged a wake up call into my temples. But, I did not wake up. I was not dreaming. I was fully awake and my ears were not deceiving me. My next question arrived. "Was Laurie wealthy?"

"Wealthy? Please. Hell, no. Laurie didn't have a pot to piss in. She used to beg me for money all the time. Laurie was a con artist from way back and a pathological liar. She owned a restaurant called Mondays, that some married man left to her. I heard it burned down years ago. They say his wife was mad about him leaving it to his mistress. Surely the wife burnt the sucker down. Heck, she may have had Laurie murdered, or at least there were rumors but no proof. What's wrong, son?" He stared at me as though I wasn't listening. Oh, but I was.

My glance was stuck. No matter what, I couldn't unglue the deliberate aim of my eyes. I continued to take in this photo that had to be more than twenty-five years old. The youthful image of my lover, Monday, a.k.a. Laurinda, as the woman called her when we exited that sex party, stared me in the face as she stood next to her attractive mother sporting the same old gap in her teeth, with an ass so fat you could see it from the front. The stare finally broke. "Nothing, Dad. Nothing. I've gotta go."

I pressed the footrest down and stood up, placing the picture and the box on top of same octagon coffee table I used to wax back in the day with lemon Pledge.

"Hold up. Where are you going? You don't need to leave so fast. At least stay for the night. Erskalene had a celebration planned for tomorrow since your birthday is almost here."

"I can't." I snatched up the keys to my rental car.

"Makkai." Dad tried to sit up but his cane fell onto the floor. He looked at me. I didn't budge. He then sat back and lowered his shoulders.

"Goodbye, Dad," I said as I took a last glance at him sitting in his chair. His mouth was open, his forehead crinkled, eyebrows raised. I was sure this would be my final snapshot of him for the rest of my life. This rolling stone whose daughter I'd impregnated.

He spoke to my backside. "Makkai. Are you coming back?"

"Not this trip."

I closed the front door behind me with a snatch and then backed out of the driveway in that rented Cadillac Catera in what seemed to be a millisecond.

The sound?

A prolonged screech.
The smell?
Burning rubber.
The feeling?
Absolute disgust.

Chapter 44

My words were directed to my speakerphone as I drove north on the 405 freeway as soon as I picked up my car from the LAX parking lot the next day.

"Monday, I'm coming over. I need to talk to you." The conversation moved as fast as my ride.

"Why?" Monday asked loudly from the road.

"Because."

"Because what?"

"Where do you live?"

"In Palos Verdes."

"What's the address?"

"I'll come to you," she insisted.

"No, I'm nearby now. Just give me your address."

"Fine, Makkai, I'll meet you at the Starbucks on PCH near the pier."

"Be there in twenty."

The upstairs strip mall coffeehouse was bustling. The scent tickling patron's nostrils was a mixture of rich Colombian beans and aromatic spices. I stepped up and got in line, looking around for Monday as I perused the crowded room. She sat in a corner, way in the back by the rest room, legs crossed, wearing a short jean jacket with her belly protruding. She had on a green wool scarf, wrapped tightly around her neck. She looked over at me without blinking, sipping bottled water through a straw. I waved. She did not.

"How are you feeling?" I asked as I approached after being handed my white chocolate mocha.

"I'm fine." The word bland was swirling all around her words.

"You seem bitter," I told her as I pulled out a chair and sat down, scooting the chair farther away from her. I searched her face for evidence of our father's genes. I saw none.

"I'm not. You seem irritated."

"I'm not."

"I'm not either," she replied unconvincingly.

I took a cautioned sip. "Are you still pissed because I wouldn't give you the money for the furniture?"

"No shit."

"Anyway, what's going on? Is everything okay?"

"Not sure."

"Why?" I asked my sister.

"That doctor friend of yours is concerned. She called and wanted to see me so that I could go ahead and take the ultrasound sooner, so I went on in."

"I'm glad you did. And she's not my doctor friend. She's just a coworker. Did she give you a delivery date yet?"

"No? But, maybe you should be able to tell us the exact date that the condom broke and add forty weeks to that. I mean you were there too. Besides, like I told you before, and like I told the doctor, I was skipping periods, which had really been happening on and off for two years ever since what I thought was menopause was trying to creep in. But, I guess the one lucky egg got shot by your potent arrow."

"Monday, why are you out and about? Shouldn't you be off your feet like Dr. Marshall said?"

"I would be, but you wanted to meet."

"You were out anyway. I could have come to your house."

"Blah, blah, blah." She looked around the room as though searching for anyone else to talk to other than me.

I wrapped my hand around the sleeved cup, pretending it was her thin neck. "So, what's the final word on what you're going to do?"

"I think at this point I'm having it." Sarcasm was her middle name. She flashed her teeth my way with a fake grin. There was suddenly nothing sexy about her gap anymore.

"Funny, I mean as far as us?"

"Oh, like I have a choice. Like you would run off to Vegas with me and make me an honest old pregnant lady." She sipped her water.

"Can't do that."

"That I know. Wouldn't wanna do that. I have no idea. Hell, just give me money every month and take her every other weekend. I won't fight you on anything."

"Monday, where's your family? Don't you think the baby needs her maternal side of the family?"

"My mom had a small family."

"And?"

"And what?"

"What about your dad?"

She sipped her water again and then twirled the straw. "I don't have one."

"Of course you do."

"Don't know a thing about him and don't care."

"Surely you do."

"I assure you, I don't."

"Monday, have you ever experienced a man who didn't let you down?"

"Stop trying to be a therapist, Makkai. And what does that have to do with this little baby girl coming into the world? You just make sure you don't let her down. Otherwise we can find a family who won't."

"Oh, I won't, so don't even go there. We just need to have her tested."

"For what?"

"Just when she's born, you know, the normal things they test for."

"Okay, Doctor. So do you have another doctor buddy who's a pediatrician who you play golf with maybe? Tell him or her to check the baby out. Just sign the dang birth certificate and I'm fine."

"And I'll want a paternity test."

She slammed the water bottle onto the table. "Makkai, I was waiting for that. Shit, aaaw, damn." She looked down between her legs and her mouth opened wide. "Fuck, my water just broke."

I sprang to my feet. "Let me take you to the hospital now."

She put both hands on her belly. "Oh, damn. It hurts like hell."

"Get in my car." I helped her to a slow stance.

"I can't. My baby, Soul, is in my car."

"Your dog?"

"Yes." We took slow-motioned steps.

"Let's drop him off at home."

"No, we'll have to take him with us. Come on."

I held open the door, placing my hand behind her back as she crouched over. We stepped outside. "Let's get him so you can get in my car."

"No, drive mine. Please. He's used to my car."

"Okay. Where is it?" I looked around.

"You know, it's the Jaguar right there." She pointed to her car, which was right in the front, and she handed me her key ring.

I opened the passenger door to let her in. The car was packed with things. The palomino backseat was floor-to-roof with filled Hefty bags, and the floor on the passenger side had a faded dog blanket and broken dog biscuits. Black dog hair was everywhere, and the car wreaked of something . . . a combination of urine, hair spray, and old pine tree air freshener, all mixed with Kibbles & Bits.

"Why in the hell don't you clean out your car, woman?" I asked as I sat in the drivers' seat, starting the engine.

"Makkai, I'm in labor in case you haven't noticed. Just drive," she said as she rested her head back, and Soul jumped in a small space in the backseat, whining as he looked at her.

"We'll be pulling up in about three minutes," I told the ER nurse and then ended the call.

We parked at the entrance to the emergency room. Two employees briskly walked out, one with a wheelchair and one with a clipboard. The gentleman held out the admittance paperwork toward us both.

I said, "I'll take it. I'm the father." He handed it to me and nodded. As they wheeled her in, I took a pen and began to write. I asked, "What's your address?"

She sat in the wheelchair, not appearing to be in pain, just looking down with her hands under her swollen breasts. "Just put yours."

The curiosity was driving me nuts.

By the time I sat in the waiting room, having filled out as much information as I could, a nurse came out. "Dr. Worthy, we're going to keep her. She'll be in labor and delivery for a while. We don't want this baby to come yet, so we're getting in touch with Dr. Marshall to see if we can give her ritodrine to stop labor. But, it looks like that baby really wants to come soon. Do you want to come in? Are you her labor and delivery coach, too?"

"You know what? I'll be right back, but page me on my cell if you need me." I briskly headed straight back out the door to the trunk of her stinky car.

The first thing that greeted my vision was an old dirty brown suitcase. It had a rusted numeric lock that was busted. Opening the case revealed papers that were filed away neatly. I pulled out a bunch of them. Most looked to be mailed to a post office box in

Long Beach, addressed to Laurinda Askins. She had love notes
from a guy named Paul. But, the one place she had the most mail
from was the Salvation Army. She had training sheets on how to
serve as a holiday bell ringer, and pay stubs at seven dollars per
hour. And she had page upon page of literature from an alcohol
recovery center in Palm Springs and an envelope from a space she
was renting at Public Storage. Also, there were copies of her release papers from a Tracy, California, prison in 2001, including
copies of a recent release from a facility in Lancaster, California,
for the past four months for petty theft. So that's where she'd
been.

Most of what remained in the trunk was boxes and blankets and
pillows, and a few empty bottles of cheap wine. I went around to
the passenger side and looked in the front seat, only to find a
cracked drinking glass from a motel. Inside of the glass were den-
ture cleaner packets. And leaning in toward the backseat, as Soul
wagged his stubby tail, sniffing my arm, on the floor there were
about three different colors and styles of wigs shoved into a plastic
shopping bag. Who the hell was she trying to be? My sister, my
baby's mom, is living in her car. My sister, my baby's mom, is homeless. I tossed the bag with the wigs back onto the backseat, and a
six-pack of miniature whisky bottles, all rubber-banded together,
fell onto the passenger seat. And, my sister, my baby's mom, is an
alcoholic.

"Hey, Laurinda. How's it going?" I asked, taking a seat in the labor
room where she lay, hooked up to monitors and an IV.

She had one hand over her eyes and one on her belly. "Not right
now, Mr. Super Investigator. Don't you dare be so cruel? I'm laying
here about to have your baby."

"Are you drunk right now? Was that gin in that water bottle you
were sipping from earlier?"

"Get off my case."

"Oh, but we will talk about it again. You put this child at risk." I squinted my stare.

She yelled out, pointing toward the exit. "Put my car keys with the rest of my things and get the hell out of here. Nurse," she struggled to yell toward the door. "Dammit," she said as the uterine contraction monitor indicated that another contraction was about to strike.

I responded anyway. "I'm not going anywhere. I'm here for this baby."

"Ooohh, damn. Get this baby out of me, now."

The RN came running in as I remained standing. She slipped her gloves on to give a quick dilation check. "Ma'am, you'll be fine."

She spoke into the tiny PDA mobile phone device, which was hanging from her neck. "Lori, tell Dr. Marshall the baby's head is crowning. And that the fetal heart monitor indicates distress. We have a second trimester patient with an incompetent cervix about to deliver and we need the doctor over here now. Miss Askins is early but she needs to deliver, now."

A team of nurses and an anesthesiologist rushed in. Two nurses began to wheel Monday's gurney into the delivery room. As I stood in the doorway, Monday managed to look over and cut her eyes at me, as she shouted, "He cannot come in the delivery room."

"Calm down, ma'am." The nurse then told me, "Dr. Worthy, I'm sorry." She closed the double doors in my face.

I spoke to the hardness and thickness and coldness of the delivery room doors. "Fine, I'll be waiting outside."

I looked at my watch, making note of the fact that in ten minutes, it would be my birthday. I began pacing back and forth just outside of the door. Hell, I was in the delivery room for Georgia's baby and here I was, unable to watch my own child being born.

A voice rang over the loudspeakers. "Dr. Worthy, please all extension 3211. Dr. Worthy, please call extension 3211."

I stepped over to the wall phone near the waiting room.

"Hello. Someone paged me. This is Dr. Worthy."

"Yes, Dr. Worthy. This is Lori, in Dr. Marshall's office. How are you?"

"I've been better. Isn't Dr. Marshall in delivery with Ms. Askins right now?"

"Yes, but she asked me to call you to tell you that we checked with King Drew to try and get Ms. Askins's previous OB files, but they have no record of her as a patient there. From what they tell me, she has not been seen by any doctors at King. And there's no Dr. Taksa at that hospital at all. So we have no information regarding her prior ultrasound."

Why was I not surprised? "Oh really?"

"Yes, Dr. Worthy. And, the results from the ultrasound we performed did show that she has an abnormal cervix. We're surprised that she was able to carry the fetus beyond seventeen weeks."

"Oh, my God. But, she did come in when you called her about scheduling the ultrasound prior to the original appointment date, right?"

"Yes, Dr. Worthy, she did. But, it looks as though she's had no pre-natal care other than when she came in to see Dr. Marshall with you last week. Perhaps, all of this could have been prevented."

"Thank you, Lori."

Chapter 45

My daughter, my niece, my father's daughter's daughter, Baby Girl Askins, was born on my birthday, August 3rd, at 12:24 in the morning, just as I received a page from the trauma unit that a male athlete had been airlifted after suffering an aortic valve dissection and needed emergency surgery. I immediately made a call to refer it to another surgeon. Then I passed another doctor while exiting obstetrics. My tiny daughter was fourteen inches long, and weighed only 2.7 pounds.

"Dr. Lambert. I need to talk to you. It's extremely important." I walked alongside, shifting into fifth gear to keep up. The young black doctor looked more like a male model than a physician.

"What is it, Doctor?" He was always no-nonsense.

"It's about the preemie girl that was born about fifteen minutes ago in delivery room number two. I need your help. I need a paternity test done right away."

We were stride for stride as we hit the south corridor. "That's up to the parents to agree on, Doctor."

"I am the parent. I am the father. Or at least I think I am."

"Dr. Worthy, the mother has to agree, you know that. We haven't even gotten to the point of having the legal documents filled out." He picked up a chart as he whisked by the OB nurses' station. "Who's her regular OB/GYN?"

"Doctor, please."

He looked up at me with low-set, thick eyebrows. "Dr. Worthy, what's up with you? Give it to me straight."

"We dated. She's in no position to provide for this baby, so I think we're going to battle. I just need to make sure for a couple of reasons. It's very, very personal."

"Well, Doctor, first things first. We're doing the usual screening for hepatitis B and HIV, and we're checking for any developmental abnormalities, mainly neurological at this point. And as you know, we're also testing this baby for traces of alcohol in her system which could have affected her fetal development, not to mention that she's extremely underweight, even considering her term."

"Dr. Lambert, I understand that, but for a very important reason that could definitely weigh heavily upon the infant's health, I need to know if this is my child."

"Why, Dr. Worthy? If this baby's medical prognosis is at stake, I suggest you cut out the pride act, because you're wasting my valuable time. What is going on?"

"For reasons that . . . this could have been an incestuous affair. This woman, as it turns out, could be my half-sister."

"Go give a blood sample to the lab. I'll get back to you."

With those words, and without flinching, he quickly entered a patient's room and left me standing before I could say, "Thanks, Dr. Lambert," expressing myself to another closed door.

"What are you doing back here?" asked Mary Jane. We started to pass each other in the hallway as I left the lab. "I thought you had a patient to see." She looked in a rush.

"I'm a father, Mary Jane. The newborn girl with the last name Askins that was just born . . . she's mine. I'm fairly sure that she's mine."

"No way." She stopped.

"Yes." I stopped.

Her eyes gave me a slap in the face, but she was all business. "Well, then you'd better get over to ICU with me because she's got some problems."

"What? Mary Jane, I'm not allowed in there until the mother gives her approval."

"What in the hell did you get yourself into?"

"All I know is, right now, I'm headed to the chapel."

"I'll keep an eye on her. And Dr. Worthy, Makkai, for what it's worth, happy birthday." Mary Jane dashed off again.

"Thanks."

Dear God,

I don't get to talk to you enough. Or should I say I don't make enough time to talk to you like this. I know that at times we go through hell and high water so that we'll come to know you for ourselves. I know you want to know me more personally, and I want to know you, too. Believe me I do. I have been through a lot, and I know it's all been my own doing, greed, lust, stubbornness. But, the bottom line is you've been so good to me. You've given me more than many people get to experience in two lifetimes. I thank you for all of your blessings and for the gifts you've given me . . . the gift of the skilled hands of a heart surgeon. And I know that there are times when I totally dishonor you and your name. But, here I am, kneeling in your name. They say through you all things are possible.

And so I'm asking for my daughter to be healthy in every way. She shouldn't have to suffer for her parents' indiscretions. She's fighting, but deep inside, I know she's not alone on her day of birth, my day of rebirth. I always remember the saying from Footprints, and how when we get weary, it seems there's only one set of footprints. Well, I'm weary. And I know, with all my heart and soul that you will carry us through. Your footprints are in the sand, taking this journey right along with us. We're never alone.

You brought this beautiful little life into this world. And I pray and ask you to keep her here for a long time. Say, one hundred years maybe. Mom always said that loss births a desire for change. Well, my desire is to change, but I pray that it's without the loss. I have faith. I know she'll be okay, I believe that she is okay as I speak to you.

And by the way, tell my little sister I was talking to you. She'll be happy about that. Or is it true that in heaven, bliss is a constant? No disappointment. Well, that's good to know.

So, thanks for your time. And when you get ready to come and get me, I'll be ready to come home to you, standing before you as a child of God. That much I promise. But, could you give me some more time to pull it all together? And some great years with my little one, please? I ask you to come into my heart and my life and bless this little girl, and her mother, and me. I also ask for peace of mind. Because I do feel that you are drawing me near. In your name, I say, Amen.

I came to a stance, bowed my head at the altar, and immediately headed out of the chapel and straight to the special care nursery unit where I stood over the incubator that held my miniature newborn daughter.

Because of her low birth weight she was susceptible to heat loss, so they put her in a double walled warmer, wrapped in warm blankets to help her retain her body heat. She was hooked up to a heart respirator monitor. The many tubes were coming out of and going into more places than any one human being should ever be expected to stand.

Years of seeing patients take their last breaths were painful, but here I was taking in the sight of my very own child fighting for her life. Her petite hands, about the size of a half-dollar, were shut tight. And her pale, slim body was a little larger than the size of my hand, yet it was sweet and beautiful.

"We've got her, don't worry," Mary Jane said, speaking from behind me.

"This is hard."

She put her hand on my back. "I know it is. She's going to get through this, Makkai. You have to know that."

"If she's given a chance at life, then all of my prayers will have been answered."

"Makkai, you need to let us do what we do best. But, it's all in God's hands from here."

I held my skilled hands out toward my baby girl. For the first time in my life, they were unsteady "I've never felt so helpless before in my life. And these hands can't do a thing about it."

"I understand. You can't save her yourself. She has to turn that corner. And she will . . . soon. Just have faith."

I thought, *Faith. Belief in all that is unseen.* I pulled my gaze from my daughter's face to Mary Jane's face. "Mary Jane, thank you." I placed my hands around her hand.

"I'm proud to be able to be one of the ones looking after her. She's beautiful, and she's very special."

"Yes, she is," I said as we looked over at her.

"Have you named her yet?"

I turned toward Mary Jane. "I need to explain some things to you."

"No, you don't. This is between you and her mother. I'd seen her around before but didn't know you knew her that well. But, Makkai, that's not the priority right now."

"Thank you for understanding."

"Nothing matters more than this little one's life right now."

"Amen. I'll see you later."

"Okay."

"Dr. Worthy, I've been trying to reach you." Dr. Lois Taylor approached just before I could walk away. "Oh, excuse me, Nurse Cherry," she said.

"No problem."

Dr. Taylor and I stepped away toward the nursery door. "What's up?"

"I wanted to know if we were still on for tonight to celebrate your birthday."

"Uh, no. I've had an emergency come up."

"That's too bad. What's going on?"

"That newborn named Askins over there in the neonatal care unit is my daughter."

"Your daughter?"

"Yes."

At first, she cut her eyes, but then she looked at me and simply dropped her words where they lay. "You know, Dr. Worthy, people have talked around here about you being Casanova Brown ever since I got here. I guess what they've been saying is true. You have gotten yourself in a lot of trouble."

"Dr. Taylor, right now, I really don't care what people think. My baby girl is fighting for her life."

"What's wrong with her?"

"I've got the pediatricians on it. She'll be fine."

"Good. You know, I truly do wish you luck. You take care of yourself."

"Thanks."

She turned back around after taking a step. "Is Dr. Lambert one of the ones attending to her?"

"Yes."

"Then she's in good hands. I've got to get going. Happy birthday."

"Thanks, Dr. Taylor."

"Call me Lois."

"Thanks, Lois."

I saw Mary Jane standing over my little daughter, half looking at me through the thick glass, half watching her boss, Lois, swish her way in her white skirt through the doorway and down the hall.

Mary Jane then glared at me. I could read her mind. Surely she was thinking, *So much for the not dating a coworker rule,* or thinking she couldn't believe my nerve. I couldn't blame her for her bullet-ridden stare. She, of all people, didn't deserve to be played.

*   *   *

Two mornings later, after having never left the hospital other than to take that flea-bitten mutt to the boarding kennel around the corner and bring back a claim receipt which I gave to Monday's nurse, I finally decided to put on my white coat and see my post-op patients. I felt pretty bad about taking that dog, but shoot, even the pound would have been better than living in that nasty car, and she didn't feel bad about not letting me see my baby being born. Anyway, the attending physicians had done a great job with my patients.

Just as I was standing before the post-op, male athlete whose aortic valve had been repaired, I heard Mary Jane's voice over the speakers, "Dr. Makkai Worthy, please come to the OB nurses' station, stat. Dr. Worthy, please come to the OB nurses' station, stat."

I walked the short distance with a purpose to my step. Mary Jane stood outside of the nursery looking flushed.

"Doctor, Ms. Askins left."

"She left?" I breathed like I'd sprinted eight hundred meters.

"Yes, she's nowhere to be found. She asked one of the nurses about some dog and then the next thing the nurse knew, she was gone."

"Where's my baby?" I held my breath.

"Makkai, relax. She left without the baby. And she left this sheet of notebook paper on her pillow. It's addressed to you."

Makkai,

You really are a total and complete jerk. That's the first thing I want to say. Yes, you found out that my real name is not Monday. My real name is Laurinda. Laurinda Askins. I am the mother of your baby, and I drink a little bit, and I'm homeless. But, I'm sure you've already verified all of those facts.

Attached you'll find the signed birth certificate form, listing you as the father. Don't be an even worse jerk. Sign it to confirm the paternity. And please, please raise this little girl to do and be better than I was and did. I drank, screwed, lied, stole, scammed, schemed, and wasted my life away. I didn't appreciate family, except for my mother, and I didn't actually learn how to love. It would be a tragedy for me to raise any human being. I barely know how to raise a dog.

I, Laurinda Marie Askins, grant full and uncontested custody of Baby Girl Askins to you, Dr. Makkai Worthy, her birth father.

I don't know where I'll end up and if I'll ever even get it together before I die. My only prayer, aside from seeing my mother again in heaven, is that this baby girl is healthy and happy. And for some reason, I believe that you can do that for a baby, even though I don't believe you'll ever be able to do a damn thing for any woman. But, aside from that, aside from what I think I would have liked to have seen from you other than screwing me regularly, I pray that you end up happy and that you settle down one day. I hope our paths don't cross again, but then again, you never know. You just never know.

And by the way, I pawned everything you ever bought me, just like I did with every fool ass, rich trick I scammed.

> *Goodbye,*
> *Laurinda Askins*
> *aka "Monday Asskins"*

I looked up as I folded the paper in half. I had an enormous lump in my throat. Standing next to Mary Jane and a security guard, was my mother, coat and purse in hand.

"Are you okay, Makkai?"

I stood as though my feet were bolted to the floor. "No, Mom, I'm not."

My mother walked over to me, and I reached down to hug her tightly.

"Everything will be just fine."

"If you say so." My eyes felt sweaty.

"Don't give me that, son. You'd better know so."

"You're right."

We broke from our embrace.

"What did the doctor say?"

"From what I know so far, she's just underweight."

"Thank God. Son, I'm here for you. I need you to know that."

"Thanks."

"Can I see her?"

"I've got to talk to the doctor first. Mom, Monday left her. I need to find out what to do next."

"I'll be sitting right here in the waiting room until you're ready to go."

"It might be a while."

"Have you been home?"

"No."

"Then you're coming home with me. I'll be sitting right over here."

"Mom, at least wait in my office."

"No. I want to sit out here so I can see what's going on. You go. I'll be fine."

Mom was always there. In all ways.

Chapter 46

"Hey. How are you?" I asked the man who had long been my stepfather as I walked inside Mom's house that evening.

"I'm fine. Congratulations." He stood with young-looking jeans and a Dunlap tee-shirt. His beer belly did lap over his belt, and he needed to let what little bit of receding hair he had left, go. Just let it go.

"Thanks," I said.

He leaned against the sink. "Your mom tells me she's a cutie. She was happy to get to see her."

I sat at the kitchen table. "Yes, we worked it out so she could take a peek. She is a pretty baby."

He pointed to the refrigerator. "Can I get you something? Water maybe."

"How about a beer?" I suggested with hope that they had one.

"Make it two," my mom told him as she walked in the room, already into her house shoes and robe.

"You've got it."

"Come into the living room, son," my mom told me. "Let's talk before I start dinner."

He came in from the kitchen behind us and placed the cold cans on the coffee table, as Mom and I sat on the sofa. He then went on into the garage as usual.

"So Monday was doing what?" Mom asked, crossing her legs and arms.

"What wasn't she doing? She'd served time for stealing, in particular while she was pregnant, she had been homeless for who knows how long, she had charges against her for swindling money from a couple of elderly men, and she'd been in and out of rehab for who knows how long. The day she went into labor she'd been drinking."

"Oh, my God. That sounds like something from out of a movie."

"And, Mom, the worst part, which I still don't believe, is that her mother dated Dad."

Mom's jaw dropped. "What was her mom's name?"

"Laurie Askins."

"That's one I don't remember. Wait a minute, you said she dated your father. Please don't tell me she got pregnant, Makkai."

"She did."

"Oh, Lord. I just know this woman is not that woman's daughter? This woman is your sister?"

"This baby is my niece." I sat back, taking a cold sip from the can.

She put her hands to her mouth. "Makkai, oh, my God, I can't believe you and her, I mean, you didn't know, but, how'd you find out?"

"I saw her picture at Dad's house when I went to the reunion."

"Oh, good God. You just never know. But, Makkai, can't that cause medical problems, when the parents are related? I saw a show on TV about that."

"It could have, but so far, I don't think it did. We've gotta keep an eye on her, though. We just needed to make sure she wasn't born an addict. And she wasn't."

"Oh, Lord, thank you for that. And she hasn't tried to call you after she left?"

"Not yet."

"That's so cruel. What kind of woman would leave her own newborn baby?"

"A troubled one."

"You know how people are going to be. People can be so nosey, sitting around wondering about this sweet baby's mother. They'll surely call, asking a bunch of questions."

"Like what?"

"Like how you and Monday met, and are you two getting married, where Monday's from, and things like that. That's the first thing we're going to get asked."

"Mom, don't be paranoid. If you're thinking that people will find out, I'm not even tripping off of that. I just want this baby to stay healthy. Nothing else matters."

"I definitely agree. I mean, that goes without saying. But, come to think of it, this is not something that anyone has to know anyway. As far as I'm concerned, it's actually none of their business."

"I really don't care who knows."

She sipped her brew, too, and said, "What I mean is, what about the mother's name on the birth announcements? You are sending birth announcements, right?"

"I can't even think about that right now."

"Oh wow, I am still in shock. So, you're not worried that that crazy woman could show up at any time and run her mouth and try to take that baby away, or even try to get money from you."

"First of all, I have her letter. And besides, with all of the crap this family has been through and all of the scandal Dad has brought with his running around, I'm not sure that anything could embarrass me. This is just an extension of his womanizing ways. Besides, Monday doesn't even know we're related. But, please tell me something, Mom. And this is something I've always wanted to know. Did you know that Dad used to have women in the car and ask me to not say anything?"

She answered immediately. "I knew that."

"I hated him for that."

"Surely you did. Anyone would. Anyway, is Georgia still acting up? I ignored her calls forever."

I wanted to say that the *D* drove her ass crazy. "Mom, Georgia lives with a woman now, and her ex-husband gained custody of those kids."

Mom's eyes bugged. "What? She was gay?"

"She was confused."

"Well, the way she showed up at your door, she had me worried. Maybe it is best that she doesn't have those sweet girls around her with all of her drama. A judge doesn't do that just on a whim. Not to the woman anyway."

"That's what I was thinking." We sat still, looking at a volumeless TV screen.

"Makkai, between Georgia, Monday and that woman named Serena or Sabina, you've been running into some strange folks if you ask me."

"It's Salina. And yes, I have."

"I'd say there's something wrong with your woman picker, if you ask me. I don't think you're using the right head, if you know what I mean."

"I hear you. That's part of my problem."

"And, I'll tell you something else, these women need to close their legs and watch who they sleep with. They're supposed to save that stuff for the wedding night. Sex is a celebration of a union. It's not even about the sex. It's about making love to that person. It's supposed to be shared by two people who have vowed to be together until death do you part."

The vision of Mom and Al consummating their union in that way was impossible to imagine. Can't ever think of a mom on her back doing the love celebration move. I shook the thought out of my head while rubbing my temple. "I agree. It's easy to get caught up, though."

"I've never been. Those women who slept with your dad knowing he was married got caught up. I love being with one person," she admitted.

"I see that." I glanced at the pictures of her and Al on the living room wall, surrounding pictures of Fonda and me when we were young.

"Makkai, my husband is a good man."

I spoke low. "Mom, I just want him to take better care of you."

She looked to see if he was within earshot. "How do you know he's not?"

"He's always in that dang garage."

"He has a hobby that he loves. What's wrong with that? It's like therapy for him. Just like when I'm in my garden, or when I'm sewing. I let him be who he is and he let's me be who I am, too."

"I've seen you walk around here in physical pain, and it worries me."

"It's worse for you because you're a doctor. Everything worries you. If I break a fingernail you're ready to send me to the emergency room."

"I'm not that bad. But, are you still having pain under your arm?"

She lifted her arm with ease. "No, that was only for a couple of days after I slipped in the shower and banged my side up against the shower faucets."

"And the headaches?"

"That was after I drank some red wine. You know me when it comes to red wine."

"Then why do you drink it?"

"Stubborn, I guess. Makkai, one day I want you and Al to take the time to really get to know each other. Enough years have gone by with you two being misunderstood."

"What do you mean? How does he misunderstand me?" I sipped again.

"He's a little intimidated by that fact that you give me money. It makes him feel like less of a man. It's like he feels as though he can't take care of his family. He has no kids, no brothers and sisters. I'm all he's got. And other than him, you're all I've got. I love you both so much. I have two good men in my life. Give me credit for having enough sense to be with someone who's a good person."

"You're right. And I didn't know the money thing got to him. He should have told me."

"He wanted me to tell you. And I finally understood, so I felt I'd do it now."

"So, you don't need the money?" I asked, almost giving her eyes of understanding if she did.

"One day I might, but for now, we're doing fine. We don't need much."

I nodded affirmatively. "Well, at least promise me you'll retire soon."

"I will. How's next year?"

"Promise?"

"Promise."

"Okay." I turned around and yelled toward the garage. "Hey, Al, what do you say you come on in here and have a beer with us? Tell me all about that shiny new cherry red Impala you went out of town to buy."

He yelled right back. "Sure, son. I'll be right there."

I turned back toward Mom. My eyebrows rose. "Did he just call me son?"

"I think we heard the same thing."

"Well, I'll be."

"By the way, he always comes home at night." She looked content.

"Right on, Mom. You do deserve that. Every woman deserves that."

Chapter 47

*F*irst message, received today at 11:46 p.m. "Dr. Worthy. You need to come back to the hospital right away. Dr. Taylor needs to talk to you. Just come on back as soon as you can. It's very important."

Well, how in the hell is somebody going to expect you to drive a vehicle responsibly with a message like that? Short of hiring a helicopter to airlift me, I couldn't get back to the hospital quick enough. Luckily the hospital was a lot closer to Mom's house than mine, but pardon me, Lord, for driving like a madman. Perhaps the word madman fits right about now.

"What is it?" I closed the office door behind me.

"Sit down." Dr. Taylor was seated.

"Dr. Taylor, just tell me. Don't treat me like I'm walking into patient services for the first time. What?" I slowly poured myself into a seating position. Her office was large, cold, and drab, and the upholstered chair was un-fucking-comfortable.

She leaned forward. "Dr. Worthy, now, you know that Dr. Lambert has run quite a few tests on little Baby Askins over the past few days. And I understand that her mother has left."

"Yes."

"Well, then I'll tell you. Even though we haven't determined what to do about custody, we need to make some serious decisions. And I feel comfort in the fact that we do know you're the father. The DNA test came back 99.99 percent."

"Thank God."

"That's the good news."

"Dr. Taylor, don't do this."

"Because of the baby's extremely low birth weight, being born at what we think was just twenty-eight weeks gestation, she's susceptible to complications in neonatal and beyond. Being that she's an ELBW infant, we've tested for any neurological conditions like mental retardation, and even deafness or any infections or vision problems."

"Dr. Taylor, please."

"Dr. Worthy, your baby girl suffers from a clinically significant PDA dysfunction, as you know, patent ductus arteriosus. The conduit between the pulmonary artery and the aorta needs to be closed. The ducts are not constricting. She has a left to right shunt that is causing a loud systolic murmur."

I sat up straight. My full stomach growled. "Hold up. So you're saying that a determination has been made that surgical ligation is absolutely necessary? Are you absolutely, one hundred percent sure?"

"Yes."

"How do you know for sure? I haven't even been in on any of the discussions. We can possibly try administering indomethacin and then see if it matures and closes on its own."

"Dr. Worthy, it's too late for indomethacin. More than twenty-four hours have passed. It is critical, and will only get worse. She needs an operation right away."

"Why is it that it took so long to diagnose this?"

"We've given it three days to see if it would close off automatically, and it hasn't. It's a grade 2/6."

"I thought you were testing for problems from her mother's alcohol intake."

She tapped her pen to the desktop. "We have not detected any long-term or short-term effects from the traces of alcohol that were in the baby's system. We've treated and passed that hurdle. However, her ELBW is more of a factor than anything. It's even more of a factor than the fact that this woman might be your sister."

I crossed my arms and sat back. "Dr. Lambert told you?"

"He had to. That is a crucial bit of information. But, at this point, that is moot. We need your permission to operate."

I sat forward again. "Dr. Taylor. I know I cannot ask you to let me do this surgery. But, please let me be a part of it in some way. Please. I've performed a ton of atrial septal defect surgeries before."

"I wouldn't even consider that for one moment, Doctor. It is forbidden from a medical policy standpoint, you know that. Way too many emotions involved. And besides, this is all about the health and welfare of this baby, and nothing else."

"I just don't want anyone else to . . . I need to know who the choices are." I stood up, walking toward the ninth floor window. Wanting to burst right through it.

"Right now, unless we go outside of the hospital, we have one extremely good pediatric cardiothoracic surgeon on staff. I interviewed him a few months ago before we hired him. I'm thinking of Dr. Thomas Purify."

I turned to look back at her. "Yes, go on."

"He's been a great cardiac pediatric surgeon for fifteen years. As you remember, he was in charge of the pediatric emergency unit set up after 9/11 when he was head of pediatrics at St. Joseph's for ten years after working at Columbia Presbyterian for five. He graduated from . . ."

"I know, Johns Hopkins in Maryland."

"Doctor, he is top notch. He has received cardiac quality awards for excellence his entire career."

"But, can't we just wait and see if . . ."

"The goal is to save her life. If left untreated . . ."

"The pressure in the pulmonary arteries might be so high that it'll induce changes on its own."

"And at that point, congestive heart failure will develop."

"But, I've seen and heard of cases where it corrects itself in a few months."

She stood up and came around to back up against the front of her desk. Her arms were folded at her waist. "Ninety percent of the cases close. Unfortunately, she's among the ten percent that won't. Makkai, she needs surgical closure. Time is not on our side. Now, I know I'm singing to the choir here, but we don't want pulmonary edema to develop in the meantime. You need to turn this over to Dr. Purify."

"Can I see the EKG?"

"You can. But, with all due respect, as you are aware, pediatric cardiology is a little bit different. And at this point, I have to treat you like the father of a patient with a congenital abnormality, because you are. Now, I know this is tough on you, but we need to get things going."

I paced to the other side of the room. "Damn, this affects one in two hundred preemie babies, and my baby is the one."

"It is the way it is. Now, let's deal with it."

The thoughts in my brain did not match the emotions from my heart, but I had to make a choice. "Have Dr. Purify handle the procedure right away."

She walked back behind her desk and started writing as she sat down. "I will set it up right now." She glanced my way as I headed toward the door. "And, Dr. Worthy, you made the right decision. Please try and think positively."

"Right now, I can't think anything." I walked out as I closed her office door.

I leaned against the wall just down the hall, looking up at the ceiling.

God, I don't think you heard me before. This is not what I was talking to you about. I can't imagine that your will would allow for my daughter to go through this. Through you, all things are possible, right? Well, please make it possible for my daughter to pull through this. If it's not your will, I will die right along with her. Please don't punish her. I know you don't punish. You've chosen this experience for me, but why her? I never knew I could care about something so deeply in my life. Please heal my child. In Your name, Amen.

I took my phone from my pocket as I walked. "Mom, they're about to operate on her. It's her heart."

"Son, we're on our way over."

Mom and Al and Mary Jane and I huddled in the small, blue and white pediatric waiting room with another family. We barely said more than hello to them, and to each other. The television watched all of us. Some old episode of "*Mayberry RFD.*" Mary Jane, no longer on duty, still wearing her uniform, sat next to me in the adjoining vinyl seat, holding my hand, with her head on my shoulder. My concern about fraternizing seemed minute. Mom paced back and forth, having never taken off her heavy black sweater, arms crossed and head tied in a brown scarf. She clutched her small black Bible to her chest. Al sat across from us reading an old issue of *Hot Rod* magazine. I couldn't get my mind off the fact that my baby girl was hooked up to a heart–lung machine, just as I had used on so many patients before. It broke my heart.

"Dr. Purify?" I said as a question, standing up promptly as the silver haired doctor walked into the waiting room.

Looking unshaven, he had his surgical mask pulled down past his chin. He still had on his surgical shoes. "Dr. Worthy. Is this your family?"

"Yes. How is she?" Small talk was intolerable to me.

"She's tiny, and she's going to need some time in here still to gain some weight on her little body, but, we tied off the ductus and it was a huge success."

I closed my eyes, and then spoke as I opened them. "Thank you, God." I felt Mary Jane hug me around my waist.

Mom placed her hands in a prayer position as she smiled out loud. "Hello, Dr. Purify. I'm the grandma. How complex was it, I mean the procedure?"

"Hello. We made a tiny incision between her ribs and left side. You might need to watch for signs of infection and bleeding, or even fluid around her lungs can be common. Most go home in a few days, but like I said, she still needs to receive intravenous nourishment beyond the standard time frame."

I put my hand on his shoulder. "Dr. Purify, I had no idea that when you were hired, I'd be standing on this side of your skills. I thank you with all my heart. I owe you big-time." I shook his hand with fatherly appreciation.

He squeezed my hand tightly. "No problem. I have a daughter of my own. I'm sure you can see her in a few hours. She'll be in recovery, closely monitored until later. I need to head off, but congratulations."

"Thanks again, Dr. Purify."

"My pleasure."

"God really does work miracles," commented Al.

Dr. Purify spoke as he headed back toward the double doors. "Yes, He does indeed."

"Amen," said Mom and Mary Jane together.

Chapter 48

Finally, after six weeks of my baby girl living in a hospital, and after going through a complicated surgery and being pricked, poked, prodded, and cut, she was strong enough to get the green light to be released . . . to me, her father.

We had an order set by the court to award sole custody to me. And during that six-week period, each and every night, the one person who spent more time with my new daughter than I did, was Mary Jane. She was also the one person I spent more time with. So much, that she had begun moving more and more things in each time she came back over to my house. Her tender and unconditional love of children exposed a whole new side of her. Suddenly, I couldn't get enough of her.

"Baby, slow down," she begged while panting as I lay upon her in my four-poster bed. Soft sounds of "*Overjoyed*" by Stevie Wonder escorted our movements.

"What?"

Sweat covered her face. "You're going so fast, you're making me out of breath trying to keep up."

I wiped my own forehead. "Aren't you enjoying it?"

"I am, Makkai, but wait."

I downshifted. "Okay, how do you like it?"

"Slower, baby. Just slow down. I'm not going anywhere."

And slow down I did. I kissed Mary Jane just as slowly as I grinded, as we slaked our thirst together, making sure to hold her tight as she softly moaned in pleasure. We clasped hands as we moved in syncopated rhythm.

"Is that better?" I explored her, just about pulling all the way out and then carefully inserting in a circular motion from left to right, and then reversing, making sure to hit a steady pace from side-to-side, and then up toward the back just where she liked it.

"Yes, Makkai. You know how to hit the same spot over and over again. That's what makes me cum."

"I know that. You've gotten used to cuming, huh?"

"Yes, baby. And then you always do, too, right?" she asked with throaty sounding words.

"Right." As I replied, I felt her walls tighten, gripping me with a deep rush of suction while she throbbed.

"Like now. I'm about to release all over your dick, Makkai."

"And I'm about to . . . release all over. Mary Jane, I can't believe how this feels when I'm . . . dammit."

I tried to hold it, but for some reason, this time, I couldn't stop the flow from coming. I had actually lost control, and the force of my buildup was propelled from me in an instant.

I remained on top of her and inside of her while we hugged. She spoke softly. "Makkai, now, I'm not one to gossip, see, so you didn't hear this from me, but word around the hospital is that Dr. Lois Taylor is really Dr. Louis Taylor." She'd shifted gears for sure.

"Oh, please." I leaned up to look her in the face.

"Really. A few folks have commented the she is a he."

I held in a laugh and my insertion began to exit her. "I don't believe that. I'm not mad at her, or him, because she pulled through for me when it counted."

"I agree, but I must say, I did notice her massive hands and her feet. Plus she's bald. And her voice is so deep. That could explain why she looks like an NFL quarterback."

I held in another laugh. My member darted out of her opening. "I hadn't noticed."

She giggled. "So, you didn't ever get that close, did you?"

"Of course not."

"Maybe this baby saved you just in the nick of time. Hey, we never even celebrated your birthday six weeks ago."

"It's cool. We've been busy celebrating a new birth."

The touch of Mary Jane was comforting; the flickering of the fireplace was mesmerizing. The feelings sent me into a relaxed frame of mind, more relaxing than normal.

"Makkai, I need to tell you something."

"What?" I gave her my eyes in the semi-darkness.

"About Carlos."

"About Palm Springs?"

"Well, sort of . . ."

I broke my stare. "I don't want to know."

"Makkai . . ."

"Mary Jane, I don't want to know."

"I think you need . . ."

I interrupted again. "Please, I'm fine not knowing. I promise you. I know Carlos, but I also know you. I'm fine with whatever decisions you make."

"But, Makkai . . ."

"Mary Jane. Don't."

"Okay." She looked away, willing to retreat, yet as though her mind was racing.

"Just relax from this day forward. All that matters is this day forward."

"Okay. But, just hold me again, please," she requested.

"I've got you," I stated with certainty while I still lay on her chest.

That woman had definitely earned the key to my house, and probably to my open heart. If she'd started to release a confession, mine would have taken three weeks to release. And being that I all but pushed her into Carlos's arms, what could I say anyway? No matter what it was, it didn't matter. Not now. We slept together that afternoon, arm in arm, and my baby girl slept in the next room, baby monitor all set up and ready to go.

Over hearts, I have painfully turned every stone. Just to find, I had found what I've searched to discover. Life was getting sweeter.

Chapter 49

Early the next morning, I was actually sent to the grocery store, assigned to pick up diapers and formula. I strolled down the aisle with my cordless earpiece flashing. For once, my phone was quiet. No one called.

I scanned the dozens of sizes and types of disposable diapers and snatched up six packages of preemie Huggies and some natural, nonscented baby wipes and headed to the formula section.

I checked the list Mary Jane gave me just to make sure I had it right, and grabbed twenty-four large cans of Similac NeoSure Advance powder. I also picked up Mary Jane's favorite Lipton iced tea, and some bottled water.

"Did you find everything you were looking for?" the cheery, fifty-something-looking grocery checker asked.

"That and more, thanks."

She examined my items. "A new baby, huh?"

"Yes. A baby girl."

"Congratulations. There's nothing in the world like the birth of a child."

"That much I know."

"It'll make you switch up your priorities, that's for sure."

I handed her the cash and the bag boy handed me my bags. "If you understand the blessing, it definitely will."

She gave me my change. "Well, enjoy that little one."

"Forever."

"Just wait until you're a grandparent, like me." She pointed to herself.

"Hey now. First things first."

She laughed. "Have a great day."

"You too." I looked back as I stepped away. "And you couldn't possibly be a grandma."

"Six times over."

"Now that sounds like a true blessing."

Next thing I knew I was heading out for my first full day back at work, which meant I had to leave the baby. I couldn't wait to get to work and get the day over with.

I headed to the hospital, speeding down the highway, pushing the posted speed limit in my red sports car that I never get a chance to drive, keeping an eye out for the Highway Patrol in my rearview every few minutes. I was going to need to get that new rust Hummer H3 I'd had my eye on, or maybe I'll stay loyal to the Porsche line and get me that sweet new Cayenne SUV.

Once I arrived, the day ahead of me consisted of two post-op follow-ups and a minor, noninvasive procedure. I had a quick moment to sit at my desk just before a physician's meeting to discuss advancements in cardiac catheterization. My eyes scanned the many greeting cards lined up on my desk from coworkers, wishing me congratulations on the birth of my daughter. I felt a warmth from head to toe. I took a second to check my cell phone messages.

"Hi, baby, it's Mary Jane. Some woman called who did not leave her name and she did not sound very happy that I answered." Lord only knows who that was. "Carlos called. Your mom called at around noon. And then your dad called shortly thereafter. He seemed surprised that I answered your phone, but he was really nice. So, give them a call when you get time. See you later, baby." Mary Jane's voice was calming.

I spoke to my cell phone. "Call Carlos."

His casualness and boldness had returned. "Talk to me."

"Yo, man, I'm just getting back to you."

"Hey, how's everything going?"

"Cool. Very cool."

"I'll bet. I see Mary Jane is answering the home phone now."

"Yeah." I leaned back and began shuffling through diagnosis reports.

"So, it's like that?"

"It's like that."

"Good for you. Looks like we both got caught?" Carlos joked.

I joked. "You too? Who is it? Some stripper?"

"No man. She's cool, though."

"Well then who is it? Must be that superwoman with stamina named Alice. Was it?"

He seemed to hold his breath. "It's Salina, dude."

My voice dropped. "Carlos."

"No, I'm telling you, she's different, man. She had to do some hours for the false charges and she kept calling me collect every night. I guess all that time on the phone did something. I think she's changed, Makkai. I mean it."

"She is crazy, deranged, and married, Carlos. She's got a real psychological problem, man. You be careful. And, to top it off, she still has a gigantic, violent husband."

"Salina has filed for divorce. And she's now on regular medication that should help things level off. I believe she's a good woman underneath all of those layers, man. She's been through a lot. But, we're hanging. She's even going to work as a salesperson at BCBG to make some extra money. The courts won't accept her for a job now that she has a misdemeanor and now that her medical record is part of that conviction. But yeah, were talking about living together or something like that, but I'm just happy to not be running the streets anymore."

"Carlos, man, she's whipped your ass, that's what happened."

"Not me."

"Yeah right."

"Well, hell, the girl can get down, now."

"That mad wild psycho sex got you hooked. I just never thought you'd really fall for her. Not after everything that happened."

"I can't explain it, man, but I wanted you to know."

He paused.

I paused.

He paused.

I said, "You know what. I hope it works out just the way you want it to."

"Me too."

"And once you toss that black book, it should be on."

"She tossed it for me."

"I should have known. She's gonna keep a tight ass leash on you, my brotha. So what else is up?"

"Not much. Just about to head home."

"Cool. Okay well, yeah."

"Maybe I'll get to see that baby one day, huh?"

"Maybe. Man, I can't lie. I can't say that I want Salina near her or near Mary Jane."

"You've gotta know she's changed, Makkai. People do change you know?"

"I'll talk to you about that later, man."

"Okay. Later."

That one deserved a major exhale and a silent prayer.

People change huh? Maybe so, but in this case, sex is powerful and my boy, the hound, is addicted. And I, of all people, should know about the bonding power of sex.

I glanced up at the wall clock, noting that I still had about fifteen minutes. I picked up my office phone. My thoughts ranged from being hooked on sex and how the thrill of an orgasm can make us stupid, to why it's so difficult to be truly monogamous, and why it was that my mother put up with infidelity for so long.

"Hello."

"Hey, Mom."

"Hey there. Let me turn this movie off. It's *On Golden Pond*." Sounded like she dropped the phone and then picked it up just after the volume of the television decreased. "Sorry about that. That Henry Fonda was good until his last days. Hey, how's that little one? I can't wait to see her next week. Mary Jane said she's drinking almost more than a few ounces in one feeding already."

"Yes, she is."

"That's good for a preemie."

It was as if I didn't hear a word she said. "Mom, were you over Dad?"

"Oh, Makkai, too over him, long overdue, over him. Why do you ask that?"

"Just wondering what was the real reason why we left so suddenly and came to L.A.? Was it the woman who called you on the phone that day?"

After I asked the question, I reminded myself that after what my mother had gone through, I didn't want Mary Jane to ever have to deal with any woman calling my house again. I was going to have to change all of my numbers.

"Wow, what brought that up?"

"Mom, please."

"Well, I guess I knew you'd ask me that one day. Aside from having to get away from that serial cheater of a man who called himself your father, and the father of half of the population in the South, I knew a couple of things."

"Like what?"

"I knew he took you to *her* house that night. And I knew why. It was written all over his face, and yours, when you came home. It's just something a mother knows."

I turned my chair so that my back would be to the door. My heart sped up. "Mom."

"Makkai, my life changed that night. It was one of many straws that broke the camel's back. Your dad talked about you possibly being gay and was bound and determined to 'turn' you straight. I called that woman's house that night and pretended I was his Aunt Ethel. She told me that Roosevelt was on his way over with his son, and I knew. You know, sometimes, you just know. If you'd come back in a few hours, I could have thought that the two of you simply stopped by. But, all night long? And I'll never forget the guilty look on your face as you got out of his car. I sat in my rocking chair in the front window and damn near cried myself to death. It was pitiful. It was a look of shame and excitement on your face all in one. It was as if you'd both fooled around on me. Roosevelt even smelled of her. He usually did. And he had the nerve to climb on top of me as soon as he hit the bed. I nearly threw up. The only thing that kept me from literally snapping was knowing we were leaving."

Instantly, my right hand soothed my warm forehead. "Mom, I'm sorry."

"It wasn't your fault, Makkai. It really, truly wasn't your fault. And she was the one who called my house not long before we left. She told me her first and last name and all I did was look her up in the phone book and call her back."

"I had no idea."

"Well, Makkai. You know what? I'm just going to get it all out today. It's long overdue. Remember when Fonda found out she was pregnant at only thirteen years old?"

"Yes."

"I had no idea that would have caused her to die or else I would have pulled hell and high water to get her an abortion. Instead, two lives perished. Especially knowing in my heart, in my gut, and in my soul that the baby your sister carried could have been your father's."

I tried to speak right after hearing her hellified words, but even though my mouth was open, my voice wouldn't obey my mental commands. I cleared my throat twice and gulped my saliva, clearing my throat again. "Mom, you've got to be kidding me. That cannot be."

"And why couldn't it be, Makkai? Your father climbed on top of anything with a hole, whether it moved or not, and I'm not so sure that men and animals were excluded." She sighed. "I asked your sister and she just started crying. I told her I knew, and she just cried some more. That's why I left, not just because of anything with other women, even though that was unforgivable and bad enough. Maybe I'd just resolved myself to that. And I guess I didn't even really leave because of the threesome he involved you in. I left because I had to take you two away from a pedophile. I knew my husband was sleeping with my precious daughter. The confrontation happened just before I left and moved us to California. It's just something a mother knows."

Chapter 50

"**W**here's Fonda?" He asked about no one else but Fonda.
He'd been out, just getting in of course. He'd stopped in the restroom and then to the door of your room. He approached me as I stood firmly in front of the doorway to my bedroom. I reeked of intolerability. He smelled of brandy.

I was packing a butcher knife. I gripped it, flashed it so he could see it, and stood just far away enough so that I could insert it deeply if need be. Only one word could have led the way. "Why?"

He pointed to your room where you slept. "Makkai is in there. But, where's Fonda?"

"She's in what used to be our bed. She's sleeping with me tonight."

He peeked over my shoulder, but the door was closed shut. "What in the hell is she doing in there?"

"She's there so that I can keep an eye on her."

He had the nerve to demand, like he had the upper hand, "Get her out of there so I can sleep."

"Get her out of there so you can do what?"

"I need to get to sleep, woman. I'm tired."

"Why don't you sleep in the garage on that mattress?"

Anger was engraved on his face. "I'll be damn if I sleep in the garage at my own house."

I did not blink. "You fuck on it. Why not spend the night on it?"

"Woman, I'm telling you. Get that child out of that bed so I can go to sleep. Now."

"No."

"Corrine." His eyes darted down at what my hand was choking.

"If you so much as raise your voice, not to mention your hand to me, as God is my witness, I will cut your throat so deep you won't be able to say another word in life."

"Have you lost your mind?" His glare was menacing.

"I swear fo' God, I will lose my mind if I don't get me and these kids away from you. Now since you're looking at me like you're gonna do something, it's your choice . . . your popular dick or your tired-ass throat. Because I know one thing, if I get hurt tonight, I'd rather you kill me, but everyone will know I tried to kill you first. That's the only way I'm leaving this earth, is if I know I don't leave them to you."

He leaned his upper body in the direction of the bedroom door. All I wanted him to do was take one single solitary step. I wished he would. I raised the wide blade of the knife even higher, bracing my stance just in case he tried to grab it.

"Corrine."

"Don't take a step toward that bedroom. I will cut you and then call the police. Now I don't have proof, yet, that that baby inside of that child's belly is yours, but once that baby is born, I will find out. And if it is, you will die in jail. So you enjoy your pathetic life for the next four months. And as of tonight, you are either sleeping in that garage, or at one of your hoe's houses, but you will never spend another night under the same roof with these kids again. Do I make myself clear, Roosevelt? Now get the hell out of this house."

His frown lines deepened. "You have lost your mind. I've never laid a hand on that girl. I would never . . ."

"I'm counting to five. 1, 2, 3, 4 . . ."

"Your father wasn't as dumb as he looked. He reluctantly but quickly walked straight out of the back door. I bolted and chained the door, propped and secured a chair up against the knob and packed up what I hadn't packed over the previous six days. And then I sat back and sipped straight from a bottle of vodka. It was a tall, friendly bottle of Grey Goose. It was all I could do to not become an alcoholic. Thank God his car was gone the next morning."

After Mom told her story, my shoulders dropped and I felt like my body was on pause. My mouth would not snap out of its paralyzed state. My blood pressure was surely off the charts. My words suddenly slipped out. "Mom, I'm so sorry. That stupid asshole is really sick."

"That's an understatement."

I breathed out through my nose with a burst of forcible air. "Sorry to curse, Mom, but I can't believe that I didn't know sooner that this punk of a man did this crap. You let me travel to see him all those times without knowing that he raped my baby sister. If I had known, I would have literally killed him."

"That's why, Makkai. I knew you would do something that would end up ruining your life. I had years of spiritual counseling later on to deal with my anger and guilt, and I prayed to God every single day, but really decided to leave it a family secret. It was a hard decision to make, but I had to let it go. So many times I've wanted to kill him, but it's as though something inside of me told me not to. He'll get his. I think it's a generational curse from his twisted side of the family. But, being that my one and only daughter has been dead for so many years, and all of this has happened with Monday being your sister, I think it needed to be said. You be careful around him with your daughter, Makkai. And around your woman."

"That man is so damn pathetic! He's a sick pervert! Mom, I have to go. I'll just keep disrespecting you with the words that are popping into my head faster than I can think. That man actually would have fathered his own granddaughter." A long, slow-motioned pause dribbled by on each end. "But, Mom, if you really think about it, how much better am I with a daughter who's my very own niece?"

"Oh, now please, don't you go doing that to yourself. You didn't know who that woman was. Son, you are a father, in every way, not just biologically. You are a father who has decided to show up and answer the call. And nowadays, many men don't do that. But, you are so unlike your dad that it's not even close. It's not what they call you that matters, Makkai, it's what you answer to. Your worth is not determined by one act. And you're definitely not a rolling stone like he is and always has been."

"I wouldn't give myself that much credit." I stood and shot my sights out of the window, capturing a view of the twin building next door. I just stared.

"You didn't know you two were related, first of all. And secondly, you didn't fool around on women who you were committed to. You never have. You weren't married, out there running around like a chicken with its head cut off. And this is your first and only child. You can't compare him to you, son."

"Mom, but I've always had at least four women at a time, ever since I was in high school, and I just barely escaped a false rap for rape."

"Makkai, now I do believe you must be responsible for your actions. But, somehow, you haven't repeated that, not from where I sit anyway. Years ago, you immediately became the man of our house and you have always been a great son. You put your sister and me first in every way."

"I saw what his ways did to you, and there was nothing I could do about it."

"Then do something now. Do what you can to raise this baby with Mary Jane. Please. Enjoy that precious little grandbaby of mine, and keep your family together. And, son, think about really settling down one day and marrying that girl. I told you before that you need stability. Today is the day you can break the pattern and begin a lifestyle for your children to emulate. God has blessed you with that opportunity. The opportunity to have peace of mind. Don't waste it, Makkai."

"I've really got to go now. I'll call you later. And thanks."

"Thank you, for being a constant in my life, Makkai Jerome Worthy."

"And you as well. I love you, Mom."

"I love you back."

*   *   *

A soft knock met my door.

"Dr. Worthy."

My back faced the door as I spoke. "Come in."

A young nurse opened the door and peeked inside. "You know your patient whom you referred to Dr. Lois Taylor? The patient with advanced metastatic lung cancer."

"Mrs. Reynolds?" I replied, slowly turning to face her.

"Yes. Dr. Worthy, are you okay?"

"Yes. What's up?"

She held a file in her hand. "Mrs. Reynolds passed away today. We need you to sign off on the original referral form."

I simply exhaled and stood.

"I'm sorry, Doctor."

I could only blink.

She approached me. "It's right here. Just sign anywhere on page four." She was silent as I flipped to the authorization page and scribbled my name. "Are you sure you're okay? Did you know her?"

"No. It's just that . . . it's just that . . . thank you, Carol."

She walked out and gingerly shut the door behind her.

It's just that . . . I promised her she'd be okay. I wanted her to be okay. Who am I to tell anyone they'll be okay? For every new life that comes into this world, another life exits. And besides, death is a part of this whole doctor thing. You cannot get attached. And so, I have to change my thoughts to something else.

But, her words, "You promise?" were all I could think of . . . think of, as my eyes welled up with tears.

I am not a machine. I am a man. A man with feelings.

Chapter 51

"**D**ad, what's up? Mary Jane said you called."
I returned to my desk toward the end of a long and grueling day. I was mentally absent from two meetings, and I assigned a last minute annuloplasty surgery to another doctor. I took a seat, clenched my office phone with one hand, and had a firm squeeze on an antique handgrip exerciser that my mother had given me when I first started medical school.

"Hey, son. I found your home number and gave you a call. That sweet little lady of yours put the phone to the ear of that precious little one. I still can't believe you're a father. You've got a lot of catching up to do."

My tight stomach flopped and twisted and turned. "Dad, I'll pass on that achievement. What did you want?" My jaw was clenched.

"What did I want? There you go again. What's wrong with you, boy? You were like this when you left the house in such a rush when you were here. Are you still mad because I didn't call to thank you for sending me that check a while back? Whatever it is, is that any way to greet your father?"

Hearing him speak the word father made my heartbeat accelerate. The fury from my anxious-to-be-spoken words burst from my lips. "It's the perfect way to greet Roosevelt Worthy, the lowest, most pathetic, motherfucking father on this earth." I clutched the grip even tighter.

"What in the hell are you talking about?"

"First of all, I will no longer call you Dad. I will no longer call you anything. You need some serious help and you always have."

"Boy, what is your problem, disrespecting me like that. I am your father. Don't tell me you haven't gotten over that night back years ago when we got with Erskalene. I thought we already talked about that crap back when you were here."

Instantaneously, I propelled to my feet and began pacing, still squeezing the grip, imagining it being my so-called dad's throat. I focused on my breathing pattern, which was far too irregular for me to get a hold of. "You son of a bitch, and I mean no disrespect to your mother, but what in the hell happened when your parents were raising you that would make you sleep with your own daughter? And I just know you did this more than once."

"What are you talking about? That's ridiculous."

"Oh, please. Your head is so twisted that you run around screwing everything that moves, including your own children? I promise you it'll be a cold day in hell before you ever come around my daughter. I'll tell you now, if you even so much as think about dialing my number or coming around my family, I will have you fucking killed. Now, I hope you got that. Yeah, and I just threatened your pedophile ass. You need to do time for incest and statutory rape."

"Makkai, I see. I know it was your mother who must have put some stuff in your head. She's always resented the fact that you and I have been in touch through the years. She's just trying to turn you against me."

"And you know what? How dare you even have the nerve to try and call my mother a liar? She let you off the hook for far too long. My own sister died while giving birth to your baby girl, that she named Rosie, after your tired behind. We ended up losing them both, and you never ever said a word about either one."

"I was at the funeral, even though everyone there treated me like dirt. And besides, your sister was sleeping around long before . . ."

I instantly threw the exerciser up against the side of the book-shelf. It bounced against the hardwood floor with a loud clang. "Long before what? I dare you to finish that death sentence state-ment." I gripped the phone with every ounce of my strength.

I heard this fool's nasal breathing, fast and forceful. "Fonda was hardly a virgin. She knew who her baby's father was."

I rapidly inhaled through my nose and exhaled through my mouth, blowing out each bit of air with force. I fought to catch my breath. It felt like a massive heart attack was brewing up to take me out.

"Yes, she did. She took that to her grave. You need your ass locked up for the rest of your tired life. I don't know how your wife stands the sight of you. You never would have seen me at that re-union if I'd known about this. I hope you didn't put your hands on those twin girls of yours. But, either way, you can bet that you'll never see this son again, unless it's in court, testifying against you, if the damn statute of limitations hasn't run out. You can take that to your damn grave, which I hope is where you lay your deranged ass soon. Not that you don't have hundreds of other offspring to taint with your sickness. Hooking that many women with your dick. Get the hell off my phone."

With monstrous feelings running all through my head, clanging around in confusion, I slammed down the phone and stood still, wanting to bang my hand through the windowpane, or kick the small, innocent trash can toward the ceiling in a forceful field-goal fashion, or toss every single one of the files in my desk drawer down the hall and stomp on them.

I took a seat again in my chair and placed my feet firmly on the floor and spoke out loud with my eyes closed. "God, you're the center of my joy. All that's good and perfect comes from you. You're the heart of my contentment, hope for all I do. God, you're the center of my joy." I repeated these words over and over again. My hands were balled up in my lap, my shoulders were back and I again concentrated on consistent breaths, in through my nose, out through my mouth. I focused to relax my hands, and was still.

After a moment, I grabbed a couple of things from my desk, my cell phone, some of my expenses I needed to review, and in particular, I picked up my nameplate, and tossed everything into my briefcase.

I then exited my office, cutting off the lights and carefully shutting the door, focusing on slow and easy, for a moment, and then walking ninety miles an hour past the reception area and into the elevator without even blinking.

Oh, yes, actually there was one particular long blink of my eyes just as the elevator doors joined together. A single, slow-moving tear that ran from the outside of my left eye rolled on down my cheek, to my chin, and down my neck to somewhere around the left side of my chest area. It stopped there.

I sniffed for a quick second, rubbed the right side of my nose with my hand, centered my shoulders and headed on down into the parking lot to my awaiting car.

I spoke out loud to the heavens as I pulled off onto the freeway and into the night air, the darkness and the stillness of the night.

"Fonda. I'm still talking to you, baby sis. I miss your big eyes and big smile and big laugh and big hugs. You did everything big. How horrifying it must have been to have your own father lie on top of you and attempt to violate your existence. I'm so sorry that I didn't know. I had no idea. Your life was so short and so tragic, yet so memorable. I won't rest until he pays for what he did. We were born to a man who had some serious problems. That was not your fault, any more than it was mine. I miss you desperately. I think of you always. I think I stay busy just so I don't think about how much you not being in my life has affected me. Hey, I have a little girl now. She's beautiful, with big eyes like you. She was a little sick, but she pulled through.

"I will love her like I love you. You will be proud of the father that I will become. Watch me. And I will see you again. That much I know. I'll talk to you again soon. Your big brother loves you.

I stopped myself just as I was about to pop in a CD when the Stevie Wonder song that played on the local radio station from my car speakers was *"A Place in the Sun."*

I smiled at the sensation of the words and the melody. The tune took me back to the many memories of the good times I had when I was a child. Back to putting on funky dance shows for Mom to some Jackson 5 song as she sat in her peach-colored button-up house robe, and coming home from school eating syrup sandwiches on fresh white Wonder bread, or having first dibs on the old-school banana pudding Mom would make, and playing tag and then playing Twister with Fonda after school in our stocking feet . . . back to the days when my life was simple and my childhood was innocent.

I accelerated down the road, with my personalized license plate following behind me as a moniker that I couldn't shake, reminding me and the world of who I was.

In spite of that, and even though I wasn't proud of where I'd been, I was finally feeling really good about where I was headed. My taillights disappeared into the night as I sped down the main highway, on my way home after one quick stop.

Chapter 52

"Hey, baby, how'd it go today?" Mary Jane asked as I stepped into a house that finally smelled like a home. Mary Jane was rinsing out a few glass baby bottles in the kitchen sink. She was wearing a peach-colored pair of silk pajamas. An old school Aretha tune played on the CD called "*Natural Woman.*"

"Okay." I put down my briefcase and car keys. My first stop was to plant a kiss on Mary Jane's cheek and hand her two dozen roses.

Her face beamed my way as she reached out to accept them. "Oh, Makkai, thanks. But, you didn't have to." She thanked me with her wide, ebony eyes.

"Yes, but I wanted to."

She sniffed a freshly blossomed bud and hugged me. "They're beautiful. I love red roses. Wow, Makkai." She inhaled them again. "I'll put them in some water." She kissed me on the lips, gave a lingering release of her lips from mine, and headed toward the sink. "Hey honey, my brother called today. He and his wife want to drive down from the bay area so that my niece, Yardley, can meet the baby. He's so happy for you, for us, for all three of us, and he wants us to spend some real time together. If you have time, that is." Her eyes searched for approval.

I nodded and gave a green light smile. "I'll make time for that. Just set things up and make sure they know they're welcomed to stay here."

"That's nice of you, baby."

"You're my girl," I said as I turned from her, headed straight over to the white wicker bassinet in the family room. I peeked in and carefully picked up my tiny bundle of a daughter, who was cradled in a pale yellow receiving blanket with tiny white lambs throughout.

I smiled lovingly toward Mary Jane and then smiled close to my tiny baby's face as she slowly opened her eyes, trying to focus while coming out of her newborn slumber. She yawned and stretched her teeny arms above her head. "She looks so peaceful and innocent." I inhaled her baby powder scent. "Hey, little-bit."

Mary Jane placed the burgundy flower vase onto the kitchen table. "She's such a calm and sweet baby. She just eats and sleeps all day long." She again smelled the blooms.

I looked down at my daughter. "Oh, good girl. And how's her scar coming along?"

Mary Jane told me, "It's fine. I just put some antiseptic on it and changed the bandage. Just keeping it clean is working wonders."

I spoke close to my baby's little face, touching her soft, peachy chin with my index finger. "That's good. Just a physical reminder of what a little miracle you are." I could have sworn she smiled at me in confirmation. My smile was automatic.

Mary Jane kept her sights on me as she heard my home office phone ringing repeatedly. "Baby, that's your emergency line."

I tried to tune out the demanding sound. It rang on and on like an annoying, unrelenting tap on my shoulder.

I stepped toward the reclining chair. "I need to just sit for a minute. Just need to sit with my baby daughter for one minute, Don't I?" I took a seat, protectively and carefully cradling my little one in my arms.

"Dr. Worthy's line," Mary Jane said after she took the initiative that I should have taken, pressing the speakerphone button.

"Is Dr. Worthy available?" a female voice asked. "This is the head ER nurse."

Mary Jane immediately picked up the cordless. "Sure, hold on." She swiftly brought the phone to me. "Here, honey."

I carefully adjusted my hold on my little bundle of joy, carefully releasing my grip as Mary Jane accepted the handoff. My baby girl began to whimper. I inhaled and then exhaled. "Her breath smells like peaches." I told Mary Jane. And then I put the phone to my ear. "Hello."

The nurse asked, "Dr. Worthy, sorry to bother you at home. I tried your cell but immediately got voice mail. You're on call tonight, correct?"

"Yes, I am. I must've had my phone on silent in my briefcase. What's up?"

"We have a pregnant woman. Actually, she's nineteen years old and going into premature labor after just twenty-four weeks. The OBs are here, but the young woman has had mitral regurgitation for years and it's worsened recently. Her mitral valve is not functioning, and we need to do valve replacement surgery as soon as possible. She's being sustained artificially."

I immediately responded, "I'll be right there." I hung up quickly.

Mary Jane inquired as I took a step toward my car keys, "You have to go?"

"Yes. Prosthetic valve surgery on a young mother."

"Oh, my goodness." She shook her head and smiled down at the baby. "This is your daddy's life, so get used to it. The life of a life-saving surgeon."

I stepped back toward them. "I'll be back," I told my lady. I looked down at my new daughter. "Did you hear that? I'll be back." I spoke in baby talk.

"We'll be here." Mary Jane took a seat in the recliner.

"And, Miss Cherry, I want you both with me when I join Pastor Smith's church on Sunday. And, if you have time tonight, when I get back, we have to talk." I patted Mary Jane on top of her head.

She aimed her eyes up at my face. "Okay. But, about what?"

"Just about some things. And hey, did you ever get approval for that leave we talked about?"

"Yes, it's all done, starting two weeks from Friday. Your mom said she'd baby-sit until then."

"Good. I love you."

Mary Jane's eyes expanded. She looked down and cleared her throat and swallowed an audible gulp. She glanced up toward me again and then down again at our baby girl while tightening her embrace. She postponed her response as though sheer shock had locked down on her tongue. Her delayed reply was accompanied by a soft smile. "You too, Makkai."

I urgently needed to leave but seemed to linger. I gently rubbed my daughter's tiny head full of thick, dark hair. I spoke into her miniature ear. "And Daddy loves you, little Fonda Corrine Worthy. I'll never stop talking to you, little Fonda. Never stop talking to you. We've gotta get you a little brother."

Little Fonda eyed me without even a blink.

Mary Jane didn't blink either. Her face played tattletale. It was as though she was willing words to pop into her mind, at least enough to form a quick sentence, if only to distract from my comment. And so she asked, "Hey, did you ever call your dad back?"

"I did."

"And? He seems nice."

I put my foot down with my words, looking her square into her eyes. "Nice, huh? Well, he's never allowed to call here again. And I mean that. Never. If you so much as see his name on the caller ID display, I want to know about it."

She absorbed my expression. "Okay, honey."

My face spoke louder than my words. It read serious and no-nonsense. I suppose wisdom told Mary Jane it was best to not push her man, and to let it go. Sensibly, she shifted into another train of thought. She was feminine. I liked that about her.

"Wave goodbye to Daddy." She took Fonda's little hand and motioned toward me.

I leaned down to kiss Fonda's tiny cheek. "Bye, my child."

"I'll be waiting up when you get home, Dr. Feelgood." Mary Jane's eyes were provocative.

"Oh, that reminds me. Trash this before I get back home." I reached into my briefcase and handed her my nameplate while kissing her on the forehead. "And please remind me to get new license plates as soon as possible."

"Yes, Makkai. We will." My lips met hers and sounded a smack not once, but twice.

My new girls.

Out of the front door I stepped, glancing at my wristwatch, and then taking a split second to look back, snapping a visual of what would be awaiting my return. I locked and shut the door, turning the knob to make sure.

The image was etched in my mind as I approached my car that was parked in the circular driveway in front of Mary Jane's silver Acura. A muscle flexed along the side of my mouth that spelled pleasure and contentment, and I allowed that smile free rein.

I adjusted my earpiece and took an incoming call.

"Hey. What's good, man? I'm just reminding you, when am I going to get a chance to come by and see that sweet little daughter of yours?"

"Hey, Carlos, man. Soon enough. Look, I'm headed out on an emergency. I'll call you when I'm done."

"Godfather's okay with that. You know you my nigga, they don't get no bigga."

"Fa sho. Peace."

The chirp of my auto alarm sounded just before I opened the driver-side door to toss my briefcase over upon the passenger seat. What caught my eye was something resting upon my windshield, tucked behind my driver side wiper. It was a dingy white envelope that looked like it had been through hell. I shut the door, mindful of my need to get to the hospital, and snatched it from its place.

On the front of the worn, torn envelope, written in what looked like pale purple chicken scratch, these words greeted my eyesight as my heart bounced like a rubber ball in my chest. For the second time in my life, my normally cool hands were shaking. With enlarged eyes, each word saturated my brain.

I will get my daughter if it's the last thing I do. This I promise you, Dr. Feelgood. This I promise you. Love, Delicious.

DR. FEELGOOD

MARISSA MONTEILH

ABOUT THIS GUIDE

The suggested questions are intended to enhance
your group's reading of this book.

DISCUSSION QUESTIONS

1. Dr. Feelgood, as successful and fine as he is, is a player. Author Marissa Monteilh set out to not only explore the mind of a player, but the mind of the women who are hormonally bonded to his bedroom skills. Did you feel sympathy for any of his women? If so, which ones? If not, why not? Would these women have acted this way if Dr. Feelgood was not rich and famous?

2. In the opening scene, Dr. Feelgood is literally getting the life choked out of him. If you were in Salina's position, and your mate was attacking your lover-on-the-side, how do you think you would react? Do you think that Salina's mixed emotions were justified, based upon Dr. Worthy's denial of her existence?

3. Monday was an independent, sexually confident woman who proudly explored her sexual boundaries. She also refused to complain about getting used, because she was getting hers as well. Do you believe this type of sexual mentality is healthy for single women who tend to bond to men too quickly? Should more women cease using the victim angle if they allow men to bed them down without a commitment, or are women justified to complain when a man who is not into them wants to be a sex-only partner?

4. Mary Jane was definitely into Dr. Worthy, but she tried to convince herself that she could simply enjoy her newfound sexual freedom with him every now and then, until Mr. Right came along. Did you see Mary Jane as a good girl who simply enjoyed Dr. Feelgood's skills, or as an undercover bad girl who took a chance on dating Dr. Feelgood's friend as a way to get back at the man she really wanted?

5. Wild and wet Georgia had an obvious issue with men. She bonded deeply to the skilled doctor and her extreme jealousy eventually reared its ugly head. Did you feel sympathy for her when she confronted Dr. Worthy, or did you believe from the start that she had some major issues?

6. Makkai Worthy's relationship with his mother was a good one. They were and always had been very close, and she tried to motivate him on a spiritual level. Do you think this relationship contributed to his view of women as individuals who were there to please him? Do you think he was a mamma's boy?

7. Makkai Worthy's father was definitely a rolling stone. And, just like his father, Makkai had a serious bag of sexual tricks. Do you believe what happened to Makkai when he was younger contributed to his view of women as sex objects? Do you know of any men, with similar fathers, who appear to be a chip off the old player block?

8. Carlos was always living in Dr. Worthy's shadow. He seemed to gain self-esteem by being able to bed down the same women as his best friend. Do you think that Makkai should have kicked Carlos to the curb early on? Do you know of many men who have friends like Carlos, men who have no problem dating women who their friends have been with?

9. Spicy Salina, the player, got played. Do you believe she really loved her husband and was jealous of his new ghetto girl, or do you think that she really wanted Makkai instead? Her addiction to black men seemed to always distract her. Do you think there's a difference between black men in the sack, and men of other races?

10. Have you ever met a man like Makkai who totally turned you out, yet you couldn't have him? Do you believe that good orgasms make women bond? Do you know of anyone who is sexually addicted to a lover?

11. As Makkai began to narrow down the women, do you think he would have continued seeing them if they had not started tripping? Do you think he ended up making the right decisions once he began to understand his past? Could you feel his desire to be closer to God?

12. As author Marissa Monteilh develops her stories, she says that understanding what makes people tick is a passionate desire. Once you finished this novel, did you feel that you totally understood why Dr. Feelgood was such a womanizer? Did you enjoy hearing his point of view? Which female character did you enjoy the most and why?

AUTHOR'S NOTE

I hope you enjoyed the ride inside of the life of a playboy! As you can tell, this story is part of a series trilogy. *Dr. Feelgood* is to be continued, so please stay tuned. The tentative titles are, *Chain of Fools* and *Freeway of Love*.

For now, this story ended right where it needed to, but I do have an idea of the types of wild twists and turns that will take place in the lives of Makkai, Mary Jane, Monday, Georgia, Salina, Carlos, Corrine and Al, Roosevelt, and even Erskalene. More drama for yo' mama!

In my first novel, *May December Souls*, I wrote about a hormone called, *oxytocin*. It actually does exist, so please feel free to look it up if you'd like. It is sometimes called the *love hormone*, and it bonds us, particularly during sex. It can affect human attachment and make us sane girls, crazy girls. We end up with Mr. Wrong for years, breaking up and making up in an addictive fashion, without knowing why. (By the way, there will be a new relationship-type book that delves deeper into this theory.)

With *Dr. Feelgood*, I wanted to show how these four women, who'd definitely bonded to him sexually, behaved while possibly under the influence of an oxytocin bonding. So, even though Dr. Makkai Worthy has his own set of problems, these women had their own issues, too. It's not just the men who trip, okay?

Today, I heard it said that *to love is to risk not being loved in return*. Unrequited love or a relationship that ends is hard to handle once we've bonded. Sometimes, people literally trip out. And characters, just like real folks, are flawed and rejected and loose and dishonest and horny and caught up, all the while, hopefully searching for peace of mind. That is what brings about the fiction friction, as we authors call it.

I promise to deliver much more dramatic fiction, and even some sexy new erotica. Just give me some time to bring it all to you. And,

I'll definitely bring back more adventures of the ever popular and talented, *Dr. Feelgood*.

Please reach out to me if you can, at *www.MarissaMonteilh.com*, and sign my lovely guest book. I'd love to hear from you!

Love, peace, and hair grease!!

Made in the USA
Las Vegas, NV
02 September 2022

54554118R00187